4/28/04 B+T $23.45

THE BODY IN THE ATTIC

A Faith Fairchild Mystery

THE
BODY
IN THE
ATTIC

KATHERINE
HALL PAGE

wm

WILLIAM MORROW
An Imprint of HarperCollinsPublishers

THE BODY IN THE ATTIC. Copyright © 2004 by Katherine Hall Page. All rights reserved. Printed in the United States of America. No part of this book may be used or reproduced in any manner whatsoever without written permission except in the case of brief quotations embodied in critical articles and reviews. For information address HarperCollins Publishers Inc., 10 East 53rd Street, New York, NY 10022.

HarperCollins books may be purchased for educational, business, or sales promotional use. For information please write: Special Markets Department, HarperCollins Publishers Inc., 10 East 53rd Street, New York, NY 10022.

FIRST EDITION

Designed by Jennifer Ann Daddio

Printed on acid-free paper

Library of Congress Cataloging-in-Publication Data
Page, Katherine Hall.
    The body in the attic : a Faith Fairchild mystery / Katherine Hall Page.—1st ed.
        p. cm.
    ISBN 0-06-052529-0
    1. Fairchild, Faith Sibley (Fictitious character)—Fiction. 2.Women in the food industry—Fiction. 3. Shelters for the homeless—Fiction. 4. Caterers and catering—Fiction. 5. Spouses of clergy—Fiction. 6. Homeless persons—Fiction. 7. Massachusetts—Fiction. 8. Cookery—Fiction. I. Title.

PS3566.A334B625 2004

2003059298

04 05 06 07   08 WB/RRD 10 9 8 7 6 5 4 3 2 1

FOR LUISE AND ROBERT KLEINBERG

dear family, dear friends

The past is the present, isn't it? It's the future, too.

—*LONG DAY'S JOURNEY INTO NIGHT,* EUGENE O'NEILL

ACKNOWLEDGMENTS

My thanks to the reference librarians at the Cambridge Public Library, Cambridge, Massachusetts; Gail Pennington of Deutsch Williams Brooks DeRensis & Holland, P.C., Boston, Massachusetts; Luise Kleinberg and Elizabeth Samenfeld-Specht for recipes; Dr. Robert DeMartino; Sarah Durand, my editor; Carol Edwards, my copy editor; and, as always, my friend and agent, Faith Hamlin.

1

Over the years, Faith Fairchild had occasionally let herself imagine what it would be like to meet Richard Morgan again. But nothing like this had ever crossed her mind.

Richard Morgan. They had had a heady whirlwind affair in the waning days of the self-indulgent eighties, meeting just before Christmas and parting before the New Year. They were both living in Manhattan—the perfect back-drop for romance, especially during the holiday season. And they were both single. Children, mortgages, gray hair were all things that happened to other people—older people.

Faith had been on a city bus returning to Have Faith, the catering firm she'd started that fall. Richard had taken the seat next to hers, and as the other passengers boarded, the strains of a Salvation Army rendition of "Good King Wenceslas" filtered through the open door. Richard had started hum-ming along, Faith smiled, and he began to sing—he had a pleasant tenor voice and an even more pleasant appearance: tall, dark brown hair, and very blue eyes. "I only know the one verse," he'd told her, and she'd confessed the same. They'd talked, and he'd almost missed his stop. When he left, he'd said, "Want to trade cards? I might suddenly remember the rest of 'Good King

Wenceslas' and wouldn't know where to find you." She'd handed hers over with her own line: "True. Or you might need a caterer."

Standing in front of her now, Richard Morgan did need a caterer. In fact, he needed a meal. They were at Oak Street House in Boston, a shelter for homeless men, and Richard had just slid his tray in front of Faith, a volunteer, so she could hand him a bowl of beef stew. Stunned, she stood with the ladle in one hand, the half-filled bowl in the other. The last time she'd seen him, they'd been at the Top of the Sixes, that elegant bygone Gotham hot spot at 666 Fifth Avenue. They'd drunk champagne, Perrier-Jouët, and the lights of the city had sparkled about them like jewelry from Tiffany. Richard was drinking coffee now. A thick mug rested next to two packaged rolls on his tray. Faith started to speak, then stopped as he put his finger to his lips, shaking his head slightly.

"Hey, lady, wake up! You gonna gimme some stew or what?" The man next to Richard pushed him aside. Hastily, Faith filled the bowl and passed it over to Richard. Their hands touched briefly. His nails were dirty and his skin looked chapped from the cold. She filled another bowl—and another.

It had been thirteen years since they'd said good-bye.

Y ou're kidding, right?" Faith said to her husband, the Reverend Thomas Fairchild.

But she knew he wasn't, and he confirmed it.

"I know it all sounds very sudden, but we wouldn't go until the end of January. That's almost two months away. Classes start on the thirtieth."

"I don't understand why you can't teach the course and commute from here."

Here was Aleford, Massachusetts, a small town west of Boston, where the reverend held sway at the First Parish Church and to which locale he had lured his bride, Faith Sibley, almost ten years earlier. Faith, born and bred in the Big Apple, had had a thriving catering business and had been loathe to leave it for the bucolic orchards of New England, but she had fallen head over heels in love with Tom. That meant "whither thou goest," and she did. If you had told her at that time that in the future she would be protesting a move from Aleford to Cambridge, Massachusetts, a veritable metropolis, two words would have sufficed to express her feelings: *No way.* Yet here she was, raising an army of objections over what would be a temporary move, a sabbatical.

Tom was sitting across from her in one of the two wing chairs that flanked the living room fireplace. They'd tucked five-year-old Amy into bed, then, an hour later, eight-year-old Ben. Faith had been looking forward to having Tom home for the evening—no meetings, and maybe some bed for themselves. She'd been surprised when he said he had something he wanted to talk over with her, then slightly alarmed when he downed a healthy slug of brandy before speaking. She sipped hers slowly, figuring she might need it.

"I could teach the course and commute, but I don't want to." He sounded ever so slightly petulant, and, more certainly, blunt. "It's not just the course, although that's what started the whole thing—having lunch with Ralph and his asking me if I knew anyone who could pinch-hit for the spring semester. The guy who was supposed to do it has to have knee-replacement surgery or something like that. He can't postpone—"

"Wait a minute." Faith put her snifter down. "You had lunch with Ralph over two weeks ago. Are you telling me that you've known about all this since then? That you've been thinking about it and never said a word to me?"

Tom put his glass down, too, and folded his arms across his chest. Faith immediately did the same. If he wanted body language, she'd give him body language. For a moment, they stared at each other like Russian dancers before the balalaikas started.

"I didn't want to raise the issue until I had something definite to propose. I didn't see any reason to upset you unnecessarily," explained Tom, speaking coolly.

But that's not us, Faith said to herself. We tell—told—each other everything.

Instead of speaking her mind, she let the anger just below the surface break through and push away her regret. "And why were you so sure I'd be upset? Because you're proposing taking the kids out of school for four months? Because you've assumed I can go back and forth to the catering kitchen from Cambridge, without consulting me? Because you never told me a damn thing about the possibility of teaching at the Harvard Divinity School for a semester? Next semester?"

It wasn't worth it. She felt her anger drain as quickly as it had come, leaving only sadness and more than a little fear.

She finished in a much quieter voice. "You're going to do this—move into Cambridge and teach—even if we stay here in Aleford, right?"

That was the fear.

Tom got out of the chair and sat next to his wife on the couch, its down cushions flattened over the years, but still comfortable. In fact, the whole room had that comfortable but flattened look. The parsonage had housed many families. With the holidays near, Faith had filled the room with color—red amaryllis blooms, pine swags tied with bright tartan ribbons, and shiny silver bowls of apples and nuts. Tom seemed to be taking inventory before he answered his wife.

"No. No, I would never do anything that would take me away from the three of you. You know that." He pulled her into his arms and rested his chin on top of her head.

This is Tom, my Tom, Faith thought.

"But why haven't you said anything about it?"

"I'm not sure," he said slowly. "but I guess I wanted to have it all locked into place, so you'd have to come, want to come. A done deal. You know how restless I've been. Hell, I even thought about taking a sabbatical to do carpentry work after that summer."

Tom had worked on the crew that remodeled their cottage in Maine, and he had been sublimely happy mastering a nail gun and the art of shingling. Hints of the conversation they were having now had been strewn all over that August and again this summer as he'd fine-tuned the work—a tree house for the kids, a shop for himself. He'd been overwhelmed with parish work all fall, and the signs had increased. She'd caught him staring out his study window on several occasions—blocked for what to say from the pulpit. When he was called to the phone during dinner—a nightly occurrence—there'd been a new look of irritation on his face. But he hadn't wanted to talk about it, brushing away her attempts to find out how serious things might be. Faith had understood that. Talking sometimes made things too real—things that were meant to stay under the surface.

It was the carpenter's son, not a carpenter, who beckoned. She knew the jokes about exchanging his collar for a tool belt were just that. Tom was deeply committed to his ministry, a person of devout faith. He lived each day according to the notion of worship as "perfect service." If he *was* going to build houses, it would have to be connected with his calling somehow.

"If that's what you want to do, Habitat for Humanity has weekend and longer projects. . . ."

Tom sat up and reached for the brandy. "I'm not making myself clear, honey. I really need a break from Aleford, from the parish. The phone calls, the meetings, the paperwork—everything that is so not what I thought I'd be doing with my life."

"And teaching at the Div School—preparing lectures, grading papers, office hours with stressed-out students—is what you want to do instead?" Faith knew—and thought Tom did, too—that academia was no nirvana.

"It will buy me the time I need to try to figure things out. Besides the teaching, I'll be working as a street minister. You know we've talked about this—an urban ministry. I like the people I've met who are involved, and, more important, they really need me, especially during the cold months."

Which, Faith reflected, accounted for most of the year in New England. Spring limped in for a week or two in late May; then the summer hurtled by, stopped by the first killing frost in September.

Tom was speaking passionately. "I knew I couldn't go to the vestry without something definite. If I said I wanted to work with the homeless men at Oak Street House or go in the Bridge over Troubled Waters van to try to convince adolescents to get off the streets, they would have applauded my sentiments but thought it all too amorphous. Teaching at Harvard—well, it was like the old Groucho Marx show: 'Say the magic word.'"

Harvard wasn't a particularly magic word for Faith, but she knew that much of the vestry and congregation had a decided penchant for crimson. She started to make a comment to this effect, when she realized Tom had used the past tense: "it *was* like. . . ."

"You've already approached the vestry?" She needed to keep control of her anger this time and try to understand why Tom was acting this way. "More of that wanting everything definite so as not to upset me unnecessarily thing?"

Tom had the grace to look sheepish.

"Not formally. I haven't brought it before the vestry formally. Just mentioned it to one or two members to see if it would fly. I've never taken a sabbatical, you know. The time I took off to research the Albigensians in France was only for a month, and when I accepted the call to First Parish, they knew I would need it to finish my doctoral work."

Faith stood up and debated lighting the fire. The hearth looked so cold, the wood stacked, paper crunched, waiting for a match. She walked back and sat down. She wasn't in a cozy mood.

"Why don't you tell me everything now—absolutely everything—and someday, maybe even someday soon, you can help me understand why you haven't before."

Tom sighed. Faith felt sorry for him. Maybe he really didn't know why he had behaved this way. It had nothing to do with the way they felt about each other. She was sure of that. It was like the teenager who asks his parents if he can have a motorcycle, and when they tell him they'll have to see it first—cushioning the *no*—he says, "Great; it's in the garage."

"Dr. Robinson is on sabbatical this semester. In fact, he's already in

California. Ralph asked me if I knew anyone who could take his place and teach a course on the quest for the historical Jesus, since the man who had agreed to come had to have this surgery."

"With you so far," Faith said, reminding herself to say "Thank you very much" to Ralph, Tom's Div School pal, who had stayed within its ivy walls instead of taking on a parish ministry. She also thought with some longing about sunny Palo Alto or wherever the good doctor was. Why didn't he postpone his hiatus, and then Tom could take his place out there? If she was going to uproot herself, she'd prefer a more hospitable clime.

"Somehow, by the time we hit dessert—we met at Grendel's—I was roughing out a syllabus. I've taught the course in the parish several times, and you remember I've always said I'd like to do it on another level. I have tons of material." Tom stopped, then, encouraged by his wife's silence, went on. "There won't be any problem about housing, because Dr. Robinson wants his house occupied. Someone's there now, a friend from Germany, but will be leaving in January."

"And where exactly is this house? Will it be big enough? How many kids does Dr. Robinson have?"

"He's a confirmed bachelor, quite a character, but don't worry about space. You're going to love the house. It's one of those grand old places on Brattle Street."

"Oh, Tom, it's probably filled with antiques and I'll be terrified the whole time that the kids will break a Ming vase or something. We'll have to pack everything away."

Faith was switching into planning gear. Tom looked relieved; the worst might be over.

"And we can't pull them out of school and send them someplace in Cambridge, especially Ben." Faith had not bought into the college fast track—tutors, after-school enrichment programs starting in kindergarten so that little Ermentrude and Aloysius would get into the Ivy League school of their choice, but she did feel that continuity was important, and Ben was having a good year.

"Thought of that, of course." Tom beamed. "Pat's hours are the same as Ben's, and she lives on Fayerwether Street, literally around the corner. She wouldn't mind driving him one bit, and of course we'd pay her, although she refused to think about it."

Not even bothering to mention that Pat, Tom's devoted parish secretary, knew where Faith would be living before Faith herself did, Faith nodded. It would work. "But what about Amy? It would make a long day for her, and in any case, I'm not sure I can get two kids ready for school at the same time yet."

Mornings were not the Fairchilds' sterling moments, and cries of "Where's my red shirt? I *have* to wear red today. I'm on the red team!" or "Sweetheart, I don't have any clean black socks" were normal. Amy was the easiest, but without supervision, she tended to consider a bathing suit, a tutu, and her froggy boots appropriate not simply for school but for any occasion. She had a sort of Sarah Jessica Parker style that Faith admired, even as she struggled to get her daughter to change into overalls and a turtleneck. Amy went to the morning session of the nursery school that used the church school's facilities. In Aleford, as in most towns, you had to be five by the first of September to enter kindergarten, which was all day, and Amy's birthday was September 16. Faith felt that this arcane statute should be publicized to a much greater extent for the benefit of mothers all over the state. Three weeks earlier would have been no never-mind nine months before Amy was born. Amy sometimes stayed through lunch and occasionally attended the optional afternoon program, but it wasn't as long as Ben's school day and Pat's workday, in any case.

"Well, why don't I ask around and see what's available in Cambridge, and then we can make that decision later?"

Faith could tell that as far as Tom was concerned, this was a nonissue. She foresaw a lot of chauffeuring, because Tom would have more luck turning water into wine than finding an opening midyear in a nursery school anywhere, except perhaps Jupiter or Mars—and even then, Amy would probably start on the waiting list.

Faith's own schedule was flexible, especially since her assistant at Have Faith, Niki Constantine, had returned from an extended trip to Australia—she had met a mate, but in the long run, she had decided to return to her native habitat. "Too relaxed, too happy. Who could stand it?" she'd told Faith. They always had a lot of catering jobs through the holidays and into early January; then there was a dry spell, when no one in the area left home unless they absolutely had to, and if they did plan something, the event was usually canceled because of bad weather.

"So, what do you think?" Tom asked.

"I think it's 'a done deal,' " Faith replied, and gave him a kiss. "*Now* can we go to bed?"

Tom smiled at his wife. He was going to be able to keep his "motorcycle."

Sleepless later, turning her pillow over to try to find a cool, smooth spot, Faith couldn't shut her mind off. The trick of going through the alphabet and naming her favorite foods wasn't working. Her husband was having a midlife crisis, although at thirty-seven, this was a bit premature, what with life expectancy on the rise these days. Still, it had midlife, adolescentlike soul-searching written all over it, plus finding oneself, and the subsequent questioning over what one had found.

He'd done something about his angst, though. Taken action. Walked out on what he didn't want to do right now to do just what he wanted instead. New turf, new challenges.

Maybe she was envious.

Artichokes, brioche, caviar, dark chocolate, eggs Benedict . . .

Scratch the *maybe.* Tom was taking his turn; when would it be hers?

Foie gras, gumbo . . .

Faith had expected her best friend and next-door neighbor, Pix Miller, to sympathize with her. She was wrong.

"Sure he should have told you what he was thinking about, but you're the one who's always going on about men being so bad at communicating. I believe you told me the last time I complained about Sam that if women want long heart-to-heart talks with their spouses, they have to marry other women."

It was hard when your words took on a life of their own. Faith remembered the conversation well, especially since she'd cribbed most of the ideas from Niki, who had given the speech to Faith when Tom was being even more reticent than usual. "That's why women have friends and lunch," Niki had pointed out. "You don't see us bonding in silence in front of some televised sports event. We're the ones in the kitchen, laughing."

"It will be good for you, too," Pix continued, relentlessly cheerful. "You could use a change. Lately, I've begun to think you might even prefer Aleford over New York."

"Bite your tongue," Faith protested. She was still an expatriate in her own mind. She moved on to another topic. "What have you picked up around the parish? You know how the wife is always the last to know—especially so far in this case. What are people saying?"

"A few grumbles about short notice, but much more about letting Tom do what he wants to do, so we don't lose him for good. Besides, he'll be on call for weddings, funerals, and dire emergencies."

"These emergencies better be pretty dire. They're the ones that have driven Tom to this. You know, 'Oh, Reverend Fairchild, such a catastrophe! Mrs. Baxter is proposing that the children sing carols before the pageant, when you know we've always had them afterward,' or 'I wouldn't have troubled you, but this is a crisis. The blue altar cloth has gone missing!' Examples from true life, I kid you not."

Pix was laughing. "Between George and Kesia, I think they can head these off at the pass and keep Tom safe."

George Albert was the divinity school intern serving at First Parish before his ordination, and Kesia Wilson was the longtime Religious Education director. Both of them were made of strong stuff, and it was their presence that had allowed Tom to consider his plan. The full burden of preaching would not fall on George's shoulders. Tom had lined up a number of guest preachers, and Pix had told Faith earlier that it would be interesting—"Like getting one of those Smith and Hawken flower-of-the-month kits. Some of the blooms are gorgeous and some don't quite make it." Pix lived for her garden and tended toward horticultural metaphors.

Faith still wasn't feeling anything like the enthusiasm Tom was for the move. The idea of packing—and packing away things in the Brattle Street house she had yet to see—loomed, insurmountable.

"I hate the thought of packing," she complained.

"What's to pack?" asked ever-practical Pix. "Throw a few things in a suitcase. When you need more, you can come out and get them. No one will be in your house. Think of it as a closet twenty-five minutes away."

"The place will be terribly musty when we get back. It's musty enough now, even with us in it."

"I'll come over and air it religiously," Pix promised. "Now, come on, what's really bothering you?"

Faith pushed her thick blond hair behind her ears to keep it away from her face. She'd let it grow almost to her shoulders. It hadn't been this long since her early twenties.

"I'm used to Aleford and Alefordians. For better or worse—maybe worse. I don't know anyone in Cambridge, apart from a few people in Tom's biz and at events I've catered, but I was most definitely the help then. Although the same can be said about a lot of the ecclesiastical gatherings—just add *mate* on the end. New England has been hard enough in a small dose like Aleford, but Cambridge, Cantabrigians—all those academics. I don't even know what to wear."

This last admission signaled what a cataclysm this was. Faith always knew what to wear.

"I mean"— she cupped the empty coffee mug in her hands —"here it's all L. L. Bean and Talbots, not that I've succumbed, but from what I've seen in Cambridge, it's neopunk in Harvard Square, Grandmamma's priceless paisley shawl over the number bought for dear Eliza's wedding or dear Richard's fortieth alumni reunion, or the

Marimekko purchased in the sixties, when Design Research was in that perfectly wonderful old house. And the only perfume I've ever smelled at these gatherings is musk oil, Chanel Number Five, and/or mothballs."

"Now, Faith, it's not like that at all. Well," Pix amended, "maybe it's a little like that—and DR was wonderful both in the old house and when they moved to where Crate and Barrel is now. If I could get into my Marimekkos, I'd wear them, too. Samantha scooped them all up the last time she was home. Apparently, they're very in these days at Wellesley. Were back then, too.

"Anyway, I'll tell you what. We'll have lunch with my Cambridge friend Bitsy. You've heard me talk about her. She knows everyone—and everything. It will be fun."

Once again, Faith realized that her idea of fun—something delectable to eat for lunch, maybe at Geoffrey's, followed by a leisurely look at what was hot in Newbury Street's galleries and shops—diverged widely from Pix's—a sandwich of an indeterminate nature tucked in a pita pocket to be eaten outdoors after something completely outré, like snowshoeing or rock climbing. In this case, since the point was to engage in conversation and not physical activity, it would be chicken livers on toast at Pix's venerable club downtown, possibly followed by a quick tour of the Sargents in the Museum of Fine Arts—lovely the first and even second or third times, but as a steady diet . . .

Fun. Lunching with two grown women named "Pix" and "Bitsy."

"I'd love to meet your friend," Faith found herself saying. "But I get to pick the restaurant."

I don't live in that part of Cambridge myself, but of course I know the house. Teddy Robinson gives divine dinner parties, and when his uncle, Ned Robinson, was alive, they used to have a brunch on New Year's Day that everyone waited for all year. I don't know why Teddy doesn't do it anymore. No work for him. The housekeeper did everything, hiring extra help and whatnot. Eggnog in silver punch cups and a

Virginia ham and biscuits. There was some Southern connection in the family. Teddy's mother? He grew up there, I believe. Uncle Ned—we all called him that—came from New Jersey, and of course we ribbed him mercilessly, as you can imagine."

Faith could. She'd been known to make some Jersey jokes herself, although since her aunt Chat had moved across the river, she was more careful. According to Chat, it was the land of milk and honey, its beauty impossible for the elite, or effete, of Manhattan to comprehend.

Bitsy continued reminiscing, "My husband and I were newlyweds the first year we were invited, and I remember how naughty Uncle Ned was saying we looked as if we'd just gotten out of bed, and of course we had. I blush to this day, and that was over forty years ago."

Bitsy *was* a mine of information—and a delight. Faith could listen to her all day. She was about sixty, her silver-streaked pale blond hair pulled back into a loose bun, what used to be called a Psyche's knot. Faith resolved that when she got to know Bitsy better, she'd ask her what she used on her skin. Her face was unlined and glowing. Her eyes were green and she looked feline, as in a kitten, not a cat.

They were comfortably seated by the window at Sandrine's, an Alsatian restaurant on Holyoke Street. "So much fun to see one's friends outside when one is warm and well fed inside," Bitsy had proclaimed, peeking over the lace bistro curtains that covered the bottom of the window. The restaurant was marking the holidays in a subdued but elegant manner; beautifully decorated wreaths hung on the dark red walls. Crimson lake, Faith had thought when she entered, remembering a watercolor paint box she'd had as a child. And cerulean blue—more paint box—trim, with plenty of gleaming copper and decorative French pottery. Arrangements of evergreens and poinsettias glistened with tiny white lights. A waiter placed an onion tartlet in front of each of them. The fragrance of the caramelized onions with a hint of smoked bacon was tantalizing. It was one of the specialties of the house, and deservedly so, the custardlike filling oozing with rich cream in a sinfully buttery crust. They were drinking a Reisling, of course, in the requisite green-stemmed white-wine glasses, and Faith was happy she'd agreed to come.

It was odd at first to hear Theodore Robinson, Th.D., referred to as "Teddy," but just as Faith could not imagine the woman sitting across from her with any name other than Bitsy, she was sure when she finally did meet Dr. Robinson, it would be the same.

Pix—the nickname had been given to her as a tiny child and had stuck, even as she incongruously reached close to six feet during adolescence—reached for a roll as they waited for the next course. "I don't know why I don't come here more often. The food is much better than the club's, although the club is so handy when you need to pee. I couldn't just walk in here, use the ladies' room, and walk out. But about the Robinsons—I never met either of them, but of course mother did. I understand Teddy took it very hard when his uncle died."

"That's true." Bitsy nodded. Unlike Pix, her nickname must have always fit. She was small, but Faith had the feeling she was one of those diminutive women whose tiny velvet gloves housed rather powerful fists. "I suppose the first year after Ned died, Teddy didn't have the heart to have the party; then it got to be a sort of habit. The parties were rather centered on his uncle. Teddy was just a young man. What I miss, though, is the mixing of the generations. Guests from twenty to one hundred and twenty—not literally, of course, but you take my point. Everything is so segregated by age these days. Generation Y, thirty-somethings, boomers, senior citizens."

It was true. Faith prized her older friends, those much more advanced in years and those only slightly. Pix was a boomer whose children were in high school and college and working. Faith considered her not unlike Dante's Virgil, an essential guide to the perilous and often hellacious circles of child rearing. But Bitsy was right: Events tended to be segregated by age, even in the parish—dinners for those under thirty, family gatherings, senior outings. She made a note to bring it up with Tom, then made a further note to file it. The last thing Tom was thinking about these days was First Parish in Aleford.

"What is the house like?" she asked Bitsy as the waiter served their main courses. Pix and Bitsy had opted for bœuf bourguignon, and it smelled heavenly. Faith was intrigued by a nontraditional dish—porcini ravioli surrounded by roasted red pepper and tomato coulis, very pretty and very tasty.

"I've only been in the living and dining rooms, but they're beautiful. The front hall between them is quite lovely, too—a very dramatic staircase goes up to the second floor. You know the type—carved newel post and curved banister. Uncle Ned collected Chinese porcelain, and those enormous blue-and-white jars, like the ones in Sargent's paintings, are set in niches along the staircase. There's more in both downstairs rooms, all of them spectacular. Ned and Teddy took many trips to the Far East together. Ned was widowed or divorced—I'm not sure which. And Teddy never married. An unhappy love affair early on. She left him for someone else—or so I've heard."

Chinese porcelain! Faith had been right. She'd have to hire Gentle Giant, the movers, to pack it all up and store it someplace in the house.

"So it's a large house?" she asked, hoping for a good-size basement *and* an attic.

"Quite large. Not one of the Tory houses, though. A good big late Victorian built for a family with the proper number of offspring, five or more."

Ignoring the specter that five or more children presented, Faith said, " 'Tory houses'? What are those?"

Pix and Bitsy exchanged glances. Clearly there was work to be done.

Having intercepted the slightly smug look, Faith added hastily and frostily, "I know who the Tories were, and I even know that Cambridge, or New Towne, as it was called then, was the capital of the Massachusetts Bay Colony."

This last bit of information had been gleaned only yesterday from Tom, who was delving into Cambridge lore with all the dedication of a convert. The city became Cambridge in 1638, named after Cambridge University back in merrie olde England, whose graduates, the Puritan fathers, had voted in 1636 to establish a college to educate young men for the ministry. After John Harvard, a pastor in nearby Charlestown, died in 1638, he left half his estate and all of his library to the college, which promptly became "Harvard." Thus was established the inexorable, and some would say execrable, link between town and gown.

Bitsy was actually patting the back of Faith's hand in a distinct "now, now, there" gesture.

"Cambridge was a popular resort for wealthy Boston Royalists in the mid-eighteenth century, and they built grand estates with gardens stretching all the way down to the Charles River. Brattle Street was called 'the King's Highway' and led west, out toward Watertown—and Aleford. The Patriots referred to the section with these large houses, roughly from Ash Street to Elmwood, as 'Tory Row,' and it's still called that by some residents—much the same way as people in Lincoln say 'Trap-elo Road,' as opposed to the common 'Tra-pelo.' Well, as soon as the Tories fled in 1775, the Patriots seized their houses, of course, the Tory houses, and Harvard, too, which became a barracks. Washington took up residence in John Vassal's house, the most splendid of them all, and stayed there during the siege of Boston. Phillis Wheatley dedicated a poem to Washington, and he invited her to come to the headquarters, which I think was rather nice of him. It's what we call the Longfellow House now."

Faith knew it well and looked forward to actually going inside, instead of just intending to. But then, it had been closed for renovations for the last two years. The house suggested royalty, if not Tories. She'd always thought it was painted the perfect shade of yellow, somewhere between hollandaise and pâte brisée, pure butter with a bit of flour, perfect for a crust. The Longfellow House had black shutters and white trim. It must have been glorious in its day. Some of the original gardens still survived as Longfellow Park, directly across the street from the house.

"George must have been something of a stick," Bitsy said firmly. "Very principled and exactly what you want in a wartime leader, but not much fun at parties. Fortunately, Martha came up to join him. I love the description of her arrival: four horses with postillions in scarlet-and-white livery, 'Washington-style.' She managed to convince him to give a Twelfth Night party a month later, because it was also their wedding anniversary."

Faith smiled. "I can hear her now. 'Look, George, I know there's a war, but the shot heard round the world is nothing compared to what will happen if you forget our anniversary!' "

When the waiter reappeared, no one had room for dessert, but they lingered over coffee. The shadows were deepening outside, reminding Faith that the shortest day of the year was only a week away. It was a comforting thought. After that, each day would bring them a little closer to more light.

With promises to get together again after the holidays and very frequently once Faith was established on Tory Row, Bitsy left. Pix turned to Faith and said, "So?"

"So you were right. Now I have a new friend—and did you notice that gorgeous Armani skirt and sweater she was wearing?"

"No mothballs?"

"No mothballs."

Driving back to Aleford, Faith felt a pleasant sense of anticipation. Cambridge was going to be fun.

It's big. Yes indeed. No problem there. But . . ."

"But what?" Tom asked anxiously.

They were standing in Dr. Robinson's living room. The weak January sunlight struggled to find chinks in the yews and hemlocks that had grown up over the windows. Their branches pressed against the frost-covered panes. Faith snapped on a lamp. The damask shade barely permitted any light to penetrate through.

"It's dark. It's very dark," Faith said, shivering slightly. It was cold, too. The heat had been turned down after Dr. Robinson's friend left.

"We'll bring our own lamps. No problem. And I doubt we'll be spending a lot of time in this room."

Faith doubted it, too, although she could immediately see its possibilities. It was the size of the parsonage's living room and dining room put together and then some. A fireplace with an Adam mantel and surrounded by black marble shot with gold faced a series of leaded-glass windows overlooking the front yard, which was screened from the prying eyes of passersby on Brattle Street by a solid fence. It was painted brown to match the brown-shingled house. Dark. Everything was dark. Were this house hers, she'd take the wooden fence down, plant a living one, and pull up all the shrubs around the house's foundation. She'd paint the living room walls a warm color—Longfellow yellow or the rosy red of cream of tomato soup. They were covered in what had once been much brighter William Morris wallpaper, faded now to a uniform sepia, the willow pattern barely visible. There was a lot of furniture—piecrust tables, chairs from Shaker to Sheraton, and a large hairy-paw Chippendale sofa. Much was slipcovered in burgundy damask, and the overall effect was an *Antiques Roadshow* dream, but not user-friendly.

Tom crooked his arm through his wife's. "Come on, let's look at the rest of the house. There's supposed to be a library back here." He opened a door on one side of the fireplace.

It was a library—and it was dark, too, but the walls glowed with the deep rich colors of bindings—row upon row of leather-bound books. As in the living room, an Oriental rug covered the floor, but this one was brighter—reds, golds, bright blue, and even orange. The one in the living room was intricate and somber—dark blue and rose.

"Better, but still not a place where the kids can hang out," Faith said.

Tom was lovingly running his hand across the top of the mahogany desk.

"It seems like a sacrilege to put a computer on something like this," he murmured.

Faith laughed. "You were born in the wrong century, love. Okay, let's see the rest."

The rest was a formal dining room. No problem entertaining, but they'd have to shout at dinnertime or cluster down at one end of the table. Eating in the kitchen was out. It had been constructed for a cook and a maid to wait on the table. The butler's pantry was almost as large as the kitchen itself. Faith was glad to see that the stove was a gas one and had been updated. There was a dishwasher and a new refrigerator—but no place for a family of four to eat. The dining room it would be. Gracious living. The bell panel on the wall above the sink in the butler's pantry attested to it.

On the second floor, there were five bedrooms and two baths. There had been a half bath at the foot of the back stairs, off the kitchen.

"We'd better put Amy in the small bedroom that shares a bath with this one, which we can use," Faith said. "I can imagine her wandering around, trying to find the other bathroom, and getting lost on her way back to bed."

"Whatever you say." Tom was determinedly upbeat. It wasn't hard. He was looking forward to this time in a completely new place as he had looked forward to few things before in his life. He sat on the bed and patted the mattress. "Feels fine."

It probably is, Faith thought. The whole house was well maintained and comfortable. The Victorian bedroom sets in each room were back in fashion, and there wasn't even a scratch on any of the marble tops.

"We can use the room across the hall, in the front of the house, for the kid's playroom. Put their things there and maybe a television."

"Don't forget the top floor. Maybe there was a nursery there. An old hobbyhorse or two." Tom was a fan of E. E. Nesbit and A. A. Milne.

"Let's go see."

The stairs to the top floor were not as elaborate as the main staircase, and no niches lined the wall. Faith had been relieved to note that the professor had had all his porcelain packed away himself and that the niches were blessedly empty, as were the living room shelves and the dining room sideboard.

Unlike the rest of the house, the third floor was warm—airless, but warm. Dust filtered through the light as the Fairchilds opened the doors, which revealed a totally different way of life: tiny bedrooms for the servants, an antiquated bath, and a small kitchen that dated from the forties at least. One door opened into the attic. It was filled with packing crates—the porcelain and other items Dr. Robinson had had placed out of harm's way. Faith stood in the doorway. There were old trunks and piles of newspapers, a dressmaker's dummy, an empty birdcage, chairs whose seats needed caning, bureaus with chipped paint. On the bureau nearest the door, someone had long ago affixed gummed red-bordered paper labels on the drawers. In a spidery hand, someone had written "Gift wrap, tissue paper, and string" on one. The next read "Dust cloths, mending yarn," and the last said "Ornaments, tree lights." She knew exactly what each drawer contained: wrapping paper ironed to be used again, tissue smoothed, string too short to be saved, threadbare cloths, carefully tied snippets of yarn, ornaments that needed hangers, and lights that needed bulbs. It was the quintessential New England attic. It could have been her in-laws', right down to the smell of cedar. She closed the door, feeling happier than she had downstairs in the land of wealth and privilege. Up here, the servants had been free, or at least freer. Their rooms were small and the mattresses straw—she'd tested one—but when they'd come up here the day's work was done.

At the opposite end from the attic, a door did indeed lead into a nursery.

"See, I was right. Look at the toys. Wow, this Lionel train must be worth a fortune! It looks brand-new, but it has to date from the fifties, or even earlier."

There was a window seat that stretched beneath the windows overlooking the front yard. White pines towered above the house and their branches beckoned to any child brave enough to go out the window and climb down. Ben was that kind of child, but that wasn't what made Faith decide to locate the children's playroom down a flight and make this floor strictly off-limits.

What decided her was the feeling she got as soon as she had opened the door—a feeling so palpable that she was sure Tom must share it, but from the look on his face as he examined the train, it was clear he didn't. It wasn't just the air, which had an acrid shut-off smell from the room's obvious disuse. The feeling was coming from something she couldn't define. She shook her head in a vain attempt to get out from under it, but, like a blanket during a nightmare, it smothered her.

Something horrible had happened here. She was certain—and she was afraid.

It was the last day of January, a Friday, and the Fairchilds had moved into the Brattle Street house the day before. Tom's parents were taking the kids for the weekend—picking them up after school—so Faith could settle in. Tom had started teaching the previous day. He'd been working with the Urban Ministry through December, whenever he could spare some time from the parish. Oak Street House was one of his main assignments. She knew he wouldn't be able to help her at the house—and there really wasn't much to do, since she'd taken Pix's advice and packed only what they'd need until the weather got warmer, by which time they could be home, given the usual state of affairs in New England. And, after surveying the *batterie de cuisine* in the Robinson kitchen, she'd packed up her own cookware and utensils. Still, they'd managed to fill both cars with bags and boxes, which were now scattered in various rooms. She was grateful to her in-laws for the chance to organize it all in peace. She was also grateful for the time alone with Tom, a rare commodity. Faith was hoping for dinner at UpStairs on the Square and maybe a movie at the Brattle. She was eager now to plunge into her Cambridge experience. The restaurant was in the heart of Harvard Square and the venerable movie theater, the favorite of generations of Harvard students, was just down the street.

She'd turned the radio up loud. The house was unnaturally quiet without the kids, and she was unpacking clothes to *The Buena Vista Social Club* sound track when the phone rang.

"Honey, I hate to ask you this when you have all that unpacking to do, but could you come down here and help serve dinner? We're short a volunteer, and the line is already stretched around the block."

"Of course. I'll be there as fast as I can. I hate to think of those men waiting in this bitter cold. See you soon."

A light snow had been falling off and on all day, covering the frozen piles that the lowest temperatures in one hundred years had failed to melt.

Faith grabbed her coat and walked to the Harvard Square subway — T—stop, happy to be out of the house. Her initial uneasy response had intensified on two subsequent visits. It hadn't been a happy house. She was sure of that, despite Bitsy's ebullient descriptions of the soirees the professor and his uncle had thrown. And it was also dark—very dark this time of year, when it seemed as if night fell shortly after noon. She was glad for the excuse to leave.

The shelter was in the South End, a quixotic section of Boston. It had been an elegant neighborhood at the turn of the twentieth century, then had become so again at the turn of the twenty-first. But quixotic because the remnants of what it had been in between still existed on its fringes. Oak Street House was one of them.

The men had started lining up outside well before 5:00 P.M., dinnertime. When Faith arrived, the first group was sitting at the tables in the large dining hall. There was no happy preprandial buzz of conversation. No conversation at all, save for an occasional mutter. The table where those too disabled to get their trays themselves sat was served before the others. Tom did this. Unlike the men gathered here, he was full of conversation, greeting them often by name, greeting them as human beings. He was sublimely comfortable in this role; she had never seen him act like this before. He had jumped into his new life with all the fervor of a proselyte—or a man released from captivity.

The first group approached and Faith started filling bowls, her hands sweating under the rubber gloves. Tendrils of hair slipped from the paper hat she wore, a hat that seemed more suited for a 1950s carhop. She blew a strand out of her eye. Next time, she'd bring a hair net. A low glass partition separated the servers from the served. The bowls were placed on a stainless-steel shelf along the top. No contact. She knew it was important the food be protected, that she be protected. But it went against everything she believed about the way food should be offered. Only this wasn't about presentation. This was simply about survival. For many in the room, it was the only food they'd had all day— or even longer.

When there was a lull, she looked up, struck as always by the diversity and contrast among the men who passed before her. Caucasian, Hispanic, African-American, Asian. Men in business suits, men in rags. Clean men, filthy men. Young men—some in their teens even—old men, although age was hard to guess. Life on the street added years quickly. One man had a copy of Thomas Hardy's *Jude the Obscure* in the back pocket of his corduroy trousers. He had a wool crewneck on under his parka and looked like an academic. May have been an academic. She smiled and he smiled back. More often than not, her smile brought no response, just vacant eyes or manic eyes, bloodshot and glassy.

Occasionally, a scuffle broke out and the entire room tensed up while the shelter employees defused the situation. They'd come close to a real fight tonight when an elderly man, refusing the stew because he was a vegetarian, asked for extra rolls. As the volunteer complied, the man behind him demanded the extra portion of stew. Faith knew she couldn't give it to him. The rules were strict. Everyone had to be served, and then if there was anything left, they could give it out. But they all knew there wouldn't be, even as they told the men asking for larger portions to come back at the end. There was never anything left at the end except some cartons of milk and the rolls. There was always an endless supply of rolls in varying degrees of freshness. The doors closed at six o'clock, and during the previous hour on a night like this, three to four hundred meals were served. Oak Street's greatest fear was not having enough. The first time she'd volunteered, Faith had been quickly ordered to be less generous. "You don't want to see what happens if we run out," a man serving next to her had said.

It was close to 6:00 P.M. now and the doors would soon be shut. If you hadn't come in time, you wouldn't be fed. Tom had finished handing out the milk and juice and was sitting at a table, quietly talking to one of the men. Some had tickets for the shelter's all too few beds. Others would stay as long as they could before returning to the cold and trying another shelter—or, failing that, an ATM enclosure or a doorway near a heat vent.

"Are there any rolls left?"

It was Richard. She had watched him come toward her from his place at a table near the door. The first shock gone, she saw that he was wearing a heavy dark green wool jacket and carried a small knapsack. Under the jacket, he was wearing what looked like several layers, topped by a Polartec pullover. His eyes were still very, very blue. His smile, revealing good teeth, cared-for teeth, set him apart from almost everyone else.

"Yes, there are. Would you like some butter, too?"

"That would be nice. Thank you."

She placed the food on top of the counter.

"Monday. One o'clock. Trinity Church."

His voice was so low, she almost missed it.

He moved away and looked back over his shoulder when he sat down. She nodded.

Someone came up behind Faith and grabbed her by the waist as she was bent over, scrubbing out one of the containers that had held the stew. She whirled around, opening her mouth to scream—and saw Tom. Of course, Tom.

"Sorry, honey, I didn't mean to startle you." His face had been glowing, and now it became contrite.

She kissed him. They were alone in the kitchen, and that was one reason why she had reacted so strongly. She didn't mind serving at Oak Street, but it depressed—and frightened—her. All these lives that had started somewhere else and ended up here. In a blink, your life could change.

"I said I'd stay for a little while longer in case anyone wanted to talk. I'll be in that small conference room for the next half hour. You can go along home, or wait for me and we'll grab a bite somewhere."

The idea of going back to the large, dark, empty house in Cambridge by herself was not appealing. Hanging out in the Oak Street kitchen wasn't much better, but she could wait in the car, listen to music, and get to have dinner out with her husband. Just the two of them.

"We're near Chinatown. Why don't I wait in the car and we can go over to New Shanghai?"

"Great. You have your keys?"

Faith did, and after wiping down the counters, she turned off the kitchen lights and slipped out a side door. The other volunteers had come from a church in the suburbs, all traveling together in a van, and had had to get back. She didn't mind cleaning up, but her shoulders ached slightly. As she closed the car door, turning to WCRB for a classical music fix, she thought of her own hearth in the suburbs with a slight pang. Ravel's mournful "Pavane" filled the air with its piercingly sad melody. It fit her mood precisely and she wallowed away.

Richard Morgan. Homeless. She could hardly bear to think of it. A brilliant writer, he was five or six years older than Faith. His byline had appeared regularly in the *New York Times*, *The New Republic*, and other publications. A foreign correspondent, he'd given her a moving eyewitness account of what it had been like to be in Tiananmen Square. It seemed there wasn't an inch of the globe he didn't know intimately— where to eat in Kuala Lumpur and the best pub in Dublin. His dream had been to be the first journalist to travel in space. He had been taking a break, working in the city on a profile of a rising star in the Republican party for *The New Yorker*, when Faith had met him. The star had imploded and was currently wearing New York State–issued jumpsuits instead of Savile Row attire. It appeared something drastic had happened to Richard also. The last time she'd seen him, he had told her he was working on a blockbuster work of fictionalized nonfiction. He was going to dedicate it to her. She'd been thrilled, but then his next sentence—that he would be away researching and writing it for many months—popped the balloon. After that, she had had a couple of funny postcards from various places in the South, and once FedEx had shown up with a Stuckey's peanut roll, but she'd never seen Richard again. Tom came along a few months later, and that was that.

Abruptly, she switched stations. Magic 106.7. Motown, Marvin Gaye. Better than Ravel. Much better. "I Heard It Through the Grapevine." But Faith hadn't. Hadn't heard anything about Richard on any sort of grapevine. It was odd. Her sister, Hope, a year younger than Faith, had asked her last summer if she knew what had happened to Richard Morgan. At the time Faith met Richard, Hope had just begun a meteoric rise to her present lofty career on the Street, a career that seemed immune to the vicissitudes of the market. Faith occasionally wondered whether, despite their ecclesiastical upbringing, Hope hadn't contracted with Faust. No Black Tuesdays—or any other days of the week—for her little sister. Hope had met Richard several times that long-ago holiday season. That last knell for the eighties had been one long party. "Fay," she'd said—Faith was still trying to figure out a way to tell her sister kindly that she hated the childhood nickname—"whatever happened to that hunky beau of yours who wrote for *The New Yorker*? Richard something? Wasn't he supposed to end up on the best-seller list?" Faith had told her what she knew—nothing. What she didn't tell her, and rarely admitted to herself, was how much she minded not knowing. It wasn't as if she was still in love with him. Of course not. Motown changed to disco and Faith turned the radio off. It was like reading a mystery and discovering that someone had ripped out the last chapter. It was the not knowing that had bothered her. That was all it was. Well, now she knew.

And Monday, she'd know more.

How hungry are you? Fish or that beef dish?"
     Faith turned her attention to the menu. She loved New Shanghai. It was where the Boston chefs gathered in the wee hours, after their own restaurants had closed. Faith had heard about it first from Julia Child, now living in California and greatly missed from the local scene.

"The shredded beef in garlic sauce, with the scallion pancakes." It was what she'd had on her first visit and she was feeling nostalgic.

"Okay, then how about the dow miow—the pea-pod stems—some rice, and maybe the bean curd to start?"

"Perfect." Faith poured some tea and Tom ordered a Tsingtao beer.

The bean curd arrived quickly. It had been delicately deep-fried, so that only a thin, crisp layer surrounded its silky interior. The two textures exploded in your mouth. So simple, yet so complicated. Faith realized she was very hungry, and three of the morsels disappeared from the plate. There was a dipping sauce of soy, ginger, and scallion, but she liked them au naturel.

Tom reached across the table for his wife's hand.

"I can help you unpack tomorrow morning. We could go to a movie tonight. It's still early."

It was only seven. It just felt like midnight.

"That would be wonderful. There really isn't much to do. If you take care of your clothes and we both do the kitchen, it shouldn't be long."

"I knew this would work out, the whole Cambridge thing. Happy?" Faith detected the slight note of anxiety behind Tom's question.

She picked up another square of bean curd with her chopsticks.

It was a hard question to answer.

Logistically, it *had* worked out. Tom had taken Ben to the parish secretary's house early Thursday morning and Pat had deposited him back at their Brattle Street doorstep shortly before 3:30 P.M. Ben was thrilled to be a commuter and was clamoring for a briefcase to replace his knapsack. He and Pat had been friends before and now appeared on the brink of an even-greater friendship, one to be tested in traffic and tried by weather. Tom had sworn to find a spot for Amy, and with the luck that comes only to those who know not the impossibility of the quest, he had snagged a place immediately in one of the top schools, which was several streets away. They needed a five-year-old girl to balance the class after a sudden unexpected move (a tenure-track offer from Stanford and the Harvard assistant professor was off like a shot, fully aware of his chances where he was—roughly the same as that of finding a parking place within walking distance of Harvard Yard). Amy had been stunned at the notion of not only a new locale—"What about my bed?"—but also a new school. Faith's falsely cheerful "Guess what? You're going to have so much fun. There's a school just around the corner and it has a playhouse right in the classroom, and a bunny" produced divalike histrionics on the scale of Maria Callas. Dragging her recalcitrant child by the hand for the interview, Faith prayed for a miracle and just this once got one in the person of Miss Margaret, the head teacher. Whether it was some kind of drug slipped into Amy's milk or plain old magic, the child reluctant to go in was instantly transformed into a child reluctant to go home.

Yes, Tom was right: It *had* worked out. And she was happy about that. Happy that Tom was so blissfully happy, too. Yet, she still felt dislocated—and she didn't like the house. "Nonsense," she could hear Pix and any number of other people saying. "You've only been in Cambridge for two days. When it comes time to leave, they'll have to pry you away." There was some truth to this notion, and she reached for Tom's hand.

"Of course I'm happy," she replied once she'd swallowed the tofu and sipped some tea.

She'd get out to Have Faith's kitchen in Aleford when she needed to and could spend the rest of her time as a proper Cambridge lady. Or an improper one.

The main dish arrived. As she ate, feeling the spicy sauce go directly into her bloodstream, Faith listened to her husband, responded appropriately—and was very, very much aware of the fact that she hadn't said a single word about seeing Richard Morgan at Oak Street House. Or about meeting him at Trinity Church in Copley Square on Monday.

Faith brought the cocktail napkin to her mouth and palmed the crab cake she'd popped into it a moment earlier. Fake crab and slightly off remoulade that the caterer had tried to disguise with an excess of chili powder. She grabbed a glass of white wine from the tray of one of the servers who was circulating about the room at the speed of light. Possibly a member of the Cold Water Army, more likely acting on instructions from the host to stretch the supply. She took a gulp to wash away the taste of the faux crab and walked off in search of a trash receptacle. Another server waved a tray of what appeared to be pea pods stuffed with anchovies under her nose. Declining, she drank some more wine. It wasn't bad. A good California Chardonnay, maybe Geyser Peak. She knew she'd better drink it quickly and get another glass before they switched to the stuff with a screw top. Any illusions she'd had about Harvardian entertaining were fast disappearing. Not only was the veil torn from her eyes, it was being ripped asunder. Noting to herself the appropriateness of the slightly ecclesiastical references, she deposited her glass and napkin on an empty serving tray, tailed the wine sprinter, scored another glass, and sat down next to a very large potted plant. Faith was not good with plants, either growing them or knowing them, but she'd seen this species before—in dentists' offices. It was a ficus and, unlike the one in her current dentist's office, had retained most of its leaves, although it was sadly in need of dusting, or whatever one did with plants. The ficus provided some welcome cover from which to observe the scene in front of her, and Faith settled back into the straight-backed chair, her spine connecting with a hard little needlepoint cushion. She was just in time. Someone was clinking a glass with a ballpoint. Nothing to eat so far had required utensils, and Faith was pretty sure it was going to stay that way. Talk died down, and after a few stray coughs, the speaker seemed to decide that he had sufficient attention.

"First of all, I'd like to say a hearty hello to all you new folks and hope that you are as happy to be here as we are to have you. It should be an exciting semester. I'll just take a minute to introduce a few of the reasons why I've been down on my knees giving thanks, but first a toast to my good lady wife, who keeps putting these little gatherings together for us term after term with such success."

The man, who Faith knew was some sort of dean—but not *the* dean, whose presence was required elsewhere, Tom had explained on the way over—raised his glass to a tall woman who bore an uncanny resemblance to Dame Edith Sitwell, flowing, slightly theatrical garb included, and everyone said, "Hear, hear." She nodded, her elaborate dark hairdo sliding across her cheeks and moving perilously close to her beaklike nose.

The dean then went on to introduce the new faculty—and on and on. When it was his turn, Tom toasted his colleagues. Her husband had always liked a good party. From the moment they had given their coats to a Harvard student hired from Student Agencies, whose tux was better than the one hanging in Tom's closet, Faith could see Tom had decided this would be a good party. No, make that a great party. She had tried staying with him, but he was in one of his "working the room" moods, which she never was. Maybe being a caterer maxed one out partywise. Maybe it was just this party.

It wasn't long before Faith noticed that there were far more men than women. Sensibly, wives were at home watching *Sex and the City* reruns and eating takeout. Or it might be that celibacy had been either chosen or thrust upon the males present. In a few cases, it wasn't hard to determine the latter to be true. If there were Beautiful People in Cambridge, and Faith was sure there must be, they weren't here. This was a corduroy crowd, both trousers and sports jackets. A number had kept their mufflers around their necks as an accessory, holding on to the dangling ends when making a point. There were also the occasional navy blue blazers and chinos—the preppies—and their mufflers were the woolen ones from Oxbridge—Magdalene or Oriel. Anglophilia was alive and well in Cambridge, the People's Republic of Cambridge apparently finding no contradiction in support for the monarchy. The interior of the house could have been a twin to the one on Brattle, down to the Chinese vases and plethora of books. The Orientals were worn enough to proclaim their worth. It was, however, in a different neighborhood and was brick, not cedar-shingled.

Faith took a stuffed mushroom before she realized what she was doing, but fortunately the wine guy dashed by again, and she was able to wash it down with the same Chardonnay. Light-headed, she decided she'd better not have anything more to drink unless someone came by with edible food. Ah . . . edible food.

She'd been excited that morning, when, in the midst of their unpacking, Tom had slapped his forehead, dashed out of the kitchen, and returned with a stiff envelope.

"I just remembered! We've been invited to a party tonight. This was in my mailbox Monday. I RSVP'd and then completely forgot about it. I'm sorry, honey, but I think you'll enjoy it. Everyone will be there. A great chance for you to finally meet the people I've been boring you silly talking about."

"Nonsense," Faith replied, lying. "You haven't been boring me at all. I'd love to meet them. This sounds like fun. I'm glad I brought some good clothes."

It is always boring to hear about people you don't know, especially ones you assume you'll never meet, unless it's particular juicy dish. Tom's enthusiasm had been running along the lines of "The man is the incarnation of Buber" and "She spent seven years in Somalia working to eradicate famine, and she'll be going back as soon as she gets her degree." All would be changed at the party. She'd have faces to go with names, and the conversations were bound to be interesting with such an intelligent, humanitarian bunch. Faith had dressed with care. The invitation had been a formal one, but it didn't indicate this was a black-tie affair. Faith settled on a black jersey two-piece Krizia number that she could vary by exchanging the black top for a fuchsia one. And she pulled her hair back into a sleek French twist. Her grandmother had taken a diamond brooch she'd always hated and had it made into pairs of earrings for Faith and Hope. Faith had fastened hers before the bathroom mirror, marveling at the way they caught the light, then arrived at the party to discover she was overdressed and the only other thing sparkling was the seltzer water.

But Tom was having fun. She relaxed, took the pillow, which was giving her a backache, put it on the floor, and sipped her wine. There were a few students in attendance, and they were clustered about her husband, listening intently as he discussed the pros and cons of a parish ministry. A very pretty girl was perched on the arm of his chair, and if she leaned any closer, she'd be dipping her long sixties-style straight hair into Tom's drink. Tom was, of course, oblivious. As the girl casually laid her arm across the back of the easy chair, Faith watched the way one watches a boa constrictor approach a mouse.

"Fascinating, isn't it?"

Faith turned to look at the woman who had just spoken. She was an attractive woman, who appeared to be in her mid- to late forties. She was wearing the uniform: a loose-fitting dress, with beads—in this case, nice amber ones—looped around her neck. A brightly colored voluminous silk scarf had been tied there, too, possibly at one time centered on her rather large bosom, but now decidedly dipping toward the left shoulder.

"I'm Natalie Compton. You must be one of the wives," she said dryly. "Your apparent need for protective foliation gives you away."

"I must be and it does," Faith replied. "Faith Fairchild. A pleasure to meet you."

The woman hopped down on the floor and sat cross-legged on the rug. Faith wondered if she was supposed to follow suit. She hoped not, since she'd just had her outfit dry-cleaned.

"I say *fascinating*, because parties always are, don't you think? Everything so serene on the surface, such normalcy. But underneath, seething passions and gut-wrenching anxieties."

"At the Div School?" Faith was amused. Apparently, Natalie was a Danielle Steel fan, or at least spoke like one.

"Of course at the Div School. All that repression, that holier-than-thouness. And I should know."

Faith waited for elucidation, but when none was forthcoming, she asked, "And why is that? Have you been associated with it long?"

"My whole adult life. I teach Greek. So of course I know what's going on."

Wishing for another drink but afraid she might start to giggle uncontrollably as the retort "That's odd, because it's all Greek to me" sprang to her mind, Faith refrained from questioning the oracle further. Natalie switched topics abruptly.

"Has anyone asked you what you do?" She turned a piercing gaze on Faith, as if calling into question a source.

"Not specifically."

"Aha! I thought not. It's Harvard or MIT. Or any of the rest. My husband's at MIT. No, he's not here tonight. We have a pact. I don't make him go to my dreary functions and he doesn't make me go to his. But we did in the early days. You are married, correct?"

Faith was about to remind the professor that she had already guessed that, but she caught herself up.

"Of course you are. To that handsome young man that girl over there is trying to seduce. No, I stopped going to those MIT parties years ago, but it was fun in the beginning. One of the other wives and I would bet each other that no one would ask us what we did or speak to us except to say hello. It got so neither of us wanted to take the bet. The outcome was so predictable. So, what do you do?"

"I'm a caterer."

Natalie was astounded.

"You mean food? You cook?"

Faith definitely wanted some more wine. The glasses had been pretty small, and not filled up at that.

"Yes . . . I cater parties like this one— well, not like this food—and weddings, events, all sorts of things."

"Good God. I can't imagine how you do it. It's all I can do to boil a three-minute egg. A cook. That's certainly a new one."

She struggled to her feet, grabbing the arm of Faith's chair for support. Faith, feeling a bit like Mrs. Bridges and definitely downstairs, was about to extrapolate on the nature of her job—the necessity for business acumen, public-relations skills, human-resources savvy—but before she could get the words out of her mouth, Natalie was moving out of range.

"Best of luck to you, my dear. I have to dash. And do keep an eye on your husband. That little minx is in his class."

The next morning, with only the very slightest of headaches to remind her of the night before, Faith enjoyed the luxury of staying in bed child-free. She got up just in time to shower and dress for church—somebody else's church. Harvard's Memorial Church, with the Reverend Peter Gomes preaching. If Faith was happy, Tom was ecstatic. No dawn sermon revisions, no sweaty palms on the way to the pulpit. Starving after the party the night before, they'd taken home and devoured an entire pizza from Emma's, justly fabled for its thin crust and unusual toppings. Tom, still high from the party—and on very little to drink—had listed all the benefits not having to preach the next morning entailed.

The second day of February, while not as cold as the prior month, was keeping a tight grip on winter, dumping a messy, heavy snowfall in the early hours of the morning. They'd bundled up and trekked to church—Faith looking for signs of a Saint Bernard with a cask of hot coffee—then emerged an hour later under clear skies with a hint of sunshine. They shook Dr. Gomes's hand and walked off through Harvard Yard.

"When I hear someone like him or Carl Scovel or Bill Coffin, I wonder how I dare face a congregation," Tom said.

"Well, you don't have the voice," Faith said. Peter Gomes had the rich, plumy accent of a Victorian Oxford or Cambridge don, although he'd been born in Boston and raised in Plymouth, Massachusetts. When Faith first heard him, she realized what people meant when they said someone could read the phone book and make it sound riveting.

"But you do have the conviction. Please don't belittle what you have accomplished. You've preached some outstanding sermons, and I'm not saying this just because I love you."

In fact, Faith found it hard to concentrate on most people's sermons, and had since childhood. There was so much distraction in church when you knew everyone there, and even when you didn't, it was hard not to speculate. Plus, there were one's own thoughts that kept intruding. Yet, more often than not, she could stay focused on what Tom was saying. She considered this no mean achievement, but she didn't quite know how to tell him without confessing to her woolgathering shortcoming.

He kissed her.

"Very nice of you to say, and I believe you, but still . . ."

His words chilled Faith slightly. Day after day, he seemed so happy to be freed from his prior responsibilities. Was he considering leaving First Parish, leaving a parish appointment? And why did it matter so much to her? Was it Aleford? She couldn't believe she was feeling so torn at the prospect of leaving. Really couldn't believe it. She wouldn't think about it now. She'd think about it when and if it happened.

They passed the bronze statue of John Harvard, firmly seated, gazing across Harvard Yard with the utter composure and total self-confidence the surname implied.

"Did you know it's called 'The Statue of Three Lies'?" Faith asked, waving her hand toward Daniel Chester French's work with its inscription, "John Harvard, Founder, 1638."

"I think I did know this once, but do tell," said Tom, smiling at his wife.

"First of all, it's not him, or do I mean 'he'? Anyway, there were no portraits of John Harvard, so French used a Harvard student—Sherman Hoar from Concord—as his model. Next, the college was founded in 1636, not 1638, and not by John Harvard, as you well know."

"You're becoming quite the Cantabrigian."

"Thanks to you and Bitsy. She and I had coffee at Au Bon Pain on Thursday. I must have forgotten to tell you. Widener Library is named—"

"For poor Harry Elkins Widener, who went down on the *Titanic*. He might be with us, it's said, if he hadn't gone back to his stateroom to retrieve his first edition of Bacon's *Essays*. His mother not only endowed the library but also insisted on the pillars."

They crossed Massachusetts Avenue and headed down Brattle Street.

"It seems everywhere you turn, there's a memorial to somebody. Mem Church, Memorial Hall," Tom mused.

The Fairchilds attended the Christmas Revels in Memorial Hall's Sanders Theater every December and had now started taking the children. Faith loved the gaudy late–Victorian Gothic structure adorned with stained glass, crests, busts, and pennants and crowned by towers, finials, and the odd gargoyle. Twenty-eight marble tablets in the grand interior hall recorded the names of Harvard's Civil War dead—the 136 *Union* dead, that is. The Confederate graduates who fell had not been immortalized. Memorial Church was erected to commemorate those graduates who had died on European soil in World War I.

As they passed by the Longfellow House, Faith was tempted to relate some more of the lore that Bitsy had regaled her with—about Longfellow's wife, Fanny, who was the first woman in the United States to demand anesthesia during childbirth, having noted its effectiveness in dentistry. Later she met a tragic end when her gown caught fire from a spark. Although her husband had rushed into the room upon hearing her cries and rolled her up in a rug, smothering the flames, Fanny Appleton Longfellow, the love of the poet's life, died at age forty-four.

It was all fascinating. Aleford, too, was steeped in history. The parsonage faced the green, where shots had rung out on that "famous day and year." But somehow Aleford lore was all too Millicent Revere McKinley—an Aleford resident who proudly traced her lineage back to the master silversmith himself and wasn't shy about proclaiming it. Aleford was inbred. Cambridge, in contrast, had been through many incarnations, resulting in a spicy mix of Tories, literary lions, academics, pockets of ethnicity like East Cambridge's Portuguese community, and more than a few members of the People's Republic of Cambridge from the sixties. They cohabited quite nicely. Faith decided to save the story of Fanny and the other Longfellow tidbits Bitsy had mentioned for another day. They were almost at the house, and there was still a great deal to do.

By the time the elder Fairchilds dropped their grandchildren off, the house was in order. Faith took Marian on a tour and tried to convince her mother-in-law to stay for supper, but Marian refused.

"It's a grilled cheese and tomato soup night if I ever saw one. You'll do something more elaborate if we stay, and you've already put in enough work for one day. Besides, Dick wants to go to the Union Oyster House."

Faith's father-in-law always wanted to go to the Union Oyster House. The oldest continuously operating restaurant in the United States, it was located in what had been the Haymarket section of Boston, now the Faneuil Square Marketplace. It was where he had proposed to Marian, and aside from the nostalgia, he knew he could count on the restaurant to offer the same meal he'd had that night and still considered the ideal meal out—a dozen Wellfleets on the half shell, clam chowder, and baked scrod.

"A rain check, then?" Faith took her mother-in-law's arm. She'd liked Marian from the first. "Please don't call me Mother Fairchild. It sounds like some kind of dreadful patent medicine," she'd told Faith. And Faith's regard for Marian had increased each year.

"Love to. It will be fun to eat in that dining room. The house is wonderful, Faith, although a bit dark for my taste. You were lucky to get it. I've always wanted to live in Cambridge, and Brattle Street is just about as Cambridge as you can get."

Marian and Dick lived in Norwell, down on the South Shore. They still owned the same house they'd bought when Tom's older sister, Betsey, was born. Generations of Fairchilds had lived in the area, seeing no reason to leave such a perfect spot. Marian, from nearby Little Compton, Rhode Island, was considered an exotic. It was highly unlikely that Marian would ever get her wish to live in Cambridge, even though Dick was virtually retired from the family real estate business. Faith resolved to invite her mother-in-law for a good long visit. Brattle Street it would be.

Now that she'd stowed her own lares and penates away, the house seemed more cheerful, and Faith was starting to feel at home. Marian's approval helped, too.

"It *is* a grande dame of a place, an elegant dame."

"The yard should be lovely in the spring. Unless I miss my guess, that's a star magnolia by the fence."

Marian, a life member of the Evergreens, the local garden club, never missed her guess—especially when it came to horticulture.

After her in-laws left, Faith did indeed make toasted cheese sandwiches, but she offered her family a rich butternut squash soup instead of tomato. One of their favorites, it had a slight hint of nutmeg, perfect for a wintry night (see recipe, page 218). She knew her father-in-law would be having Indian pudding for dessert, but, lacking the time and inclination to whip up a batch—it was one of those New England dishes she'd never acquired a taste for, like boiled dinners—she slid some grapefruit with brown sugar under the broiler. Affirming her belief that young children were not whimsical but totally illogical, Ben would eat the citrus fruit done this way and no other. He'd convinced his sister to follow suit, and unmasking the Easter bunny and Santa were sure to follow, despite Faith's threats: "No television ever again until you have a job and can buy one yourself."

The children went to sleep early—visits to their grandparents were strenuous, what with the multitude of nearby Fairchilds showing up for pickup games of touch football or soccer. Faith was getting into bed herself when she realized that what with one thing and another, she still hadn't mentioned Richard Morgan to Tom. Hadn't mentioned that she'd seen him at the shelter and hadn't mentioned that tomorrow she'd be meeting him at one o'clock in Copley Square.

It took her a long time to fall asleep.

She woke up cold. This house absorbed fuel oil the way dry skin did Oil of Olay; it was almost as bad as the parsonage when it came to drafts. It was cold at night and stayed cold all day. Buried under their down quilt, Faith was inclined to let the alarm keep ringing. Maybe home-schooling Ben, at least for the winter months, wasn't such a bad idea. Then the boy himself appeared and jumped on the bed.

"Come on. Get up, Mom. Pat will be here any minute. Can you make pancakes?"

Faith shoved her feet into her slippers and pulled on a robe.

"Okay, and don't worry. You won't be late." She gave Ben a hug. He was as warm as a potbellied stove. Both children seemed to have inherited whatever gene that was from Tom's side. "Don't wake your sister, and I'll be down in a minute. Do you have everything you need for school?"

Now was the time for revelations of science projects or school play costumes. None were forthcoming, and Faith felt the day was getting off to a good start. She'd made Ben's lunch the night before and there was plenty of time for pancakes. Basking in the glow of a potential nomination for Mother of the Year, she started down the back stairs to the kitchen. It would be warm there, and even warmer once she started cooking.

"Mommmeee!" a small voice cried out.

"Go back to sleep, sweetheart. It's too early."

"But I have a scratchy throat." Amy's voice was filled with tears.

Faith rushed into the room and clamped a hand on her daughter's forehead. No fever. She checked her glands. No swelling. Amy had had a slight sniffle the night before. Postnasal drip. A little decongestant and she should be right as rain and ready for school. It was Monday. She *had* to go to school today of all days. Richard would be waiting. It would be too terrible if he thought Faith was brushing him off because of his homelessness. That was it. She couldn't let him think that. This was why she had to go. If need be, she'd take Amy with her, bundled up. No, that wasn't a good idea. But she *had* to go. What would he think? She could call Pix and drop her off there. But what would she say? I'm leaving my sick child with you to meet my former lover?

Amy swallowed the medicine.

"You close your eyes, and when you wake up again, all the scratchiness will be gone," she told her daughter.

Down in the kitchen, Tom and Ben were standing by the counter, utensils in hand. There had been no way to wedge even a small table into the kitchen, which must have been constructed for servants who ate standing up. They were using the dining room, and Faith had unearthed the table protectors, which she'd then covered with a bright cloth from home.

"I'll only be a minute. Start on your juice, and Tom, honey, push the button on the coffeemaker, will you?"

Then everything fast-forwarded into a typical school-day morning. Pat pulled up, Ben couldn't find his mittens, and Tom realized he had an eight o'clock meeting with one of the TAs.

"You couldn't possibly pick Amy up from school today, could you?" Faith asked Tom's retreating back. "I'm meeting an old friend. . . ." There. It was out. She'd said it and was prepared to elaborate.

"That's nice, dear, but no can do. If you knew what was on my plate today . . ." The door closed behind him.

If only you knew what was on mine, Faith thought.

Amy had reawakened without a trace of scratchiness. Extreme guilt impelled Faith to fetch a flashlight to make sure; then she took Amy to school and signed her up for the optional afternoon session that ended at three o'clock. Amy was thrilled. This was a rare treat.

Back home, Faith cleaned the kitchen, made beds, and went through her wardrobe. She searched through Tom's, too, looking for a sweater or some other article of clothing to give Richard. For herself, she decided on a pair of black wool pants and a gray cowl-necked pullover sweater. Realizing that it might be difficult to explain to Tom where the puce cashmere sweater his sister had given him for Christmas went—he hated it, but he'd have to wear it next time Betsey was around—and aware that handing out one's husband's castoffs wasn't even noblesse oblige, but just plain tacky, Faith left the house for Copley Square empty-handed.

She emerged from the subway and the wind hit her head-on, stinging her face, blowing her hair, and penetrating straight through her shearling coat. She'd rejected her Pillsbury Doughboy down parka, along with the warm hat that invariably produced cap hair. A homeless man, not Richard, stood on the corner with an empty Starbucks cup held out in front of him. His face was red with cold, and a deeper red network of broken capillaries covered it. A shopping cart filled with cans and what appeared to be old quilts was shoved behind the subway entrance.

"Couldja spare some change for a cuppa coffee, lady?"

Faith fumbled in her purse and put a five-dollar bill in the cup. The man's eyes widened and he said, "God bless you, ma'am."

She hoped he would use it to get something to eat, but whatever he did with it, it would take away the cold for a while. Take away the cold and maybe reality, too. Self-medication. She sighed and her breath made a frosty trail in the air. The WALK light flashed on and she crossed the street. Madness in Boston not to wait for it. Drivers here *would* run you down.

Faith loved Copley Square. It was anchored by some of Boston's most noble edifices, their architectural styles spanning the nineteenth and twentieth centuries: The grand Italian Renaissance facade of the Boston Public Library was directly across from H. H. Richardson's Romanesque Trinity Church; then the Gothic New Old South Church diagonally faced the Copley Plaza Hotel—beloved by Faith, since the same architect, Henry J. Hardenbergh, had designed her Plaza: the Plaza Hotel in New York. Rising behind Trinity was I. M. Pei's sixty-story glass marvel—a rhomboid that served as a mirror of Copley Square and the surrounding streets. But today, her mind wasn't on these architectural triumphs—all the more impressive for the fact that not too far down, you hit water. The area wasn't called the Back Bay for nothing. Starting in 1857, carloads of gravel—as many as 3,500 a day during the peak period—were dumped into the mire for over thirty years to create the landfill. Today, her mind was on one thing only: Where was Richard?

The wind had discouraged tourists and natives alike from lingering on the benches along Copley Square. In the good weather, they were filled, and there was even a small farmer's market on one side from May through November. Faith hurried toward Trinity, wondering if Richard had meant in front of the church or inside. She didn't see anyone remotely resembling the man she had seen Friday night. She climbed the stairs and was starting for the heavy carved doors when she heard someone call, "Faith! Faith, over here!"

She had walked right by him. Right by the stylishly dressed, good-looking businessman carrying a Mark Cross briefcase in one hand and a bouquet of roses in the other.

3

He kissed her cheek and she smelled his familiar cologne, remembering she'd never gotten around to asking him what it was—clean, fresh, lemon with something else, something slightly spicy. They were both laughing. He was speaking, but she couldn't take it in. She was completely bewildered. It was like watching a film, a film of your own past. Richard looked older, of course—his face had filled out a bit and there were streaks of gray in his dark hair. But he had changed very little. For an instant, she was Faith Sibley again—young, carefree, single.

"Let's go someplace warmer," Richard said, handing Faith the roses and tucking her arm through his.

Her mind stopped spinning and she agreed, following him to the Copley, where they checked their coats and settled into Copley's Bar, not as elegant as the hotel's Oak Bar with its wood paneling and coffered ceiling, but, unlike that whiff of "Inja" and the Raj, open.

Faith couldn't stop looking at him. Couldn't stop wondering.

"Richard, what's going on? Friday—"

"Friday, I was a bum and today I'm—well, I'm not." He motioned to the bartender. They had the place to themselves.

"Champagne, I think," he told the man. "That's what we were drinking the last time we were together, if memory serves. Perrier-Jouët—is that still your favorite? Oh, and find some hot hors d'oeuvres to go with that, will you? I'm starving," he added, turning to Faith.

"Please, don't keep me in suspense any longer," Faith begged.

"It's simple. I'm working on a book about living on the street, about being completely homeless. Interviewing people wasn't working, so I realized I'd have to join them. It's been an extraordinary experience."

"But why Boston? Why not New York? I assume you're still living there."

"Yes, I am, and that's why I couldn't take the chance of being recognized and having my cover blown. No one knows me here—or so I thought." He grinned, and Faith remembered the way his smile extended all the way to his eyes. Those very blue eyes. Now that they were indoors, she could see his face was lined and the skin around his neck looser, but these signs of age did not diminish his attractiveness. To the contrary: His youthful handsomeness had matured, making him more attractive than ever. Richard had always been someone you'd looked at twice in passing; now besides his appearance, he had an air of someone who had been—and was—living an interesting life.

He took her hand in his. He wasn't wearing a wedding ring. She was. He traced it with his finger.

"Someone's a lucky guy. I hope he appreciates what he's got. Any kids?"

Faith filled him in, the champagne arrived, and before she knew it, it was after two.

She jumped up. "I have to get back to Cambridge and pick my daughter up from school. My son will be coming home soon, too."

"Okay, Cinderella, I'll walk you to the subway," he said, signaling for the check and handing over a Platinum Visa card. He'd told her how he kept a suitcase in a locker at the bus station for switching identities— he traveled down to New York to meet with his agent every so often and see his family. He'd lost both his parents over the years, but his sister still lived in Westchester. When he couldn't get a shower at one of the shelters, he went to the Y. Besides the record cold and the constant search for where the next meal would come from, keeping clean was a huge problem. He'd never take a steaming stream of hot water for granted again.

He helped her on with her coat, then let his hands rest on her shoulders a bit longer, "Letting you get away was the biggest mistake I've ever made. I was a jerk. Maybe I can explain it to you better next time. But there's no excuse for the way I left you."

"It was all a very long time ago, Richard, and you never promised me anything. We were just two people having some fun during the holidays."

"If that's what you think . . ." He paused. "Lunch Thursday? Or let's make it brunch. More time. How about eleven by the church again? We'll figure out where to go from there."

She agreed to meet him, then spent the entire ride back to Cam- bridge trying to figure out where to go from here. She'd been attracted right away to Richard all those years ago. Hearing his voice as he described the plight of the homeless, his hopes for what the book might accomplish, she remembered how much his passion for his work, and, well, just his plain old passion, had captivated her younger self. She'd listened to him today with the same intensity and heard herself sound not uninteresting in return. But that young Faith Sibley was long gone. She was a real grown-up now. A grown-up with a husband and kids.

Ben knew where the key was hidden in the small detached garage, but she didn't want him returning home to an empty house. Pat would probably stay with him until someone arrived, but Faith didn't want that, either, so she got Amy into her snowsuit in record time and arrived home—to find lights on downstairs.

"Ben? Ben, where are you? Ben?" She was sure it was too early, but maybe traffic had been light.

"In here," Tom called. "In the study."

Amy had to pee and Faith was in a race with time. The Rugged Bear outerwear seemed to be clinging to Amy like a pelt. Just in time, the snow pants came off and Amy raced to the small bathroom off the kitchen. Faith went toward the study and collided with a figure coming out. It wasn't Tom. Too short and way too curvy.

"Hello; you must be Mrs. Fairchild. I'm Mindy Connors, one of Dr. Fairchild's students."

Faith recognized her immediately. The last time she'd seen the young lady had been Saturday night, when she'd been draped across the back of Tom's chair.

"I've been trying to convince Reverend Fairchild to be my thesis adviser."

Faith was sure Little Miss Mindy was adept at convincing anyone endowed with a Y chromosome of just about anything, but this time she'd be out of luck.

"I'm sure my husband has told you that he doesn't have the time. This is a temporary appointment, and Harvard is only one of the places he's working just now."

"Oh, yes, but he's going to think about it. I'm sure we'll be able to work something out."

With the confidence killer good looks, brains, and being in one's twenties give, the graduate student let herself out with a slight wave of her hand.

"See you."

Faith shut the door behind her. Firmly. Before she could confront Tom, Ben and Pat arrived at the back door. Ben was carrying a large stuffed bear and Pat had Ben's knapsack.

"It's my turn for Bernie," Ben announced solemnly. It was a sacred trust, not unlike the Olympic torch or Frodo's ring. Faith knew all about

Bernie. The teacher had explained it on Parents Night and had followed that up with a letter detailing exactly what having Bernie as a houseguest for the week entailed. It would have been easier and much less revealing to have a member of the CIA move in, especially these days, preoccupied as the agency was in turf wars with the FBI. Essentially, Ben was to write up an account each night of what Bernie had observed of Fairchild family life, taking Bernie along during any afterschool and weekend activities for a bear's-eye view. Faith knew families who planned whole outings around the bear, treating him to the IMAX at the Museum of Science and Young People's concerts at the Longy School of Music. One family managed to squeeze in an educational trip to New York City, complete with a visit to the Statue of Liberty. So far, Faith's plans for the weekend included grocery shopping and buying new boots for Amy—it was getting to be too humiliating tying Baggies around her daughter's feet to keep her socks dry. She could see now that she'd have to throw in something else, like building a cyclotron or, failing that, sculpting a model of the Taj Mahal out of soap. She thanked Pat profusely and, on impulse, gave her the roses that were still wrapped and lying on the counter. Pat had indeed refused any payment for her taxi service, insisting she loved doing it. This would mean flowers and candy—Pat was partial to Burdick's chocolates—from time to time. Explaining to her husband where the roses had come from was not an issue at all, not why she was giving them away, Faith told herself as Pat oohed and aahed at Winston's exquisite blooms.

Tom had appeared to say hello to Pat. She was sensible enough not to mention First Parish, and he didn't ask. He greeted her warmly, but with the air of an addressee unknown.

Faith steered the kids upstairs to the room she'd deemed the playroom and, for Bernie's sake, settled them in front of a tape of Bill Nye The Science Guy. Then she went back downstairs to Tom.

"What on earth can you be thinking of?" She was having trouble keeping her voice down.

Tom looked up from his laptop.

"What do you mean?"

"Mandy, Mindy, Missy . . . whoever she is. You. Alone in the house with her. Don't you read the papers?"

Tom leaned back in his chair. He loved this room. The beautiful big desk, the books, this comfy chair.

"I think you're overreacting, Faith. Miss Connors is a graduate student, an adult. She missed my office hours and dropped by to see whether I'd agree to act as her thesis adviser. She was on her way to her aunt's house farther down Brattle."

"Her aunt, my ass," Faith said. "Did she tell you the address?"

"Of course not, and I wouldn't have asked her. It wasn't an inquisition. And what you're suggesting is absurd."

"Tom, I saw her at the party Saturday night. She was almost in your lap. Natalie thought it was inappropriate, too."

"Natalie? Natalie Compton, the Greek professor?"

"Yes, the professor of Greek." Faith was feeling nitpicky.

"Ralph tells me she's the biggest gossip in town. I wouldn't put any stock in what she said."

"Forget Natalie. I saw what was going on myself. You have to be careful, Tom. I know this type of girl. The moment you give her a bad grade or tell her her thesis is a pile of *merde,* she'll yell sexual harassment so loudly, you'll be lucky to get a job ironing collars, let alone wearing one again."

Her husband squirmed uneasily. "You really think that's what she's after. Me, I mean?"

Faith groaned. Men were so dense. Tom had his First Parish groupies: "Oh, let me get Reverend Fairchild's coffee." "No, it's no trouble, and I was here first." This an actual conversation, overheard by Faith as two women grappled over a cup by the coffee urn. They all believed that they were the women truly destined by God to be Tom's handmaidens, especially as Faith was obviously woefully inadequate. It would be funny were it not so irritating. They'd drop off books, preserves, soup, and knitted mufflers at the parsonage, and Tom, unfailingly polite, would offer sincere thanks, which only added fuel to the fire.

"Yes, you, you big lug." Faith came around to his side of the desk and kissed him. She considered the subject closed. "Garlic chicken, roast potatoes, and new asparagus from California sound good to you for dinner?"

"Yum." Tom ran his hand through his wife's thick hair. "Garlic with the asparagus, too?"

"Okay, since we all know each other. I'll roast it in the oven. You know—with olive oil, high heat on a baking sheet. The kids like it that way."

"Little gourmands."

"Thank goodness." Any vegetable that had come Tom's way in childhood had been courtesy of Birdseye, unless his father had decided to plant tomatoes in the backyard that summer.

Faith started out the door toward the kitchen. She'd tell Tom all about Richard later, when the kids were in bed. The fireplace in the living room was large enough to roast an ox and the log carrier was full. She'd been wanting to try it out, sitting in front of the flames with some cognac, since they'd arrived. Tonight was the night.

"But Faith . . ."

"Yes, love?"

"I still think you're totally wrong. Miss Connors is a serious biblical scholar and I'd learn a great deal acting as her adviser, besides being of some help to her. I'm going to accept."

"Fine. I'll call you when dinner is ready," Faith said. She pressed her lips together to keep the words *And don't say I didn't warn you* from springing out.

Tonight wasn't going to be the night after all.

———

Y ou seem different."

"What do you mean?"

Faith and her assistant, Niki Constantine, were packing the food for a small luncheon Have Faith was catering. Pix, who kept the books for the firm, was in the corner with the ledger and her calculator. It was Niki who'd made the statement and Faith who'd countered with the question.

"Preoccupied. Moody. Up one minute, down the next. You've been this way since you moved into town. What's going on?"

Pix got up and joined them, but she didn't say anything.

"I don't know. Maybe I'm as bad at transitions as Amy. You know, leaving block corner for story circle is kind of like leaving Aleford for Cambridge."

Faith was attempting a lighthearted tone, but it was hard. Both women were looking at her with a mixture of concern and skepticism on their faces.

It had been over a week since she'd been at the Copley with Richard, and they had met twice more. The second time, he'd been in his shelter clothes and they'd sat drinking coffee in a McDonald's on Tremont Street, Richard blending right in. He'd told her that he'd been scooped on the big book he'd been working on. The one he'd been sure would head straight for the best-seller list. The one that was just a little too similar to the book that came out just as he was getting ready to have his agent start sending his around—came out, jumped to the top of the list, and, what was worse, remained there for literally years.

"I was so depressed, not just at having lost the chance for fame and fortune"—he smiled wryly—"but at expending all that effort. I took off and bummed around South America for a while, picking up work as a Reuters stringer here and there. It's pretty easy to lose yourself *and* track of time in paradise. You have to go to Brazil, Faith—and Peru and—"

She had been losing track of the time again—it seemed to be becoming a habit—listening to him talk about the places he'd been and people he'd met, imagining herself there.

When he had returned to New York, many of his connections had moved on—up or down—as happens in the revolving-door world of publishing. He'd decided to try another book. This time, he went out to Montana to work, taking a job with a newspaper there.

"Let's just say I'm no Jack London. The book fizzled, but I liked the open spaces."

He'd come back and try New York for a while, get itchy feet, and then take off again.

"I needed an anchor," he'd told her. "And unfortunately in a witless moment, I'd thrown her overboard without holding on to the end of the chain."

He'd been wearing a suit when they'd met the day before and had whisked her off for a perfect lunch at Radius, one of the hottest restaurant in town. Faith could almost imagine herself back in the city. Back in the city with Richard.

"Okay. I guess I do have something on my mind. It's Tom," she told Niki and Pix. Well, it's true, she said to herself. He *was* on her mind, and if her words weren't followed by a string of toads, it was because she really wasn't lying. She just wasn't telling the whole truth.

"Tom?" Pix sounded alarmed. The Millers lived next door to the Fairchilds and were members of First Parish and their best friends. The two families also both had cottages on Sanpere Island in Penobscot Bay, off the coast of Maine.

First, Faith told them about Mindy Connors, divine graduate student.

"I can see her now. I always hated girls like that," Niki said. "Want me to have a chat with her? Put her in the picture?" Niki came from a large, totally respectable Greek family in Watertown, but she liked to play the bad girl and enjoyed giving the impression that she'd been raised by a Greco-Soprano family.

"No, not yet anyway. I'm hoping Tom will come to his senses. He did tell me he wouldn't have her to the house anymore."

"I don't know whether that's good or bad," Niki commented reflectively.

"Sorry, I can't help it, but it reminds me of that old joke." Pix giggled. "You know the one where the sexy female student comes into her professor's office, sits down, hikes up her skirt, and says, 'I'll do anything to get an *A* in your course, Professor. *Anything.*' 'Anything?' he says. 'Yes, *anything.*' He gets up from behind his desk, lowers the blinds, and locks the door. Then he tells her, 'Take off all your clothes and lie down on the floor.' She obliges. He kneels next to her and whispers in her ear, 'Study.'"

When they'd finished laughing, Faith said, "It isn't just Mindy, although I will certainly tell Tom the joke. It may help put things into perspective. It's that I can't figure out what's going on with him. He's so happy."

"Oh, too bad. Very tragic," Niki said. Pix responded differently. She was married; Niki—to her mother's dismay—wasn't.

"You're not sure whether he's happy, as in 'I'm having a kind of vacation here in Cambridge,' or happy because 'I'm never going back to Aleford or a parish ministry again.'"

"I know it sounds absurd after all the time I spend complaining about the way living in the parsonage is like living in a fishbowl and that Aleford becomes Stepford with a mere swap of letters. Being married to a member of the clergy is like being married to someone in the armed services or someone climbing corporate ladders. You know you're going to be moving. It comes with the territory. My family was an exception, and not moving was the deal my mother struck when they got married."

Faith's mother, Jane, had made it very clear to the newly ordained minister who came to be interviewed by her father—a deacon—for the position of assistant minister and stayed to court the charming young woman who answered the door that she had no intention of living in a parsonage or of moving out of New York City. Jane's family had deep roots in Manhattan, stretching out from a tree heavily laden with Schuylers and Stuyvesants. To hear Jane, a real estate attorney, tell it, her forebears had been the ones who urged the 1626 deal: "Twenty-four dollars' worth of blankets may seem like a lot, especially when we throw in the beads, but amortize it over two hundred, three hundred years, say, and it's a steal. Sure it's an island, but bridges are a helluva lot easier than dikes. You put them up and they stay there. Nobody has to stand there with a finger plugging up a hole." Hence, the Upper East Side duplex where Faith had grown up. When it was her turn to marry, she didn't have the option or leverage. Tom was already installed in First Parish when he and Faith had met; plus, he was most definitely of the "It's a nice place to visit, but . . ." school when it came to the Big Apple. He still seemed to find it hard to believe that his in-laws had actually raised a family there. "Where did you play?" was one of the first questions he'd asked his future wife, and he appeared unconvinced by her rhapsodic descriptions of the glorious opportunities presented by Central Park, the museums, and every ethnic neighborhood under the sun.

"Being reluctant to leave Aleford doesn't sound absurd—and don't worry, we won't cast it up to you next time you're crazed by Millicent or the lack of selection in the produce aisle at the Shop and Save," Pix said. "You've built a life here—friends, your business—and the kids are happy in school."

"Plus, you go down to the city for a fix whenever you can," Niki chimed in. "Are you sure you're not just depressed because Balducci's closed?"

"You had to remind me," Faith said, slumping dramatically onto the steel table. She *was* depressed about the landmark food store's closing. The original store had opened in 1946, and when it outgrew that space, it moved to the Avenue of the Americas between Ninth and Tenth in 1970. Aside from the fantastic fruit, vegetables, meats, fish, cheeses—you name it—there would be no more of their wonderful homemade pastas. And no more Mama Balducci's Corner: no more peppers stuffed with spinach, ricotta, and pignoli, no more calzone Barese with leeks, sweet onions, golden raisins, anchovies, and black olives. No more Balducci's! It was like losing a friend.

"What has Tom been saying?" Pix persisted. "He told the vestry he'd be back at the end of May."

"He hasn't been saying anything. That's one of the problems. Whenever I bring up future plans or even try to talk to him about what's going on now, what he's feeling, he avoids the issue. That's when I get two minutes with him. Between his teaching and his work with the homeless, we barely see him. Thank goodness I read Bernie's diary before Ben handed it in. I made him take out Bernie's remark that 'The Fairchild children don't see much of their father, who is not home often.'"

Pix and Niki knew all about Bernie.

"Bears never know where to draw the line. They are soooo judgmental," Niki said.

Faith had also edited out Bernie's biased description of Ben's role in an argument with his mother over whether a third-grader was old enough to go to Newbury Comics in Harvard Square alone. Bernie's line about "Ben's mother's face looked like a squished tomato" had really stung.

Pix put an arm around Faith's shoulder. "Tom is just enjoying the change. He's always said he's committed to a parish ministry. We know he'll be back in May. He would never break his word."

"It sounds like you just have to hang in there, sweetie," Niki said with all the nonchalance of someone whose only responsibilities were rent, car payments, and fines for overdue DVDs. "Your best bet is to wake Tom up in the middle of the night and put it to him straight. He'll be so hot to go back to sleep, or so hot not to, that you're bound to get an answer."

Faith thought this was a pretty good idea and said so. As they packed the rest of the things, she thought about moving. Although she had made changes to the parsonage since her arrival there as a new bride, she was always aware that it didn't belong to them. Maine was their real house, small as it was. There, she knew the marks she made on the wall with the kids' heights would stay and not disappear under a new coat of paint or be scrubbed off by someone else's hands. If Tom wanted to leave Aleford, so be it. Whatever Tom wanted. She hoped it would be what she wanted, too. And exactly what was that these days?

The luncheon they were catering was one of the Uppity Women's Club's. The members were a small group of Aleford women in their forties. The club had grown out of a luncheon given by one of them, who thought the others ought to know one another. Professional women, stay-at-home moms, and all sorts of variations, the Uppities now met every other month to "keep ourselves sane," as one of them had told Faith the first time Have Faith catered. For today, Faith had tried to duplicate the onion tart appetizer she'd had before Christmas at Sandrine's with Pix and Bitsy. She thought she'd succeeded, caramelizing the onions, using a small amount of a strongly smoked bacon, so it wouldn't overwhelm the dish, and folding it all into a creamy sauce before pouring it into the crust (see recipe on pages 219–220). To warm everyone up on arrival, there would be *vin chaud*, with spiced pecans and cheese straws to nibble on. The tart was the main course, accompanied by a pear, endive, and frisée salad. One of the Uppity Women was always avoiding carbs or trying some other diet, so Faith stayed away from pastas and sandwiches. She was taking along some lentil soup in case the tart was rejected because of the crust or cream. Dessert was something else, never turned down—a just this oncer—and it had to be chocolate. She was giving them thick, moist old-fashioned brownies with buttermilk sorbet to undercut the sweetness. Faith, Niki, and Pix packed everything into insulated bags and loaded the van. It was Faith's gig today, although Niki got such a kick out of the group and vice versa that she was an ex officio member. However, she needed to stay behind and prepare for a dessert buffet they were catering; pastry was her forte.

The Uppities liked to use their own dishes and cutlery, as well as supplying the wine. All Faith had to do was serve through dessert, load up the dishwasher, and leave them lingering over their coffee. She got into the driver's seat and pulled away, waving just as she turned out of the drive.

"So what is it she isn't telling us?" Niki asked Pix.

"Beats me," Pix said.

The Uppities were as much fun as usual, and they insisted Faith have a glass of wine with them as they ate. They'd been through children and spouses and were listing maxims to hand down to the next generation of women.

"You'll never find a great-looking pair of shoes that won't kill your feet," Sandra Katz, today's hostess, said.

"Amen—and while we're on the subject of appearance, how about this? 'You will never be able to blow-dry your hair the way your stylist does without a full course at whatever's Academy of Beauty.'"

"But of course," joked a tall woman with graying hair. "We don't want to depress them too much. Here's one: 'There will always be someone on the beach with more cellulite than you have.'"

"That's assuming you go to the beach. I haven't appeared in a bathing suit in public for years!" said a short, trim woman, laughing.

"Elaine, that's crazy! You have a great figure! You've been looking at those CK ads again," Sandra protested.

"I think we need a field trip to the beach as soon as it's warm enough. We'll stand in the middle of Wingaersheek in our suits and shout, 'We're dimpled and we're here!'" suggested another woman.

It's sad, Faith thought. This was an attractive group of women—they worked out, ate right for the most part, had good haircuts, even by Faith's standards—and still they were insecure about their bodies. Maybe that should be added to the list of maxims: "No matter how great you look, you'll always think something's wrong—nose too big, hips, tummy. . . ."

The group had drifted on to more serious maxims.

"You'll never be finished raising your children," one offered.

"Or your husband," said Sandra, laughing.

"Why, in the vernacular, is it that men are always boys, but women are only girls after their teens?"

"What's our position on adultery? Pro or con?" asked Martha or Mary. Faith could never remember which woman was which.

"Hmm," Sandra mused. "That's tough. You've been quiet, Faith. Any thoughts?"

Yes! Faith thought immediately. First, why ask me? Then, is it adultery if you've already slept together, say a long time ago? Wouldn't it be more like being really, really good friends? But she said, "Not at the moment. What about you guys?"

"Too hurtful to be worth it. I mean, sex is sex," the short woman said.

"Maybe that's the point," Mary or Martha said. Faith was beginning to think the woman had a hidden agenda. Did she want permission from the group?

"Okay," Sandra said. "This is just me, but I think Cindy's right. Sex *is* just sex. If you're drawn into an adulterous relationship, it means something is wrong with your marriage and it's not just the sex, or maybe it is, but that's a symptom. We all lust in our hearts, just like Jimmy Carter. You might fantasize about Antonio Banderas, Sean Connery, the cute guy behind the counter at the deli, but having an affair is something else. It's a weapon."

"What about a fling? Men have them all the time," protested Mary or Martha.

"I'm talking about men, too," Sandra answered sharply. "The rules are the same for all of us. Am I sounding too preachy?"

Everyone laughed.

"You always sound preachy. That's why we love you. But in this case, I agree. Having an affair is saying 'You're not enough,' and that's too painful." Cindy made a face. "It happens, people stay together, but I'd imagine it would always be there like a particularly unwanted houseguest. Besides, one man is enough to have to deal with, in my opinion."

"Anyone want some brownies?" Faith asked, leaving her wine untouched. Her mind was muddled enough.

As she drove down Route 2 toward Cambridge from Aleford after leaving the Uppities, the toast one of them had made at the end of their conversation on cheating stuck in Faith's mind: "May you kiss whom you please and please whom you kiss, but love only the one whose lips you would miss." They'd toasted Faith and her food, too.

Faith felt lousy. Why hadn't she told Pix and Niki that she'd met someone she used to date and they had gotten together to talk over old times? Niki would laugh and kid her. Pix would—well, Pix wouldn't laugh and kid her. She might say something like, "Do you know what you're doing?" Maybe not in those exact words, but that's what she would mean. Faith hadn't bothered to turn the radio on. Her own thoughts were noise enough. Despite the Uppity Women's table talk, the thought foremost in her mind was that she was driving five miles over the speed limit—not to pick up her daughter at nursery school, but to be home when Richard called.

When they'd parted the day before, he'd said he was trying to find someone he'd met at the Arlington Street Church's Friday Supper when he'd first arrived in Boston. It was a fluke that he had been at Oak Street House. He was in the neighborhood and decided to go in. Usually on Fridays, he went to Arlington Street because he liked the meat loaf. The man he'd met there was, like Richard, a Harvard graduate. He'd had a house in Dover with plenty of land for his horses, plus a summer place on the Vineyard. Wife, kids, Mercedes. Then his wife left him for another man, his business went down the tubes, and his kids didn't want to know him, pretty much in that order. He told Richard he'd been on the streets for five years and was happier than he'd ever been. Richard wanted to feature him in the book, find out why he was so happy. Or at least happier. He wasn't an alcoholic, at least so far as Richard could tell, and he did seem at peace. Everyone called him "the Monk," since he seemed so calm and serene—plus, he knew something about everything. "Most of the people I've met have nicknames like this—some are ones other people have attached to them; some they've attached to themselves," Richard had told her. "And they all fit. This guy really does seem as if he'd be right at home in a Benedictine order or a Buddhist monastery. People tell him things. He knows all the secrets of the street."

The Monk had disappeared, as they all did for stretches of time, but recently someone had told Richard the man was living under the Southeast Expressway. Richard was planning to check it out, so he didn't know when he'd be able to see Faith. They'd arranged for him to call if he could today when she got home with Amy.

She turned down Brattle Street from Fresh Pond Parkway, driving past houses that charted the architectural history of the city. They ranged from Colonial to Federalist to Arts and Crafts Victorian, with one renegade Bauhaus thrown in for good measure. With the leaves off the trees, the houses stood proud, doors closed, brass hardware gleaming, knowing full well that the passing motorists were just that. She was passing through, too, Faith realized, and maybe that's why the time with Richard was something she was still keeping just for herself. It reinforced her outsider status. Yet it was more than that, much more.

It was lovely to sit and talk with him, having conversations that did not touch on how high they should set the thermostat, whether Ben would need braces, how many pounds of shrimp to order for the Porter wedding, or whose turn it was to take Amy to the bathroom in the middle of the night. Faith loved her husband, her children, and her work. But Richard noticed what she was wearing, sought her opinions—and listened to them. He made her feel smarter, wittier, and sexier than she'd felt in a very long time. And that, she told herself as she dashed into the kitchen to pick up the phone on the first ring, was why she didn't want to share him with anybody—not her best friends, not her husband. She'd stepped out of the frame and she wanted to stay there for a while with this very fascinating and, yes, as Hope put it, "hunky" guy. The eighties had been years of "Meism" and she was reverting.

"Hello," she said, slightly out of breath.

"Hello, you—is this a bad time?"

"No, not at all. I just got back from work."

"Work. That seems a long time ago. I mean putting on a suit, going to an office work."

"*You* never did that kind of work," Faith teased him. When she'd dated him, he'd owned a tuxedo and two sports jackets, no suits.

"You know what I mean."

"Yes."

There was a pause and they both started talking at once.

"Did you—?" Faith said as Richard asked, "Can you—?"

They laughed. Faith was aware it was all pretty junior high, but she didn't care.

"Did you find the Monk?"

"Not yet, but I'm heading over there now. If he's there, I'll be free Thursday and Friday. I'm planning to hang out with him for the next day or so."

"School vacation starts Friday afternoon. My kids will be home next week," Faith said, then realized how it sounded. "I mean, I'll be tied up with their friends. I like the break from the routine. It gives all of us some downtime." She was babbling.

Richard had extremely well-developed antennae. "You're a terrific mom. I don't know anyone who devotes herself to her kids the way you do. And actually, it works out, because I'm going down to the city next week to talk over what I have so far with my agent, see my sister and her kids—they're teenagers now, if you can believe it."

Faith remembered going to F.A.O. Schwarz and ordering Christmas gifts for his niece and nephew, toddlers at the time. He'd had them wrapped and sent so that he wouldn't have to carry the bulky ride-on toy and huge panda on the train Christmas Day.

"It goes so fast," Faith said, biting her tongue at her lack of originality.

"Let's hope it does. The time until, say, Friday, that is."

It wasn't all that original, either, but it worked for her.

"Friday will be fine. Same place?"

"Same place."

It wasn't until she was helping Amy out of the snowsuit she'd helped her into ten minutes earlier at school that Faith remembered Friday was Valentine's Day.

There comes a time in the course of every vacation week when both the vacationees and the vacation coordinator hit bottom. Mindful of the separation from their Aleford friends the move had meant, Faith had spent most of the week ferrying children to and fro, mostly fro. She'd taken children to the Children's Museum, The Museum of Science, the New England Aquarium, and the Computer Museum. Ben had friends sleep over twice; Amy once. In a fit of madness, Faith had agreed to take care of the third-grade class pet, a particularly repellent longhaired guinea pig that had a problem with flatulence.

It was Thursday afternoon, too cold to send the children out to play, and if it hadn't been, what would they have done? Pick up branches and twigs—all the Cambridge yard offered for active play at the moment. Tom was going to be late—again. Harvard wasn't on vacation. They'd spent the morning baking bread in animal shapes and a kind of bar cookie that Ben had instantly dubbed "Harvard Squares" (see recipe on page 222). Wondering if Ben's future would take him to Madison Avenue, Faith immediately decided to adopt the name and feature the cookies at Have Faith's next dessert buffet. The house smelled wonderful, and she was able to convince both children to take "rests," not naps after lunch. Then the minutes began to drag. Could it only be two o'clock?

"You know what I feel like doing?" she announced to her children, who even at their tender age could identify false bravado when they heard it.

"No, what?" Ben said with the world-weary look of an absinthe addict.

"Having a quiet afternoon up in the playroom watching our favorite tapes, like *The Lion, the Witch, and the Wardrobe*. We haven't seen that in awhile."

"Amy gets too scared, Mom, remember? The White Witch."

This was true, but their choice was limited by the fact that Ben and his friends had watched all the age-appropriate ones, leaving only "baby stuff" and Narnia.

"I tell you what, chickadee, if it gets scary, you tell me and we'll turn it off."

Amy looked dubious. She'd watched *The Snowman* over the holidays on Faith's recommendation and now sobbed every time she saw one: "It's going to melt and die!"

"I'll make some popcorn and it will be just like going to the movies."

This turned the tide, and Amy ran upstairs to claim what she swore was the comfier of the two identical beanbag chairs.

Lucy had just met Mr. Tumnus when the phone rang. Tom was in class, and Faith had talked to both Pix and Niki that morning, so who could it be? Why do I always do this? Faith asked herself as she went to answer it. I'll know as soon as I pick up the receiver, but I always speculate. Which brought her to Richard. He wouldn't be calling from New York. Or would he? The prospect quickened her steps.

The call was from New York, but it wasn't Richard Morgan.

"Fay?"

It was her sister, Hope.

"Hi, what's up?"

Hope never called without a reason. Not with her schedule.

"I have to be in Boston next week and I thought we could have lunch."

"I'd love to see you. Of course we can have lunch. You might want to come here. The house is definitely worth seeing, although a little cheerier in the spring, I suspect."

"I was actually thinking the Ritz. That's where I'll be, and you're all the way in Cambridge."

Hope came to Boston a couple of times a year for business. Cambridge was to Boston as Queens was to Manhattan; similarly, Aleford was to the "home of the bean and the cod" as New Jersey was to New York City—totally off the map. Hope had visited the parsonage for an overnight shortly after each child was born and had considered her on-site obligations as an aunt met. Since then, when she came north, Faith met her sister in town at the Ritz or the Four Seasons, an expense account being what it is. Hope saw the kids when Faith took them home for a visit, and she spoiled them wonderfully.

"The Ritz is fine." As Faith well knew. That's where she'd gone with Richard last Friday. He'd given her a bracelet that looked like candy hearts, with all those funny mottoes, "I Go 4 U" and "Hep Cat." Tom had given her a dozen red roses, just as he had last year and the year before.

"You haven't been there since they've reopened," Faith said to her sister. "It looks beautiful. They didn't try to change it too much, just polished it up a bit. Like having your diamond rings cleaned."

Faith had a perfectly respectable engagement ring from Tom, but Hope had a rock from her longtime beau, Quentin, that made putting on gloves difficult.

"Funny you should mention rings. . . ." Hope didn't finish whatever she had been planning to say.

Faith waited patiently, then, after some moments of dead air, said, "Why is it funny I should mention rings?"

"Oh, forget I said anything. It's not important. I'll tell you all about it on Tuesday. Is Tuesday okay?"

"Tuesday's okay, but don't you dare hang up without telling me what's going on. I know you."

Hope always finished her sentences. Something was definitely up.

"Oh pooh, you're spoiling the surprise. I was going to tell you when I saw you in person, but now I can't. I'm getting married."

Faith shrieked. She hoped she hadn't frightened the children, but apparently Aslan had them in hand.

"That's fabulous! I'm so happy for you. I assume it's Quentin."

"Oh course it's Quentin. Who else?"

"You've been going steady since Truman beat Dewey or there-abouts, so I didn't think it was anyone else, but you never know. Some Michael Douglas look-alike trader might have swept you off your little Guccis."

Hope made a noise into the phone; it sounded like "paah." "Fay darling, I would never date a trader, let alone marry one. I would have thought you'd know that."

Quentin was a corporate lawyer.

Hope continued. "So now you know, but act surprised when I tell you on Tuesday."

"I promise. What did the parents say? They must be over the moon."

After another sound that wasn't a "paah," but a heavy sigh, Hope said, "I haven't told them yet, and don't you dare breathe a word to them. Don't even talk to them about anything else. You'll give it away; you won't be able to help it."

Faith was puzzled, as this was virtually a first where Hope was concerned. Her sister was an open book, and not only to Faith. She probably kept her cards close to her chest when it came to business, but emotionally she laid them all out on the table.

"Why—"

"I've got to take this call. I'll see you Tuesday. Noon. The Ritz. Love you."

"Love you, too."

Faith hung up the phone and went back to the playroom. The White Witch was plying Edmund with Turkish delight, but Amy wasn't frightened. She wasn't frightened, because she wasn't there. Neither was Ben. Faith walked out into the hall.

"Ben, Amy, where are you?"

There was no answer. It was getting darker outside now and Faith turned on the switch to light the hall sconces.

"Kids, where are you? Answer me this minute."

She quickly checked their rooms, which were empty. She was about to head downstairs, when she heard Ben call, "We're up here."

"Up here" was the top floor, where the servants' quarters and attic were. It was strictly off-limits to the kids, as they'd been told numerous times. She went up the back staircase, angry words issuing from her lips, "How many times, have I told you, Benjamin and Amy Elisabeth, that you are not to be here!"

"In here, Mommy, in here," Amy shouted joyfully. "We think we've found Narnia!"

They were in the old nursery, and as Faith approached it, she felt the same prickle of fear that she had the last time—the only time—she'd been in the room.

"Come out right now," she said from the doorway.

"Mom, really, it's just like Narnia. I know we should have waited for you, but you were taking so long. See, there's a wardrobe. I remembered it while we were watching the movie."

Ben looked so earnest, so contrite, and, above all, so excited that Faith didn't have the heart to scold him. The big armoire did look like the one in C. S. Lewis's tale. The kids had opened the doors and found coats hanging in it—but not fur coats. These were heavy woolen overcoats, a tan Burberry, and several parkas.

Ben had it all figured out. "Every country must have different coats. Because of the different climates, right? And fashions? Right? So these must be the Cambridge, Massachusetts, USA ones."

Before she could stop him, he climbed in and pushed the garments aside. Amy prepared to follow.

Faith ran across the room. She didn't want them in the room, and she especially didn't want them in the old armoire. She'd have to figure out a way to lock the nursery door. There were a bunch of keys in one of the drawers in the butler's pantry. She'd go through them, and if none of them fit, she'd get a locksmith.

Trying to keep her voice calm, she said, "I know it looks like the same one, but there's only one wardrobe, and it's far across the ocean, in England." She pulled Amy gently away and reached in for Ben, who was tapping on the back of the piece of furniture with the persistence of a true believer.

"But you can get into Narnia many ways, Mom," he said, his voice muffled by the coats.

"This isn't one of them," Faith said firmly, and grabbed him. He was going to reek of mothballs unless she got him into a tub immediately.

"I've found something! I've found something! There's a crack in the wardrobe!"

Faith put her other hand in and tugged harder. The balance of power was shifting faster than she'd envisioned. It was hard to budge him, and he was only eight. What would it be like in a few years, or even next year?

"Wait a minute, will you!" Ben was seriously annoyed, and she didn't blame him. Thanks to her, there would be no fantastic adventures, no crown or throne.

"Ben, I'm sorry, but you have to come out of there. It really isn't one of the ways to Narnia," Faith pleaded.

Thankfully, he began to back out. She loosened her grip and he stepped onto the floor.

"It may not be the way in, but I found a secret book. It was stuck at the bottom of the crack, pushed up against the wall."

He was holding a small leather-bound book. There were no words on the cover. It was blue.

"Please give the book to me. It isn't ours. Daddy will save it for Dr. Robinson, the man who owns the house, and give it to him when he comes back. It belongs to him. He must have lost it." She reached out her hand, but Ben had opened the book and was looking inside.

"I don't think so, unless he's really old. It's got to be an antique. Maybe a hundred years old. Look at this writing."

"Ben!"

Benjamin Fairchild knew that tone of voice and he handed the book over immediately.

Schools didn't teach this kind of penmanship anymore. The words flowed across the page in perfect precision, the dark ink unfaded. A diary, but there was no name or address on the inside cover. The book wasn't a hundred years old, but it was old. The first entry was dated January 12, 1946. Faith's eyes strayed to the words below:

"If I can't get away from him, I may have to kill myself."

4

He's locked me in again until he comes back from his office, but I hid you, little diary, tucked into the waistband of my skirt, under my sweater. That sunny day last summer when I was buying my trousseau in Bangor, I had the sudden thought that I'd keep an account of the happiness of my first year of marriage to read over in old age and perhaps pass down to my children and grandchildren. I was ordering writing paper with my new name and address and selected the prettiest diary from a stack nearby. The happiness stopped early—on our wedding night—and I have not had the heart to make a single entry, but now without a soul to talk to, I must write. What is happening is real, and even an imaginary listener gives me some comfort. There are times, especially in the middle of the night when he reaches for me and there is no difference between the nightmare I've been dreaming and the one to which I awake, that I long for death. But this will only come with my escape to a better place with the Lord.

I do not mind these hours up here in the nursery, which he has stripped of anything that might help the hours pass. It is sheer heaven simply to be away from him, and it is the only time I feel safe. The *shelves that must have held toys are bare and dusty. There is no crib or small bed, only one straight chair. A faded strip of circus animals marches around the top of the walls, so I know what the room once was. I wonder if it was his nursery. I know so little about him. Before we were married, I used to tell him all about my own life, but he said almost nothing about his own. I took that as typical male shyness. Women talk so much more about themselves. All I learned was that his parents were dead and he had no brothers or sisters. "The past is often tedious to contemplate," he told me. "We need to think of our future, which I promise you will not be so." My blood chills when I remember these words, which I took to mean something so different from what has happened. But how could I have thought otherwise as we sat and he held my small hand in his large one, tracing my fingers with one of his, as if to measure them?*

There is a long window seat below the front windows, and it is here I sit, looking out at the tall pine directly in front of me and watching the life of Brattle Street beyond. There is an old woman who walks by precisely at ten o'clock, returning a half hour later with a shopping bag. She is quite energetic. I speculate on what is in her sack—what kinds of food, perhaps a newspaper? Then there are mothers rushing to keep up with their children, holding the little ones by the hand—there must be a school nearby. I have tried repeatedly to open a window, pounding on the glass with all my strength, but the leaded panes do not give way, leaving only bruises on my palms. He confiscated all my new pretty high heels, which I could have used to break the glass, and has left me only slippers to wear. I finally realized the windows are nailed securely shut from the outside. Yet even if I could attract the attention of one of the passersby, what would they do? Quicken their footsteps and tell their children not to look up, assuming I was some kind of maniac? No, help will not come from the sidewalk.

How could I have been so blind? To think I was the envy of all the girls at the inn. Almost any one of them would have changed places with me in a minute, especially when they saw the ring he gave me. Only Josephine tried to warn me.

She always was one to speak her mind. "He's a lot older than you. Have you thought about that? He may look good now, but in twenty years, when he's sixty-one and you're forty-one, it could be a different story. You'll have kids to take care of along the way and somebody who might be as much work as another one." If only he were like another child! I was used to Pa, and after Ma died, that took a lot, but I never knew a man could be like this. If I write about what he does, though, I will be sick.

I thought he would be my ticket to heaven—no more scrubbing, no more jumping up to do whatever a guest wanted no matter how tired I was. Josephine didn't think I'd fit in with all his rich, smart friends—the kind who came to the inn, but I figured it would be my turn to be waited on. That's what he promised. Oh, he promised the stars, and I believed him. But Josephine knew. That last night, she tried to talk me out of it. "Stay here. The boys are coming home now, and you're so pretty {This is what Josephine always told me, although I've never thought too much of my looks}, you're bound to get married in no time. I don't like his face, somehow." She said that a couple of times. But I didn't listen. In my mind, I was already on the train coming to be mistress of this big house, right down the street from Longfellow's old home in Cambridge, Massachusetts. Before I left school to help on the farm, we read those poems. I can still remember them and all the others we memorized. When things are the worst, I say lines over and over in my mind to block out the sound of <u>his</u> words, "This is the forest primeval. The murmuring pines and the hemlocks . . ." Our teacher, Miss Scott, had a picture of Longfellow's big house. It was a mansion. Almost as big as the whole inn, and that was one of the grandest in all of Bar Harbor. This house is grand, too, not like Longfellow's—I recognized it from out the car window coming here—but like a palace compared to the farm. I wish I were living in a shack, though—free and safe.

Josephine Royce. I wonder what she's doing now? Married to Sam,
probably. He came back whole from Europe just before I left, got in his
boat and set his traps out the very next day. Steady, calm as a clock.

He's coming back. I hear his footsteps on the stair. Dear God, protect
me. It hurts so much. It hurts every time. And then he beats me. Calls
me a whore. I never was with anybody except for him. I'm not a whore.
Just a girl who made a bad mistake.

Faith had taken the diary downstairs after getting the children out
of the old nursery and closing the door securely behind them. The first
sentence had left her trembling, confirming what she had felt about the
room, about the house.

They finished the Narnia tape and she fed Ben and Amy, who
seemed to sense her mood, behaving like such model children that that
began to upset her, too—they were like pod people. Fortunately, bedtime returned them to themselves, and Tom came home in the middle
of a raucous pillow fight. He announced that maybe he'd forgotten to
tell her, but he'd eaten already and he hoped she'd had a bite with the
kids. Well, she hadn't. On her way downstairs to put away the ingredi-
ents for a vegetable risotto and broiled pork tenderloin with fennel,
she'd grabbed the diary from the drawer of her night table. It wasn't
that she planned it as bedtime reading. From that first sentence, she
knew it would give her bad dreams, but she didn't want Ben to explore
it. He remained under the impression that the book was magical.

She had poured herself a glass of Shiraz, sat at the long dining room
table, and started to read.

"Just a girl who made a bad mistake."

Faith closed the book, leaned back, shut her eyes briefly, and knew
that she couldn't read any more now. But she would have to read more,
would have to read the rest.

Who was this tormented soul? Faith started to put together the
pieces she'd gleaned from the first entry. Recalling what Bitsy had said,
it was obvious the couple were occupants who predated Dr. Robinson

and his uncle. It also seemed clear that the writer was a young woman from rural Maine who had left the family farm during the war to go work in one of the big Bar Harbor inns. Maybe the farm had failed. Her mother had died, and so far there was no mention of any siblings. In any case, she had exchanged one sort of drudgery for another, made even worse by the shortage of both manpower and goods during those years. But the wealthy still took their vacations, and places like the inn where she had worked stayed open, even if the guests did have to tighten their belts a notch. Faith had seen these big old piles on several occasions when Pix and she had gone up to Bar Harbor for the day—Pix for the view from Mount Cadillac; Faith for the lobster rolls at the Jordan Pond House.

The woman's husband, her oppressor, must have been a guest, sweeping her off her feet and taking her far away from friends and family. Was this why she didn't leave? Surely she would have been able to get out of the house when he was there and she wasn't locked in. Locked in! Faith felt sick again. He hadn't wanted a wife so much as a sexual slave. The man had been a twisted sadist.

January 1946. The war had ended in August 1945, and Josephine was right: The boys were coming home again to the girls they'd left behind. The girls would be wearing real nylons instead of painting a seam on the back of their legs, and straight skirts would eventually be replaced by the wide New Look—yards and yards of fabric, unavailable previously, due to wartime shortages. Did this wealthy older suitor promise her an elegant wardrobe to go with the ring? Servants? A life of leisure? Afterward, was she too humiliated to go back home?

Or too frightened?

"Sorry, Faith. Did I startle you?" Tom, who'd been grading papers, took a glass from the sideboard, poured himself some wine, and sat down. The sound of his footsteps coming through the doorway had caused her to jerk her hand. Some wine spilled onto the table's polished surface, the crimson liquid beading up like drops of blood. She quickly wiped them away with a tissue from her pocket.

"What a crazy day!" he said, a smile of contentment belying the implication that he was complaining.

Faith closed the book and slid it behind the large bowl of fruit she left on the table for their snacks. Another secret—and she had no idea why.

She put her hand over his. "Why don't you tell me about it?"

G o on, this is fascinating." Richard had put his hand over Faith's, then quickly moved it back to the fork on his plate. It was the most intimate gesture he had made. The slight pressure where he had touched her was as defined as the stamps on the back of her hand made by all the museums she'd taken the kids to last week. She half-expected to see a mark appear—and wasn't sure what that mark would be.

"There isn't much more to tell yet. I've only read the first entry." She didn't tell him that she'd had neither the time nor the privacy to read on. The rest of the vacation week had telescoped into all the things they had to get done, things that they had put off—the dentist for both kids and new boots for Ben—his had started leaking, too, and there was no question of Baggie inner liners for him, what with his position as older brother to maintain. That took all Friday; Saturday was spent with her in-laws in Norwell. Tom couldn't get away, but Faith had driven down. Then Sunday was a mad after-church scramble to write "Why My Vacation Was Fun"—Ben—and "Draw a Picture of Something You Did"—Amy. Both children picked the wardrobe, and Faith had decided it was better not to make an issue of it, especially since she'd located the key to the nursery door and locked it, shuddering at the thought of its prior use. She'd dropped it back in the drawer, then washed her hands several times.

"It would make a terrific book. And it bears out my belief that nothing writers of fiction come up with can ever compare with the stories of real life. Here you have a rich wacko coming to this inn and eyeing all the young Maine maidens working there, choosing this poor unfortunate for his own personal one-woman, we presume, harem—and on

Brattle Street no less, quintessential Cambridge. I wonder if he was a Harvard professor, one of the independently wealthy ones. He'd have to have been rich to have a house like that. He was older, so he wasn't drafted. Obviously, he sat out the war in comfort. How many wives had he gone through before?"

This had not occurred to Faith. The Brattle Bluebeard. She pushed the notion far into the recesses of her mind. "She said he was at his office, but that could have been at a university. He might have been a professor."

"I don't think I mentioned it, but I took a course with Professor Robinson when I was at Harvard. He taught a class in the English Department, something like the Bible as Literature. Anyway, it's all a little hazy now, but I think I figured it was going to be a gut, although it turned out to be one of the most demanding courses I took. He was one of those typical Harvard prof dandies—bow tie, hand-tied, of course, no clip-ons, please. And every hair in place. But he was great. A bit on the serious side, even when we got to the good stuff, like the Song of Solomon."

"I've never met him, but judging from his house, 'serious' is a good description. Serious books—I haven't found a single Robert Parker or even a Father Brown. Serious artwork, and of course his porcelain collection—so serious, it's packed away, thank goodness."

They were in the Parish Cafe on Boylston; it was noisy and bustling with the lunchtime crowd. Richard had called that morning, and as soon as Faith heard his voice, she realized how much she'd missed him. When he'd suggested an early lunch, she'd agreed, then headed straight for the T in Harvard Square.

They ate in companionable silence; Richard ordered another beer for himself. It was overcast outside, the kind of day for staying in a warm place and eating good food, the kind of day you wanted to have stretch on and on. Faith returned to the subject of the diary.

"I don't think I'd be comfortable publishing it, even as fiction. It would be a violation of some kind of trust. A betrayal. I'm not explaining this very well."

"Sure you are, and it's what I expected you to say," Richard replied, brushing his hand once more over Faith's. "It was buried and would have stayed buried, except for Ben's adventuresome spirit. Maybe Dr. Robinson would have found it when and if he ever decided to move out. But still, it was never intended to be read by anyone except the writer."

"And whoever wrote it may still be alive. She was a young woman in 1946."

As Faith said the words, she couldn't help but think that no, whoever wrote it wasn't still alive. What filled that room, what was so terrifying, was death, not life. She was positive the diary did not have a happy ending.

"Those were good years," Richard said thoughtfully. "I was talking about it with the Monk. You remember—the man who has found real inner peace on the street, a peace he never had when he was making money and maintaining a suburban mansion complete with thoroughbreds in the fields. Very picturesque, he told me, like the manor house of a proper country squire. Anyway, we were talking about what everyone is talking about—this time of increased anxiety, with an orange code one day, a yellow the next. He mentioned the longing his mother had expressed once for those years between World War Two and the Cold War. There was a national optimism. We'd beaten Hitler and now could sit back and enjoy life—a TV set in the living room, a new Ford in the garage, plus all those labor-saving kitchen devices."

"Designed to keep the little woman *in* the kitchen again, forget any notions about being Rosie the Riveter."

Richard laughed. "That's true. And what's even more so is that there never were any good old days, not when you look at them hard."

"Maybe some better old days," Faith suggested. "The Monk sounds like an interesting guy. I'd like to meet him."

"I'd like you to meet him, too, but he doesn't frequent any of the shelters except to go to the Arlington Street Church's Friday Supper. Like me, he's partial to the meat loaf. It's strange. We were at Harvard at the same time, but our paths never crossed. He comes from a background similar to mine, and we even look alike. When I look at him, it's as if I'm looking in a mirror, except that his face doesn't have as many lines. The Monk, despite the fact that he owns virtually nothing, has had more success than I have, although I'm not sure our class notes in the alumni magazine would read that way."

"Absolutely not, although those columns are a crock. You're not going to write in and say that your son is trying to be the first transvestite to walk from Medicine Hat to Miami, your daughter is turning tricks in the Pigalle—at least it's Paris—and your husband has left you for a particularly attractive ewe," Faith said, producing the desired laughter. Richard was sounding so pessimistic.

"You have to go," Richard said regretfully, looking at his watch. He knew Faith's schedule, had had her relate it to him several times, and seemed sincerely interested in hearing about everything she was doing, even mundane chores like picking up Amy. The minutiae of the catering business were an additional source of interest to him: Faith's descriptions of Niki, Pix, her several part-timers, and some of their more unusual jobs—the Gila monster in the pantry sink, pet of the client's son; the Beacon Hill bride who was still trying to make one more change to the menu the night before her wedding; and the Hollywood movie crew that had been filming in Aleford and demanded seven different kinds of bottled water for each "star."

In turn, he'd told Faith about all the coping strategies the men he'd come to know used to survive on the streets—scrounging for food from the top of garbage cans, avoiding Dumpsters unless totally desperate, because some places put rat poison in them to discourage vermin. Or they'd buy a cup of coffee at a place where you served yourself, like a food court, and take the leftovers from the trays on other tables. Some of them sold the newspaper *Spare Change*; more collected cans. He'd assumed an alias, "Richard Goodman," but everyone just called him "Richie." He didn't look like a Richie to Faith, but he didn't look like Richard when he was blending in with his subjects.

The check came and, over Faith's objections, Richard grabbed it, pulling out a wad of cash from his pocket.

Seeing her surprised look, he said, "I have to put most of this in my locker this afternoon, but when I was in the city, I went to my bank. Can't be walking around with an American Express card and retain my credibility."

"We should at least split this," Faith said. "Next time, it's my treat."

"You're always a treat," he said. "Corny, very corny, but true. Now, I'll walk you to the T. Look," he said, pointing up at the light on the top of the old John Hancock Building. "We're going to get some good weather. By now I hope you've learned 'Clear blue, clear view; flashing blue, clouds due; steady red, rain ahead; flashing red, snow instead.'"

"I know what the colors mean, but I didn't know there was a rhyme. I'm a New Yorker, you know."

"Sure, sure," he said. Then as she started to go down the stairs into the subway, he stopped her. "Faith, you have no idea how much it's meant to me, finding you again. I hope we'll always stay friends."

"I don't see why not," she replied lightly, although she knew her words weren't light at all.

Tom had not reacted to the news of Hope and Quentin's nuptials with the surprise Faith had expected. But he was happy.

"To say it's about time is too trite," he'd remarked, "but tell her from me that I couldn't ask for a better brother-in-law. Quentin has grown on me much the way an itchy wool sweater does after repeated washings. You don't need to tell her that, though."

It was true, especially in the beginning, that a little Quentin went a long way. Quentin always knew where you should eat, where you should buy something, what show you should see, which people you should know—from Manhattan to Madagascar—and he was always right. Hope worshiped this quality in her beloved; others found it less endearing. But age and one or two servings of humble pie—"Damn, I was so sure about that place in the Marais!"—had indeed washed some of the itchiness out of Quentin.

Waiting for her sister in the Ritz lobby, Faith thought to herself that she was spending a great deal of time in the Back Bay these days. She was also becoming a lady who lunched. In the past, this meal usually consisted of yogurt and fruit, if she remembered to eat at all. Yesterday, she'd had an amazing sandwich, "the Blue Ginger"—all the Parish Cafe's sandwiches were created, and named by or for the Boston area's top chefs. Called after his restaurant in Wellesley, Ming Tsai's had combined grilled teriyaki glazed tuna steak with avocado, wasabi aioli, lettuce, and tomato served on scallion foccacia. Now, here she was, back at yet another yummy trough.

Her sister appeared, turning heads as she rushed toward Faith, whom she enveloped in a cashmere cloud scented with just the right amount of L'Interdit. There was a strong family resemblance, but Hope was a brunette and had deep emerald eyes. Her legs were a little longer, too, but standing side by side, the Sibley girls made lovely bookends.

"You cut your hair," Faith said.

"You've let yours grow. Now that we're finished with that, I'm starving," Hope said. The routine almost never varied, unless it was "You've lost weight" or "You've put on a pound or two."

They went to the Café; the elegant dining room with its famous Czechoslovakian cobalt blue crystal chandeliers was open only for dinner and Sunday brunch.

"I'm not going to get dinner until late, so I want a real meal," Hope announced, then quickly ordered clam chowder, steak au poivre, pommes frites, and Boston cream pie with vanilla sauce.

Realizing Tom had said he had a "working dinner"—whatever that was—Faith ordered the steak, as well, specifying she wanted hers rare. She skipped the chowder, though, preferring salad with the Ritz's appropriately rich Roquefort dressing (the recipe called for mayonnaise, buttermilk, and sour cream, plus the cheese and seasonings). She skipped dessert, too. Her sister never finished hers, so Faith could count on a few bites of the pie, which was really a cake—two layers of yellow cake, vanilla custard in between, and chocolate frosting on top.

"Would Madame like to see the wine list?" the waiter asked. Quentin knew everything about the subject, of course, and was prone to saying things like, "I believe the grapes growing on the north slope of the vineyard were better that year than the one before." Hope had been an apt pupil.

"None for me, thank you," Hope said, ordering a bottle of water. "Fay?"

"Water will be fine for me, too."

The waiter finished writing down their order and retreated, leaving the impression that their particular choices were sublime and would immediately be placed in extremely capable hands.

"Now," Faith said obediently, "what's new? Anything to tell me?"

"As if you didn't know, but you're very good, Fay. Yes, Quentin and I are getting married. As soon as possible. No tents, clouds of tulle, parade of attendants, standing room only. It would be too, too ludicrous, but obviously I want you there." Hope was tearing a roll apart with such vengeance that Faith wondered how happy the bride-to-be actually was. And why the rush? And why the simplicity? She would have thought that wedding presents alone would have been an incentive for a very large guest list. Quentin and Hope considered the word *materialistic* a high compliment. To be otherwise meant you weren't billing enough hours. She decided to approach the subject head-on. It was the only way with her sister.

"You don't seem to be jumping for joy. I mean, it's been a foregone conclusion, but still, where's that glow? And you know if you just send announcements afterward, you never get good stuff."

She regarded her sister, who was still shredding her *petit pain*, and realized that Hope did have a glow, but it wasn't that of a blushing bride. There was a slight sheen to the skin, the kind you get— The words tumbled from Faith's mouth.

"Oh, Hope. This sudden rush to get married. It's not because—"

"I'm with child? Knocked up, preggers, in the family way, bun in the oven, *enceinte*? Actually, I am. One of Quentin's stork-stoppers must have sprung a leak. Tell me you're happy for me, and *please* tell me how great it's going to be."

Faith wasn't able to tell her sister anything for a moment, because she was choking on a bread crumb and drinking copious amounts of water. The Ritz staff, the word *lawsuit* dancing in front of their eyes, had gathered en masse to pour her more water and ask, "Is Madame all right?" They looked prepared to pound her on the back or perform the Heimlich.

Madame was all right, and they slid back to their places as part of the decor.

"I'm very, very happy for you if this is what you want. You'll be a wonderful mom!" And Hope would be, especially with a nanny and a housekeeper.

The first course arrived and Hope eagerly spooned up her chowder. "I'm hungry all the time, but I haven't gotten to the throwing-up part. My clothes are starting to get tight. Did this happen to you?" She took another roll.

Faith knew she'd been pregnant. She had two children who looked like some almighty power had stirred Tom and Faith together in a genetic cocktail shaker. But she had trouble remembering the nine months preceding delivery and even the deliveries themselves. This was supposed to be a blessing, Pix had told her; otherwise, you'd never do it again after the first one. Therefore, she was a little vague when she answered her sister.

"Hungry. Yes, I do remember that, and of course the bother with clothes. You can get some larger-size Eileen Fishers that will do very nicely and then have them taken in later." But there were more important matters to discuss, although clothes were right up there. "How does Quentin feel about all this?"

"He's being totally obnoxious. Suddenly, he's superstud because one of his guys made it through a latex barrier and swam the equivalent of the English Channel. Honestly, Fay, I haven't had so much nookie in years."

That further explains the glow, Faith reflected.

"You know you don't have to have a small wedding. Think of all the people we know who've been three at the altar. No one thinks anything of it, and besides, it will be ages before you show. I mean, you did just find out, right?"

"Right, but apparently I'm three months gone. Don't look at me like that. I've been very busy. There's been a lot of stress at work, and I figured that's what was going on. Looking back, I realize there were probably some signs, but I've been working round the clock, almost literally, so I didn't notice."

Only her sister—and all the other female workaholics of the world. Around her ninth month, it might have dawned on Hope that she wasn't simply putting on the pounds from Snickers fits. Then she'd have headed off to Mt. Sinai Hospital or wherever during lunch, had the kid, and been back at her desk that afternoon.

A busboy took away their plates. As soon as he departed, Faith asked, "But why haven't you told Mother and Dad? When Quentin junior or little Hope arrives, they're bound to notice, particularly Mother."

The Reverend Lawrence Sibley didn't always take in the immediate, presumably because his mind was on a higher, less worldly plane. Nothing got past Jane, however.

"Quentin the third. Quentin's a junior." Having straightened that out, Hope waited until their entrées were placed in front of them and she'd had a large mouthful of steak before answering. The "poivre" was green peppercorns in this rendition, and the sauce was delicious.

"I sort of thought you might tell them for me. You know, pave the way."

"Oh Hope, you have nothing to be ashamed of, and they won't be upset. You must know that. They both like Quentin and have assumed the two of you would get married when you were ready to start a family. So here you are."

"Hmm." Hope chewed rumitatively. She had always hated any sort of confrontation, unless it was over a conference room table. One reason the two sisters had always gotten along so well was that Hope never even tried to put up a fight. Plus, being only one year apart, they had never known the nirvana of no siblings.

Faith pressed on. "This is not like the time you accidentally broke Mother's Steuben vase. Besides, you're a grown-up now. I think the two of you should go together to see them and tell them everything. This is supposed to be a happy time."

"I am happy, and happier now that you know. I think we'll do it in a restaurant. It's always better to tell iffy news in a public setting. Now, when we finish eating, you need to tell me everything I'm going to need. A crib or something, one of those stroller thingies, diapers—don't even want to go there—baby clothes, probably a layette from Bonpoint will cover that." She had already reached into her Kate Spade bag for her Palm Pilot.

"I'll do better than that. I'll send you some books. *What to Expect When You're Expecting* and *The Girlfriend's Guide to Pregnancy* are good ones. And I'll give you a shower—two of them."

"You're a doll, Fay. This *is* going to be fun. Two married ladies with kids. Ben and Amy will be the best cousins." Hope ate the last morsel of steak, wiped her plate with a piece of bread in the European manner, and looked her sister straight in the eye. "Now, what's going on with you? I haven't seen you look like this since the time you got all involved with Emma Stanstead when her father was murdered."

Which was the same time she was dating Richard Morgan. Was her sister some kind of witch? Faith ordered coffee and pie for herself. It wasn't that Hope wouldn't share, but judging from the way the rest of the meal had disappeared, it would have been too cruel to ask for some bites. Besides, Faith had seen it go by and it looked too good to pass up.

The dessert arrived, the waiter left, and Faith told her sister almost everything.

"I wish I didn't have to go to this meeting," Hope said after their cups had been refilled several times—decaf for Hope, who was already catering to her baby's diet. "We could go shopping—and keep talking. But I have to go, so here it is in a nutshell, Fay. You're in Cambridge, staying in a house you don't like, and Tom is all involved with his new life, which may or may not be his and your future life. You don't have Pix and all those other creatures out in Aleford to talk to. You spend your days driving kids around or cooking for strangers. Suddenly, a long-lost honey comes back into your life in what has to be the most romantic and weirdest way I've heard of yet. Of course you're going to want to see him. You're bored and nobody's paying much attention to you. What is wrong with this picture? Nothing, so far as I can see. I'm sure Tom doesn't mind that you've been meeting an old friend."

"I haven't told Tom about Richard."

Hope shook her finger at her sister.

"Naughty, naughty—or maybe not so far. But it's your call; do what feels right. I'm not an expert on married life yet, but I'd say the longer you wait, the harder it will be."

"That is if I ever tell Tom at all," Faith blurted out.

"Oh, Fay," Hope said, shaking her head now—and smiling so ruefully, the air seemed redolent with the herb.

February 9, 1946

It has been some weeks since I have been able to take pen to paper again, and I am not sure I have the strength even now. When it came down to it, I could not do it. I looked at his razor and held it to my wrist, but either I am a coward or the Lord stopped me. I do not know which, but I put it down on the sink and cried. Nor can I raise it against him, simple though it would be to take his life during the night. Prison would be nothing compared to my life here, but again I cannot take another's life, even a demon's. I could more easily take mine, but as I made the first small cut, I saw Ma's face—not the way she looked at the end, almost a skeleton from the cancer, but the rosy round face of my childhood. The way she looked when she'd read to me after the chores were done and while we were waiting for Pa. When she was finished, she'd close the book and smile at me. "Who's my best little girl?" she'd ask. I'd give her a big hug and say, "I am."

I am. I am.

My only chance lay in escape and I should have known this, too, would not be possible. Since the day I arrived, I've been looking for some way to get out of the house undetected, but he keeps all the doors and downstairs windows locked from the outside. I cannot telephone for help, either. He made a great point of showing me the only instrument in the house—in his library, whose heavy oak door is locked in his absence. The key, like all the others, is on a ring that he keeps in his pocket or under his pillow at night. Each week, I give him a list of the groceries I will need and he calls Sage's. The same for any feminine needs I have—he takes my list and the goods are delivered to him.

Desperate at my inability to end my own life and the suffering that grows worse each day, late the next afternoon I waited until I heard him go into the library, then left the kitchen and my dinner preparations, silently creeping up the back stairs to the bedroom on the far side of the house. I was able to get the window open and jumped, hoping the recent thaw had softened the grass. But high as it was, I did not clear the bushes, and upon landing in them, my foot twisted painfully under me. Despite this, I tried to run for the back gate, but the branches held me back. His hearing is so acute, I swear he must have heard the window opening, for he was at my side in a moment, foaming with rage. I never reached the gate. I have not told you, little book, that the house is surrounded by a solid high fence with a gate leading from the sidewalk to the front path and another at the rear. This last is left unlocked for deliveries and was my object. The fence itself is impossible for someone my size to scale. Dense shrubbery further lines it, and were I ever to get outside and scream, I doubt my cries would be heard. He has thought of everything. Even the possibility that I might try to set the house on fire to bring about my rescue. The fireplace matches are closely guarded and he has made me stop smoking, not a great hardship, as I wasn't that fond of it, although he takes great pleasure in reminding me

I had to give it up. His own cigars are kept in a humidor in the library and the smell fills the house with a loathsome odor.

I succeeded only in badly spraining my ankle and nothing else. We had to have a woman come for a time to do the cooking—there have been no servants, only me—and my spirits rose at the thought that here would be the means of finally getting away. But he is too clever. And I am too stupid. He told me he had hired someone, since I would be bedridden for a while—he was, of course, furious at that—then left. Like a cat with a mouse, he wanted to give me time to savor the idea of freedom, playing with me, letting me run forward before pouncing. An hour later, he was back. He drew up a chair next to our bed—monstrous words—and told me I mustn't think of trying to communicate with the housekeeper. The devil! He has gotten in touch with Pa and taken over the mortgage on the farm, plus offering a wage for Pa to work it or caretake it for the rest of his life. "It was the least I could do for my father-in-law. He was delighted to be free of his burden and scolded you for not calling or writing, but I said you were so caught up with your new friends and new life that the old had ceased to exist for you. Now, you don't want your poor father to lose everything, do you?" Even if I did—and I hope that Pa would understand the circumstances, although I am not so certain of that as I would like—I could see in his eyes that he would search me out wherever I would go and kill me. Kill me in such a way that it would look like an accident. My only hope was to write to Josephine and tell her everything and ask the housekeeper to mail it, as if that were an everyday request. I still had some stamps in my handbag and paper and pen in the writing table in the room. Even if Josephine could not save me, she would know that if anything happened to me, it would not be a natural death. And she could tell the authorities to investigate.

It is as if he can read my every thought. My pathetic little plan never saw the light of day. I waited until the housekeeper, Mrs. Morris, had been here a week. She brought my meals on a tray and helped me bathe and dress, saying little. This attention and the fact that he had had to move to the spare room made me feel thankful for my injury. I wrote the letter, addressed it, and found the stamps. I sensed the first stirrings of spring outside my windows, even though I could not touch the buds or hear the birds. God willing, I would be away from this hell by the time the daffodils were in bloom.

Mrs. Morris was always kind, smiling at me when she came into the room and once placing her cool hand on my forehead as if to check whether I had a fever or not. She was about the same age Ma would have been, and it made me long for my own dear mother, gone these many years. When I asked Mrs. Morris to mail the letter, her words were so unexpected that I thought one of us must be well and truly crazy. "You poor thing. Don't worry yourself about Josephine or anyone else. You're safe here. Give me the letter. I'll take care of it and bring you another cup of tea." Then she took my only hope and tore it up. Late that afternoon, after sobbing myself to sleep, I awoke and found he was next to me, smiling that hideous smile. "Mrs. Morris knows that you've been very, very ill, my dear. That you have delusions, one of which is that you have a friend named Josephine Royce, as well as some others, whose voices tell you to do dangerous things like throw yourself out the window. I've told Mrs. Morris, who is out now, that you believe yourself to be a farm girl from Maine who worked at an inn and did something very, very wrong, something you must punish yourself for, but actually you are from New York City. You are the daughter of a wealthy family, all of them having succumbed to the mania that is overtaking you, too. It started shortly after we were at an inn in Maine, and that is where you believe yourself to be on occasion."

I could not even cry out, although his hand moving below the bedcovers would soon make me scream. It was then that I understood the doctor's attitude the way he spoke to me as if I was a child.

I can walk now and Mrs. Morris is gone. He told her he was taking me abroad to recuperate, and she has returned to her home in Rhode Island, too far away to know whether we are here or not—and of course she would never consider that he had been lying. Such an eminent

man—and he spoke to her the way he spoke to me when we first met,
charming her to the point where she sympathized completely with him,
saddled as he is with a wife who is mad.

Faith stopped reading and marked the place. She'd picked the diary up again in the morning after everyone had left, impelled by her own curiosity, but also because she knew Richard was interested in it. He hadn't called the last few days, but she assumed it was because he was living on the street full-time. The thought was not comforting, and she wished he would finish his research soon. Aside from the cold and lack of decent nutrition, the life was so depressing. Reading the diary, oddly enough, made her feel as if she was doing something similar—and therefore staying in touch.

There were quite a few more entries, and although tempted to turn to the last one, she was ambivalent. Faith both wanted and didn't want to know how it ended—that is, if the end provided any clue as to the woman's fate. She decided it was better to read it as if it were a novel, straight through—and it certainly felt like one. The woman was a gifted writer; not just her pain and anguish spilled out on the pages but also her sensitivity and intelligence. She'd had a good old-fashioned education in that rural school in Maine, memorizing classic poetry and learning to write a clear hand, as well as construct a clear sentence. Her style was slightly old-fashioned. Faith imagined the little girl as one of the last ones up, if not the winner, in the spelling bees and an avid reader who enlarged her vocabulary as she tried to broaden her mind. Was it this that made her such an easy mark? A desire to go beyond the tiny sphere she'd inhabited all her life, to enter the wider world she had read about? He'd chosen well, her husband. The girl had been eager to leave her old life behind and had no ties except for a father she wasn't sure wouldn't trade her well-being for his. Did she succeed in getting word of her imprisonment—for that's what it was—to "Pa," and what did he do? Tell her to be an obedient wife—thinking of his own comfort—or did he save her?

When she finished reading the diary, she'd share it with Tom—
share it just before they moved back to Aleford. He had had to deal with
domestic abuse all too frequently and would feel the desperation of this
long-ago victim as Faith was feeling it now. She wanted to wait, wanted
not to cast a shadow on this time in Brattle Street that was so unambigu-
ously happy for him. Once he had read it, then they would put the book
back where Ben had found it or destroy it. There was no point in rushing to tell Tom about the diary. There was nothing anyone could do
about it now, fifty-seven years later. The woman was gone. Faith
returned to the rest of the entry.

*My days have such a sameness that without the calendar on the wall in
the kitchen and the slow coming of spring outside, I would not know
what day, month, or year it is. I awake and get out of bed before him,
although his eyes are always open, watching me dress. Then I make
breakfast, serving him in the dining room and eating my own frugal
meal standing up in the kitchen. There is housekeeping to do; then he
locks me in our room or up here in the nursery, where I have hidden
you, along with my pens and ink. Lately, he has let me read, selecting
books for me that I am sure he believes will be boring, but he does not
know that words can never be that for me and that I would be delighted
with anything. Often he leaves only the worn Bible that was my
mother's, and this is the greatest joy of all. I have learned to make my
face a mask, so he can have no indication of what gives me pleasure—or
pain. He takes his noon meal at his club, then returns late in the day to
let me out to prepare supper. Afterward, I try to take as much time as
possible cleaning the dishes, for most nights after supper, the horror
begins anew.*

The entry ended and Faith sat staring out the window at the front
yard. She was sitting on the large window seat that ran under the
diamond-paned windows. The sun shone in on the fabric covering the
cushions, picking out the blues and greens of the dark chintz. The more

she read, the more she felt that she had to find out who had written these words. There was no name in the front of the book. She turned to the back; nothing there, either. She shook the pages upside down, thinking a scrap of paper might have been slipped in—perhaps a photo or an address. Nothing. Nothing except a pressed flower, a purple pansy, translucent with age. Faith picked it up carefully and placed it back approximately where it had been.

She had to find out the woman's name—and she had to find out what had happened to her.

5

R ichard Morgan had disappeared. Or rather, he had disappeared from Faith's life. It had been exactly a week ago that
they had had lunch together at the Parish Cafe, and she hadn't
heard from him since. At the time, his parting words—about how much
she meant to him and that he hoped they'd always stay friends—suggested a long and happy future, not unlike the last scene in *Casablanca*,
although it was Claude Rains who metaphorically walked off into the
sunset with Ingrid Bergman, not Bogart. Now, after days of rushing
home to check the answering machine in vain, she was beginning to
think they had been words of farewell. But why? If he'd finished his
research and was returning home to work on the book, why not say so?
She was puzzled—and worried. If something had happened to him,
there was no way she'd find out. A *New York Times* reader, she started
scanning Tom's *Boston Globe* each morning.

She was alone in the big house. As always when this happened, she
was eager to go out, although the thin March sunshine was not particularly beckoning. And it continued to be frigid. She was also tired. The
weekend had been a hectic one. She'd worked almost all day Saturday

catering a Wellesley College alumnae event with her entire staff, plus extras; then Sunday, Tom was preaching on the North Shore and she had promised to go with him. Pix came and took the kids to Aleford for the day. Each of the Miller children had baby-sat for the Fairchilds, and Danny, the youngest—now a junior in high school—was the current, and last, sitter. Although he was a veritable god to Ben, Amy treated him as a kind of pony, climbing all over him, demanding piggyback rides, much to her brother's disgust. One did not ask such mundane things of Phoebus Apollo.

On Saturday, Niki had suggested meeting Faith in Harvard Square for lunch sometime, and now Faith decided today was the day. She couldn't get Richard out of her head, and listening to Niki would do it. Niki never had problems; she just caused them—or so she insisted. As Faith went into the kitchen to call, she couldn't help but remember that at one time there had been only one phone in the house, a phone kept under lock and key, and she quickly punched in Niki's number.

"Hi, it's Faith. What are you up to?" she asked when Niki answered.

"Not much. You?"

"The same. Do you want to meet for lunch?"

"Love to. I saw some shoes at Jasmine Sola that I need to have, so we can eat and shop or shop and eat."

"It's not even ten, so how about shop first?"

"Great. I'll meet you in half an hour, and whatever I say, do not let me buy more than one pair of shoes. Not even if the second pair happen to be boots and are on sale."

Niki was close to Imelda in the footwear count and also had T-shirts that proclaimed CHANGE YOUR SHOES, CHANGE YOUR LIFE in several colors.

"See you in a bit, then," Faith said, feeling happy at the idea of shopping. She wouldn't mind some new shoes herself.

"Ciao, sweetie."

Faith changed. It was important to look good when you went shopping; otherwise, you weren't on a par with what you were trying on. And it made the salespeople act nicer, too. Then she walked to the Square.

She lingered at Longfellow's House, wishing she could paint the parsonage the same way—hollandaise with black shutters and white trim—but the abode for the minister of First Parish had always been white with forest green shutters, and so it was destined to stay until the last trump. She wondered if the woman who wrote the diary had ever had the chance to walk by the house, or if the glimpse she'd gotten from the window of the car she arrived in had been all. Continuing past Radcliffe Yard, Faith was deep in thought when she heard someone call her name. It was Niki, walking down Appian Way. Niki lived on the other side of Harvard Square, off Massachusetts Avenue.

"We have some serious shopping to do, and then I have the perfect place for lunch."

"Great." Niki's mood was infectious. It always was, whether she was up or down.

"We are now passing the Dexter Pratt House, better known as the Blacksmith House," Niki said, gesturing with her arm. "It may look like a bakery now, but in the olden days, that's where he lived, the village smith. You know, 'Under a spreading chestnut-tree.'"

"I went to school, too, and it's 'smithy,' not 'smith,'" Faith retorted, hoping Niki wouldn't press her for the next lines. They had something to do with muscles was all she remembered, "sinews," or words to that effect.

Niki shook her head, causing her short, tight black curls, which always reminded Faith of a pot scrubber, to vibrate.

"Wrong, wrong, wrong. The 'smithy' was the place; the 'smith' was the guy. 'Under a spreading chestnut-tree / The village smithy stands; / The smith, a mighty man is he, / With large and sinewy hands. . . .' Sounds pretty hot, don't you think? Anyway, the blacksmith shop—the smithy—is gone. See? There's a granite marker where it stood. The tree's gone, too. The Cambridge city fathers had it cut down in 1876, saying it was a danger to the loads passing under it. Shortsighted, to say the least. Note: Nothing much changes. At least Longfellow got a chair out of it. The schoolchildren of Cambridge gave it to him for his seventy-second birthday. I don't think they had shop in those days, so probably somebody else made it. And I know all this—to answer your question—because I used to work as a guide for Harvard Square Walking Tours."

"Your past is a source of constant amazement to me," Faith said as they went into trendy Jasmine Sola and Niki caught her breath. Faith pictured a tournament with Niki and Bitsy, each armed with Cantabrigian lore. Niki talked faster, but Bitsy might know more. It would be a hard call.

An hour later, they emerged with the shoes, plus a halter top made from bright silk Japanese kimono cloth that Niki just had to have, and since it couldn't be worn on her feet unless things got very kinky, Faith let her buy it. She herself had succumbed to a cute, although not too cute, long-sleeved soft rose—colored T-shirt with a faded seed packet on the front and a few tiny rivets for some sparkle. She could wear it to her next Cambridge soiree. The seed packet was dated 1894.

"Now, where are we going for lunch? Henrietta's Table? I wouldn't say no to a burger at Bartley's, either," Faith said. Henrietta's was a relative newcomer, but Bartley's had been satisfying Harvard students and other Cambridge residents with their burgers and sweet-potato fries since 1960. It was virtually the only eatery in Harvard Square that you could walk by without someone bemoaning the passing of a venerable institution like Elsie's, Hayes-Bickford—"the Bick"—the Wursthaus, and Cronin's.

"A little more ethnic. You need to be in the mood for what I want your opinion about. Besides, with these temperatures, we need this kind of food."

Five minutes later, Niki stood at the counter in a hole-in-the-wall Greek restaurant, ordering lamb shish kebabs, stuffed grape leaves, tabouli, baba ghanoush, and pita bread. The food came fast, and they went downstairs, where there were tables. They managed to snare an empty one as a young man, with his nose still in his Philosophy 101 text, got up to leave.

"Yum," said Faith as she tore off a piece of bread and scooped up some of the baba ghanoush. "The eggplant is pureed, not mushed, and they didn't overwhelm the smokiness with too much oil or garlic."

"It's a good place: Look at that poster—Acropolis, sunny sky, no clouds. Don't you feel warmer, even without ouzo?" Niki enthused. "I come here a lot. Comfort food, but don't tell my mother, or I'll never get another doggy bag again."

The one cuisine Niki didn't attempt was that of her ancestors, insisting there was no way she could ever duplicate her grandmother's and mother's expertise.

"Do you have any particular need for comfort food right now? I thought everything was going great with Phil."

Niki sighed dramatically. "You know my problem. He *is* great. He's perfect, in fact, and that's my problem. He's even Greek."

Faith had met Niki's family on several occasions, and she had to agree with her assistant that *My Big Fat Greek Wedding* was a pale imitation of the Constantines. Niki had rebelled early and often, bringing home bikers, men old enough to be her grandfather, and once a practicing Buddhist in saffron robes.

"He wants to get married."

"There must be something in the air," Faith said. "My sister's getting married. Did I tell you that?"

"No, you didn't, but that's not the same. She's what—forty? And been with him forever."

Faith bristled. Niki was forgetting that Hope was Faith's *younger* sister.

"Hope is nowhere near forty, but let's talk about you." She popped a grape leaf in her mouth. Excellent. Niki might not cook Greek food, but Faith did, especially grape leaves, which were a good hors d'oeuvre.

"If he was missing even one of the things on my parents' list, it would be okay. But it's like they sent off to some perfect husband mailorder place on Mount Olympus: college graduate—Harvard M.B.A., no less; family man—if we did get married, we'd have to have it in the Fleet

Center just to hold all the relatives; nice manners—always brings Mom flowers, and me, too; chem-free; loves children—pictures of his nieces and nephews in his wallet; clean fingernails, no dandruff; and let's not forget he's—"

"Greek," Faith chimed in, and they burst out laughing.

"Obviously, you have to dump this Prince Charming," Faith said, knowing full well what Niki would say.

"I can't. I'm in love with him. But marriage?"

They'd been having a variation on this conversation ever since Niki had met Phil last summer and fallen for him hard. She swore it was before she knew his pedigree, but Faith had a suspicion that despite her protests, Niki's list might not be so different from that of her parents.

"Why don't you try being engaged? See how that feels. Sort of like working your way up from a goldfish to a dog, commitmentwise."

Niki shook her head. "I would never get engaged to someone I didn't intend to marry. If I love him enough to be engaged, I love him enough to get married. I never really understood the point of being engaged anyway."

"Well, it's like holding a place in line. Or like putting dibs on something." Niki was as much a minimalist as Hope was a materialist, so the ring and gifts argument wouldn't mean anything. If it came to saying yes, Faith would have a quick word with Phil, whom she liked very much. Diamonds really are a girl's best friend, next to her best friend, of course. A diamond can't laugh and cry with you. Her mind strayed back to the diarist. She'd had a friend, Josephine Royce. A friend who cared enough to try to save her from a disastrous marriage. Was Josephine still in Maine, married to Sam? If she'd been in her early twenties when the war ended, as it seemed, she'd be in her late seventies now. Faith switched back to Niki. A marriage to Phil wouldn't be a disaster; despite his perfection, they were a good match. They had the same quirky sense of humor, kept the same weird hours, were totally into techno music and Japanese anime, loved to travel to extremely obscure places, and were obsessed with food. Phil had seriously thought about becoming a chef before the siren song of high finance beckoned.

"Maybe he'd agree to go steady for a while," Niki mused, slathering her pita bread with some hummus she'd gone back for.

"Or you could get pinned. That would be sweet. Come on!" Faith cried. "You're not a teenager, even if you do behave like one. The numbers are wrong. You're twenty-seven years old, and twenty-seven-year-olds get married; they do not go steady, unless you're willing to trade clubbing for the soda shop and sex for heavy petting in the back of Dad's Oldsmobile."

Niki laughed. "I guess I will have to marry him. I certainly don't want him to marry someone else, and I can't imagine myself in a rocking chair on the porch with a golden-ager other than Phil. I still have to think about this, though. Don't breathe a word of it to my mother. Don't even think about it when she's around. She does that Vulcan mind-meld thing, so watch out."

"When did Phil propose?"

"Friday night. Gross-out romantic—roses, drinks at the Bay Tower Room, sparkly ring. Didn't you notice how out of it I was Saturday? I didn't want to say anything when we couldn't talk. If you hadn't called today, I would have called you."

So there was a ring. Good for Phil.

"In order of importance—you told him what, and what does the ring look like?"

"In order of importance to you—" Niki fished the chain that normally held a cross from beneath her collar and showed Faith the ring that had been added. A perfectly acceptable diamond in a Tiffany setting.

"I told him no engagement, but he insisted I take the ring. It's a sort of door prize for couples, I hear. I suppose I have to get him a watch or a boat or something."

"Your problem is that you wouldn't mind being married to Phil; you just don't want to *get* married."

"Out of the mouths of babes—you are a babe, you know, Faith. Hair looks very, very good today. However, I have a much better chance of winning Mass Millions—and you know I don't buy lottery tickets—than I would avoiding the whole nine yards, as in yards and yards of taffeta and tulle."

"Obviously, Phil did not demand an answer then and there; otherwise, we wouldn't be having this conversation."

"He told me to take as much time as I need. See what I'm up against? Mr. Perfect!"

"Sit down and make a list. You like lists." Niki was always revising her list of all-time favorite desserts and other comestibles. "What does he do that makes you crazy? What does he do that doesn't? Then compare them."

Niki brightened visibly. "It's a start. I'll do it with you and Pix. My other married friends haven't been in it for as long as you guys. You're pros."

Pros at what? Faith wondered. Being married? Tolerating someone else's foibles? Tom never shut a door—closet, cupboard, medicine cabinet. It only took her five years of remarking on the fact to learn to shut her mouth—and close the doors herself.

"I'm thinking December. Bad travel time."

"Sorry, I lost the thread here. December?"

"For the wedding, silly. Cut down on the guests, and the bridesmaids could wear red velvet. I love red velvet. You'll be my woman of honor, won't you? No way I'm having a matron by my side unless I'm in an orange jumpsuit and a whole lot of trouble."

Hope and Niki. Standing up with both of them. It wasn't a case of always a bridesmaid, never a bride. She was already married. Next to the births of her children, her wedding had been the happiest day of her life. But it had to mean something—a matron was a matron, no matter what Niki said. Faith didn't feel matronly. She never wanted to feel matronly. Niki had said "woman of honor." That was better, much better.

"I'd love to—and Phil is a very lucky man."

"Damn straight," Niki said, raising her diet Coke to Faith's.

After lunch, there was just enough time to look into the Cambridge Artists' Cooperative on Church Street before Faith left to pick up Amy and walk back to the house.

When Faith arrived at the school, Amy was tired and it was a slow trip. Faith hoped she wasn't coming down with something. The teacher had mentioned ominously that half the class was out with the flu. Amy didn't want a snack, so Faith tucked her daughter straight into bed for a nap and then headed for the answering machine. The light was blinking. She pressed the button. "You have one new message and four old messages." Faith knew what they were. She used the machine as a supplementary "To Do" list. There were days when she felt like her whole life was a "To Do" list that would never be completed, but after being with Niki, today wasn't one of those days. She was thinking about the party she'd give the couple as she pressed the play button.

"Tom, it's Mindy. I've tried your office and there's no answer there, either. I must have gotten the time wrong. Anyway, I'll stay here at Yenching for another ten minutes; then I have to go. I've already drunk so much tea without ordering that they must think I'm homeless! Call me."

Faith's first impulse was to hit the Delete button. Instead, she waited for her husband to come home. As soon as Tom walked through the door, Faith told him there was a message for him on the machine, then stood watching him closely as he played it. Much to her chagrin, she did not get the pleasure of seeing him squirm—pleasure she had been imagining in various degrees and forms since playing the message herself several times. Mindy's tactless homeless remark brought particular satisfaction. Instead, Tom seemed only mildly interested, commenting, "Too bad she had to wait. I told her I wasn't sure I could make it. She's given me her proposal, which has been approved, and wanted to show me her outline."

Resisting the temptation to point out exactly which outline Mindy intended to show him, Faith said, "She can't come to your office?"

Then she was immediately struck by the dilemma of which was worse: Mindy sequestered in Tom's tiny office or Mindy seductively feeding Tom tidbits with chopsticks in a public restaurant. Yenching was an excellent Chinese place on Massachusetts Avenue, located right where the Bick had been.

Tom replied, somewhat wearily, "Oh Faith, you've got this all wrong. And leaving a message on the family answering machine is pretty aboveboard, I'd say. She thought we could save time by combining lunch and work, which would free me up for the other students."

Why hadn't she thought of that? Mindy of Arc? Mindy Nightingale? Saint Mindy?

There was really nothing to say. Whatever she came up with would sound petty and suspicious. She was suspicious, oh yes, but not petty. And Mindy was so "aboveboard"—a pretty sharp tactic. Taking refuge in silence, Faith went to prepare an elaborate dinner. She could be a martyr, too.

Since she couldn't do anything about Richard, short of combing the streets and shelters of greater Boston, Faith decided to start finding out who wrote the diary. She'd finish reading it as she searched. The plan was pretty irrational, but she was feeling pretty irrational these days. *Dislocated*—she kept coming back to that word. *Dislocated*, not as in elbow, but as in space—and maybe her heart.

The following day, she sat with the diary in hand, thinking of the best way to proceed. She knew the woman had been working in an inn in Bar Harbor in 1945 and she also had the name of a friend. She could investigate the Brattle Street area. So far, she hadn't met any of her neighbors. The houses were far apart, and New England winters were not conducive to socializing. But Bitsy Higginson might know someone who had lived here a long time, some spry octogenarian with a mind like a steel trap. These were as common as advanced degrees in Cambridge. She'd start with Bitsy; then there must be records of some sort.

That meant going to the library. Plus she could call Bar Harbor information and ask for a listing for Royce. She had a plan, and Faith always liked having a plan. First, she turned to the next entry.

March 15, 1946

He has been laid up with gout and it has made him more demanding than ever, but not, thank God, in the worst way. He does not want me even near him. The doctor has given him some pain pills, but he has told me he will not take them and let down his guard. I sometimes wonder if what he enjoys most is having an enemy in the house to outwit, an enemy he can crush.

I have done my best to keep him clean, but after all these weeks without any exercise to speak of, I have lost much of my strength, as well. He has called the Harvard student employment agency to find someone to live here. He's offering lodging in exchange for driving, gardening, other chores, and help in the sickroom until he is better. He has told me that it is no use to imagine my freedom through this person, as he will be told the same thing as was told to Mrs. Morris—plus, my father will find himself destitute and homeless immediately. I cannot imagine that a young man would ever be able to understand the true nature of my life here in any case, so I have no hope. Still, it will be an escape from the worst of things, for surely my screams would alarm even the most naïve student. Also, he will not dare to bring another woman in—something he has done twice—the kind of woman I had never imagined existed. The first time, I was tied to a chair and made to watch. I cannot write about the second time.

I want to think about something else.

The garden. The student will be taking care of it. The winter has taken a cruel toll, and many of the trees and bushes need replacing. He has told me to make a list and a diagram, for he knows nothing about such things and cares only because the garden—the whole house—is a reflection of him, so it must be perfect. He knows I spent many happy hours with the head gardener at the inn. The gardens there were famous throughout New England. Ever since I was a child, I've loved to plant things, although there was little time on the farm to tend flower beds. When I could spare a minute from my duties at the inn, I would trail after Robert, the gardener, until finally he put a spade in my hand and I became an unofficial member of his staff. This place has a large yard and I may do as I like, except for the yews and other shrubs that grow up against the house, blocking the light from the windows. At times, I feel as if I am in Sleeping Beauty's castle before the prince came, surrounded by impenetrable vines. That is the purpose. No one is to see in and I'm not to see out, except from upstairs. Were it not for that, I wouldn't know the snowdrops have bloomed, poking up through the ivy along the front fence. I'd like to tear out all the ivy and plant delphinium—the deepest blue possible—and arum lilies, hollyhocks, and roses. In the front left corner, a large dogwood snapped during the last ice storm, and that's where I'd put a star magnolia. If only I could leave, go into the fresh air and do the work myself. I haven't been out of this house since I crossed the threshold in September.

Faith longed for one of H. G. Wells's time machines. She had such a visceral sense of needing to go back and rescue this woman—take her out into the fresh air and sunshine, restore her to life. The husband had been mad, no question, but how could it have gone unnoticed? The deliverymen from Sage's and other places, neighbors, work associates, wouldn't they have wondered at never seeing the woman of the house? But then, didn't you read about this sort of thing even now—women, children shut away, imprisoned in their own homes? She felt ill when she thought about the charade the man had conducted—a wife suffering from insanity, a family curse, and no, he could not bear to institutionalize her, even at McLean, the asylum in Belmont, at that time a well-appointed clubhouse for barmy Brahmins, where they could go insane gracefully. Faith found herself devising plots for the woman to escape, then giving each one up as she must have done. He'd been diabolical, refusing the pain medication, or disposing of it so as not to raise questions with the doctor. There was no way his wife could have put it in his food and gained some time to break a window or steal his keys to open a door, get to the phone. Even then, would she have been believed? And if she had been able to get free, would he have let her live, or, as she believed, would there have been an "accident" once he had tracked her down? Nineteen forty-six was well before the days of abuse hot lines and shelters for battered women. This was a man whose monstrous ego, whose perverted need for total control, could never have brooked defeat. Faith turned to the next entry. A week had passed.

March 22, 1946

Just to have him in the house is wonderful, even though I do not see him. His name is Phelps, a funny name. I'd like to tease him about it, see him smile. He has a lovely smile. I've seen it twice. Once when we were introduced. "This is my wife. You recall what I've told you about her," the demon said in the deep, sincere voice he uses when he wants to make a good impression. That's the voice he uses all the time now, but I do not think Phelps will be fooled. He smiled at me and said, "I'm very pleased to meet you, ma'am." The second smile was over his shoulder as he followed my husband—how I hate to write those words—up the servants' staircase. There are rooms, a bath, and a small kitchen on the top floor— at the far end from the nursery—and that is where he is to be. Before I arrived, it was often occupied by students exchanging work for lodging. Phelps—I do not know his last name or where he is from—is at Harvard, attempting to make up the time he lost overseas. He does not look like a student, but like a man, and that is what he is. He is not very tall, but I could see from the way he carried his suitcases that he is strong. His eyes are blue, blue as the delphinium I hope he will plant for me. His hair is bright red and still short from the service. He was wearing his army trousers, a shirt, a tie, and a sweater, and carrying an army overcoat. He cannot be wealthy; otherwise, he'd have civilian clothes and not need to be wearing the ones from the service. Or he could be thrifty. I remember from the inn that some of the richest people looked as if they were down to their last penny. One lady used to sit and darn her gloves, when it was a wonder she could find a place that hadn't been mended. And she owned a railroad. Phelps wouldn't be at Harvard unless he had money, although he could have some sort of scholarship. I sound like a schoolgirl, but I have to imagine almost everything about him except his name. I am not likely to have the opportunity to speak to him. My husband's gout still troubles him, but he has gone back to work. Every morning, Phelps drives him there, then goes to his classes. He does not have a key to the house, I was told pointedly. They return together at the end of the day. Phelps does the chores, then goes to his quarters. Only then am I summoned to prepare the evening meal. The devil has worked it out perfectly. His gout has prevented us from sharing a bed, but I am locked in the spare room at night, as I am up here now. When Phelps goes to the garage, I am let up here or left downstairs under lock and key. The doors are so close to the floor that I cannot even push a note for Phelps underneath into the hall. In any case, my husband would see it before it would ever get to Phelps, and I know too well what that would mean.

Just now I looked out the window and saw Phelps in the front yard! It is a warm day. I can tell by placing my hand on the pane of glass. Phelps is in his shirtsleeves. He cannot get into the house, but the back gate is always open for deliveries, and all the garden tools are in the garage. Maybe his class was canceled, the professor picking up spring fever from his students. Or Phelps could not resist the sunshine and the garden calling to him. I am as sure as I am about anything in this world that he shares my passion for gardens. He is ripping out some ivy. I know it is impossible, but I can smell the new earth as he turns it over. Is it better or worse to have him here? I feel more trapped than ever. I thought I had cried out all my tears long ago, but they are streaming down my cheeks.

Joy is mine! I put you down, dear friend, and banged with all my might on the window, stopped and banged again. He heard! He came closer to the house and looked up at me and nodded. Just nodded his head, but I knew what he meant. He knows! He knows and he will save me somehow. I know he will. The Lord has not forsaken me and the dark night will lift.

We looked at each other for what seemed like an hour. I pushed myself against the glass, willing it to dissolve. Then he waved—a simple gesture, but how welcome—and went back toward the garage to get my jailer.

Faith felt her spirits soar as well. The story would have a happy ending, but her elation did not last. The upstairs room contained misery, not happiness—more misery than the woman's incarceration. Faith had never believed in spirits other than 80 proof, but there was something that had permeated that room, leaving a permanent stain of overwhelming tragedy. Yet now, Faith found herself drawn to the back stairs, the stairs Phelps had used—not just the husband—and went up to the top of the house.

The nursery door was closed, locked, and she averted her eyes. She had no desire to go into that room ever again. Instead, she looked in the other rooms, shivering slightly. They had turned the heat down up here, and the sun provided little warmth. It had been one of the coldest winters on record and the prediction was for more cold. Tom had come home depressed the night before at the news that an elderly homeless man had frozen to death in his makeshift dwelling under a highway exit ramp in downtown Boston. Shelter workers had tried to get him to come inside, but he had stubbornly refused, insisting that he could stay warm enough in his "home." He'd lined the small hut with planks of wood, blankets, and mattresses to block the wind, and he put on layers of clothing before getting into his sleeping bag and bedding down under more blankets.

"It was his right to stay where he was," Tom had said mournfully. "I talked with him several times when he came to Oak Street. He said it was his solution to affordable housing. He was a Korean War vet and lost his son in Vietnam. He didn't have anybody else, and after he lost him, he told me, the rest of his life was just marking time."

There was so much room in this house. It was absurd for the four of them to occupy so much space, but she didn't think Professor Robinson would want them taking in the homeless—and the neighbors would complain. NIMBY—property values could be affected.

The servants had lived in tiny rooms up here at the top of the house and shared a bath. The kitchen would have been put in much later, although it was a period piece now. There was nothing in the cupboards and drawers. Apparently, the professor didn't take boarders. She wandered into the first bedroom and sat on the iron bedstead. Was this where Phelps had slept? The bed had no linens, but next to it there was a small nightstand with a drawer. A lamp on a rather dusty doily stood on top. Other than that, the room was empty. The next bedroom was even more barren, filled with boxes of books, if the contents of all were the same as those on the top. Faith went back to the first room and sat on the bed. Phelps was not a common first name. He'd have graduated in the late forties. She could find out his last name, but what would that tell her? No, she had to find out the woman's name in order to find out what had happened to her.

She opened the drawer in the nightstand. Someone had lined it with paper, but it was empty. She pulled it all the way out and it fell to the floor. It wasn't a valuable antique, but Faith was still relieved to find it was in one piece. She started to slide it back in place, when she saw an envelope stuck in the back. She reached in and pulled it free. It was blank. The flap had not been sealed, but was tucked inside. She opened it and pulled out a snapshot. A beautiful dark-haired woman stood in front of a small tree. From the look of the surrounding earth, it had been newly planted. She was smiling and reaching out one hand toward the photographer. The woman was wearing a dark skirt and a light-colored twin set. It had a wintry look for what was obviously a spring day. Her face was pale, especially in contrast to her hair, which fell to

her shoulders in a long bob, a style popular in the forties. Behind her
was the same fence that enclosed the front yard now.

Faith turned it over. Someone had written "My Dora" on the back.

She had a name. Dora.

She had to be the woman who kept the diary. The photo was not a
crisp black-and-white one, but soft brown and off-white. The edges
were serrated. It was not a Polaroid, nor were there Kodak paper marks
on the back, and it was small, no oversize print. Aside from the
woman's clothes and hair, these characteristics, or lack thereof, placed
the picture in the same time period as the book. Faith had family pho-
tos that looked like this, pictures of her mother and father as teenagers.
Holding the photo in her hand, she felt a deep sense of sorrow,
although she wasn't sure why. The woman was smiling, gesturing to the
photographer—and she was in the yard, out of the house, out of the
prison. But all Faith could think about was what had happened next.

She replaced the drawer and put the photo back in the envelope, but
she did not put it back where she'd found it. She put it in the diary,
where it belonged.

Downstairs, as she was trying to figure out whether she had enough
time to go over to the Cambridge Public Library before she had to pick
up Amy, the telephone rang. It could be Richard, she thought as she
went to answer it. He's been tied up all week and his first words will be
"I'm sorry." She was so sure that what she was envisioning was true that
it took a moment for her to realize who it was.

"Oh, Dr. Robinson. Hello," she said.

"Please call me Teddy; everyone does. Even though we haven't met,
you are living in my house, which means you know me. Besides, I have
met your delightful husband."

Faith felt she did know Teddy from his house, although it might be a
problem calling a grown man and Harvard Divinity School professor by
the same name as one of Ben and Amy's nighttime stuffed companions.

"We're very grateful to you. The house is in a perfect location." She couldn't wax eloquent about the house's charms. It was too soon after reading the most recent diary entries. She needed some distance. But she did feel she should add something. "It's a very special place." *Special*—suitably ambiguous.

"Good! I'm glad you're enjoying yourselves. I'm calling for two reasons. First of all, I wanted to make sure that everything's working properly, especially the furnace during the cold spell I understand you've been having. Nasty of me to crow about the balmy temperatures here, but I will. It makes me wonder why I've never thought to escape the inclemency before."

"The furnace—and everything else—is working fine," Faith replied.

"The other thing is a bit of an imposition, and please feel free to say no, but I wonder if you could send me a light jacket that I failed to pack. It was hard to envision the need for what I consider part of my summer wardrobe in what would normally be winter."

"It wouldn't be any trouble at all. Tell me where it is and I'll do it right now."

"You *are* kind. I know sending packages is such a bother. Though I don't think you'll have any trouble finding the jacket. There's an armoire in the largest room on the same floor as the attic, and that's where I keep any outerwear I'm not using. I'm afraid you'll encounter a strong smell of mothballs. The jacket is beige, lined with red plaid. It will be the only one like that. I suppose I could pick up a similar one here, but then I'd have two."

This would be a severe catastrophe for a New Englander, as Faith knew from her husband, who could not understand why she had so many black skirts and black pants when one of each would fill the bill.

Faith often made snap decisions, and she made one now. Teddy was on the phone. Teddy had lived in the house for years. Maybe Teddy knew who the diarist was.

"I know exactly where your jacket is, because I have very imaginative children and they thought they could get to Narnia through your wardrobe." There was no need to explain C. S. Lewis's Narnia to a professor of religion.

"They sound delightful. Were they terribly disappointed? Or perhaps they were successful." Teddy gave a little laugh. Faith remembered Richard's description of the professor as "serious." He was serious, but apparently not humorless.

"They were disappointed. I've locked the door to prevent further exploration, but I found something."

"And what was that?"

"It's a diary written by a woman who lived in the house in the mid-forties. Do you have any idea who that could have been? Who owned the house before your uncle, or perhaps there was another owner in between?"

"Hmm, I know when the house was built, but not much about the owners over the years. I imagine there must have been a great many of them in that amount of time. Uncle Ned never mentioned the name of the owners prior to him."

"Oh well, it doesn't really matter. It's just that I've become interested in this woman. She was from Maine originally." Faith stopped. Somehow she couldn't bring herself to tell Teddy about the horrors that had occurred in his house—his beloved house.

"And it was in the armoire—wardrobe, rather—you say?"

"Yes, it had fallen through a crack in the rear and was wedged against the wall. My son found it. I don't think he made the crack worse, though, but please check when you return. We'll be happy to take care of any repair."

"Please don't be concerned. I'm sure he didn't. That thing has been there forever. Don't know how it was ever moved in. At one time, we thought of making the room a game room with a Ping-Pong table and such, but my uncle said it would be too much trouble to move that great old piece, which must have had the house built around it! We put the table in the basement instead. Now, you're sure it isn't a nuisance to send the jacket?"

"Absolutely sure," Faith reassured him.

"Then thank you very much. When I get back, you and Tom must come and have supper with me. I'd like to meet those children of yours, too."

"That sounds wonderful. We'll look forward to it. Good-bye."

"Good-bye, my dear."

It really wasn't much work to pack up the jacket. Faith had a box left over from Lands' End and she wrapped it in paper and string from the chest in the attic. With a good half hour left before she had to pick up Amy, she decided to try Maine information. She could check the Net, too, to search the state, if there were no Royces in the Bar Harbor area.

She gave the city, state, and the name Josephine Royce. An actual person came on the line.

"I don't have a Josephine, but I do have a J. Royce in Northeast Harbor."

"That would be fine, thank you," Faith said. Northeast Harbor was the next town over.

She took the number down and, with an eye on the clock, dialed quickly.

"Hello." It was a man's voice.

"Hello, I'm trying to find a Josephine Royce. She'd be in her late seventies by now, and I believe she worked with a relative of mine in an inn at Bar Harbor some time in the forties."

There was a long pause. Unlike Faith, Mainers did not make snap decisions.

"What exactly do you want with her?"

This was hard.

"I'd like to learn more about my relative when she was young. I never knew her, you see." Faith hoped he did.

There was another pause. Then Faith heard the man call, "Mother, have you got Aunt Josie's address?"

"Just a minute," he told Faith. "Here's my wife."

"Well, hello. So you're trying to trace your roots. So many people are doing it these days. I volunteer at the historical society, and a day doesn't go by that we don't get somebody looking for information. Well, Aunt Josie's my husband's father's sister, and I believe she did work at one of the inns before she got married to Sam Marshall. She's in a nursing home now near Saco. Went down to be close to her daughter, but anyone could have told her that Patty and Roy wouldn't stay put, and they didn't. Florida, and now Josie's setting in a rocker downstate, but she says she doesn't want to move at her age. We see her two or three times a year. My daughter likes to go to the outlets in Freeport, and Saco's only a little farther south. Maybe more than a little, but it's family. I'm sure you know what I mean."

Faith did, and she hoped that Josie Royce Marshall would be as loquacious as Mrs. J. Royce.

"Could I have the name and phone number of the nursing home?" Faith asked.

"You surely can, but it won't do you any good. Aunt Josie is as deaf as a post unless you're right by her side and shouting."

After some more words, including a lengthy description of the two-hundred-dollar suede jacket Arlene—"that's my daughter"—got for twenty-five dollars, Faith had the name and address of the home.

It looked as if she'd be making a trip to Maine.

6

F aith still had not heard from Richard Morgan. It didn't make any
sense. Not even a postcard. Thirteen years ago, she'd received at
least that.

She replayed each of their meetings, searching for clues, but turned
up nothing. Then she forced herself to confront the fact that he might
have felt she was looking for more than lunch and it wasn't the sort of
entanglement he had in mind, so he fled. Suburban Matron Desperately Seeking Solace. But she hadn't been and she wasn't—desperate,
that is. As for the seeking part, she didn't think it had come to that,
although replaying some of their conversations, maybe she had mentioned Tom's overinvolvement in his new world and maybe she had
touched on how much kids could take out of a person. Unconsciously,
like plant pheromones, had she been projecting something—something that was misinterpreted? But *he* had been the one dropping hints
so broad, they echoed all the way to Cambridge, filling her thoughts
from each meeting to the next. And she hadn't taken him up on any of
them. She'd smiled, been flattered. Who wouldn't have been? An
attractive man—no, make that a very attractive man. The hints had

remained hints—although she had kept meeting him—and, she admitted to herself, would be still if only she knew where he was.

She was so confused.

Then she decided to be worried. When Richard had dropped out of her life the last time, it had been with plenty of—well, some—warning and for a reason. This time, there had been nothing. She went back to obsessing that something must have happened to him on the street. He might be ill, lying in Mass General or some other hospital at this very moment. What was his alias? Richie, Richard Goodman. She could call around and see if he had been admitted. Maybe she'd do it later.

The day lay stretched out in front of her. Ordinarily, a gift of time like this would thrill her with its array of possibilities. Now she had trouble generating any, restless though she might be. She could go out to Aleford and experiment with some of the new pasta recipes she was fine-tuning for their Have Faith's spring menus. The best so far was the simplest— linguine with fresh asparagus (see recipe on page 220). Bite-size pieces of asparagus were cooked for a scant minute or two with sautéed onion and garlic. Then she added a little white wine and lemon juice to the bright green pieces, piling it all on top of the pasta portions. She hadn't figured out about the cheese yet—grated Parmesan, curls of Pecorino, or maybe no cheese at all, just a bit of salt and pepper? She had also tried the mixture pureed as a filling for ravioli, and that had been delicious, too.

But she didn't feel like going to work. She was annoyed with herself. Mooning around. It was getting pathetic. Self-involvement was boring even when encountered in oneself. Tom had mentioned that they were shorthanded in the kitchen at Oak Street because of the storm that was being predicted. The volunteers who came in from the suburbs didn't want to drive in bad weather or risk getting stranded. If she wasn't going out to Aleford, she should head down there. They prepared the evening meal around 1:00 P.M. Oak Street didn't serve lunch, only breakfast and dinner. With nothing on her plate except anxiety, Faith decided to go help out. Besides, it was as close as she could get to Richard at the moment.

As she walked down Brattle toward Harvard Square, she slipped her phone out of her purse and on impulse called Bitsy Higginson. They had not been able to get together as much as Faith had hoped—and Bitsy did not seem averse, either. Concerned as she was about Richard Morgan, the woman who wrote the diary—Dora—was never far from Faith's thoughts, especially since yesterday. She had a name and a face—a beautiful young woman's face. Faith knew that reading the diary would be even more heartrending now. Dora. Dora short for Eudora?

She couldn't make a trip to Maine without major juggling, but she could talk to Bitsy about the neighborhood. Even if Bitsy didn't know anyone who had lived there in the forties, she might have asked Uncle Ned to give her a tour of the house and he might have regaled her with stories of previous owners. Women like to look at houses; men don't. It's all they can do to tour one they are thinking of buying. Faith sometimes thought one of the reasons Tom went into a parish ministry was so he wouldn't have to go around and look at houses. "Oh, that's the parsonage, fine." His own father had stubbornly refused to move from their original house in Norwell, even as an expanding family made it much too small. And *he* was a real estate agent. But women love to look at other people's houses, which is why house tours are such a success. If Uncle Ned had told Bitsy anything about the Brattle Street house, she would remember it. Unlike others Faith knew, Bitsy never forgot anything. Whatever went into her file cabinet lobe remained retrievable and cogent.

Bitsy was home, and they arranged to have lunch at UpStairs on the Square the next day, weather permitting. Faith walked more briskly, feeling her heartbeat increase. With all these lunches, she was going to have to get a whole lot more exercise. Exercise reminded her of her sister, who had called twice since spilling the beans. The first call was late on Saturday night. She'd just gotten home after she and Quentin had taken the future grandparents to dinner.

Faith had been about to go to bed, but Hope had the kind of voice that chased drowsiness away.

"Fay, you were so right. I should have told them immediately. They were so sweet. Daddy cried a little. We took them to the Post House. Daddy never gets a steak. Maybe that's why there were tears in his eyes, come to think of it. No, it was definitely the baby. Quentin ordered martinis—not for me, of course—and then we told them."

Jane Sibley's idea of dinner was a nice piece of fish and a salad or a nice piece of chicken and a salad. Hope had been astute in her choice of venue. The Reverend Sibley did not see sirloin often—plus, the Post House always had salmon for Jane.

The next call from Hope had been to thank Faith for the books she'd sent. Hope said she'd hired a new personal trainer, one who specialized in pregnant women. Only in New York—or L.A. Hope was certain all these exercises would make for an easy delivery. Not wanting to point out the oxymoron, Faith had congratulated her sister on how well she was handling her pregnancy, and then she ordered her a few more books.

When Faith got to Oak Street, there was only one person in the kitchen, and he looked pretty harried. He was preparing franks and beans, plus macaroni and cheese, for dinner.

"Can you start the water for the macaroni while I finish cutting up these hot dogs? You're Mrs. Fairchild, right?"

"Yes, but please call me Faith."

"And I'm Don."

Don was a fixture at Oak Street. Faith didn't know whether he was an employee or a volunteer, but he'd been there every time she had, and Tom had spoken of him with fondness and respect. "I don't know how the man does it," he'd said. "Whatever else is going on around him, he just keeps cooking or doling out the food, completely unflappable."

Filling the large vats with water and setting them on the stove took no time at all, and Faith started opening cans of baked beans to heat with the hot dogs. There were some containers of barbecue sauce left over from another meal to add to the mixture, which would give it more flavor. The men weren't looking for haute cuisine, but many of them were quite picky and quick to complain. When she'd been serving one night, a man's criticism of the food had almost started a riot. Several of the regulars had surrounded him, shouting, "You're not at Locke-Ober's, pal" and "If you don't like it, get the hell out of here." Someone shoved him toward the door and he shoved back. The security guards had arrived and broken up the fight, leading the man to a far corner to eat and then bundling him out the door.

"There's coleslaw too," Don said. "A donation from Star Market. It's in the containers already in the fridge."

All the food had to be things the men could eat with forks and spoons. No knives. Butter was spread on the rolls with the cardboard squares it came on. And no glass bottles of juice. They'd had a donation of flats of Snapple and had had to pour it all into pitchers. They'd had other donations, too: dented out-of-date cans, some swelling, and boxes of crackers—high in salt, high in fat—that were too mangled to put on the supermarket shelves. Then there would be the bags of food that people would drop off—Faith had unloaded one that contained a bottle of balsamic vinegar, several packages of Peek Freen cookies, and Droste's cocoa. Obviously someone winnowing out a pantry and engaging in a little noblesse oblige. Very few people donated food that was nutritious—and that didn't mean fancy health food, just peanut butter, powdered milk, canned tuna, cans of fruits and vegetables, SPAM, Dinty Moore stew. She thought about how impossible it was to stay healthy when you were homeless, even though the shelters did the best they could. Fresh fruits, vegetables, and whole grains were rarities.

Tom had told Faith that Don would often sit and talk with the men after dinner was over. Recalling that, she asked, "Have you seen a man around lately with dark brown hair, blue eyes, pretty well dressed—a green wool jacket over a yellow Polartec pullover—in his early forties? Tall, almost six feet. Clean, and no problems with his teeth." She was thinking of all the smiles that had answered hers, smiles that displayed missing or blackened teeth, swollen, sore-looking gums. "His name is Richie."

Don stopped grating cheese and looked at her regretfully.

"Sorry, Faith, They're all called Richie, if you know what I mean."

She did.

When Harvard had kicked Mary-Catherine Deibel and Deborah Hughes out of the space their restaurant, UpStairs at the Pudding, had occupied so long and so well on the top floor of the Hasty Pudding Club on Holyoke Street, Cambridge and its environs were devastated. For months, rumors abounded: They would reopen; they wouldn't. They were moving to Brookline; they were moving to the South End. Finally, it was announced that they'd reopen, but the location would remain a secret for a while. Happily, the secret was now out. The restaurant had opened its doors in November, to rave reviews. If anything, the food was better, and the decor—well, the decor had to be seen to be believed. The Pudding location had looked like the inside of a Victorian chocolate box, with enough humor to take away the possibility of cloying sweetness. UpStairs at the Square left Victoriana behind—except for the sort represented by Swinburne and St. John's Wood—for a richly extravagant gold-leafed "Klimt meets Jean Harlow" look. Faith was meeting Bitsy at the Monday Club, the downstairs dining room. Crossing the larger area, she noted a cheerful blaze in one of the two huge fireplaces at either end, adjacent to a long, curving bar. Faith stopped to admire the crystal chandeliers—each one different, each one funky. She recognized some of the furnishings from the old restaurant—the gold faux-bamboo banquet chairs, and possibly the immense ornate mirror on one wall—but the Hasty Pudding Show posters that had decorated the former space were gone. Generations of Harvardians had relished the opportunity to kick up their heels in drag and let their hair way down during the Pudding shows, and still did. Pushing from her mind the thought that she couldn't ask Richard if he'd ever been involved in these irreverent capers, she stepped through a doorway into the Monday Club's smaller room, a kind of glass-enclosed veranda across the front of the building. It was a jewel box of reds and golds, with wall-to-wall zebra-striped carpeting. Bitsy was sitting at a table by the window and seemed to be enjoying the choice view of tiny Winthrop Square in the heart of Harvard Square. Despite the cold, there were plenty of people to watch. She got up and greeted Faith heartily, a resounding smack on the cheek and a hug, no air kisses for her.

"I'm so glad to see you, and I want to hear all about what you've been doing. Do you love it yet?"

"Cambridge?" Faith had already fallen head over heels for the new Upstairs. "I'm not sure *love* is the right word. *Like* is, though. Very definitely *like*."

"That reminds me of a friend of mine. This was years ago. She'd met a man, and when I asked her how she felt about him, she said, 'I'm liking him, but not loving him.' Unfortunately, they got married. It didn't last long. So, you're still wedded to your Manhattan. It certainly can't be Aleford that has the prior claim to your affections. Well, that's perfectly fine. I admire loyalty. Now, let's each have a kir royale. This is that sort of place, isn't it?"

Faith agreed.

While they were waiting for their food, Faith plunged straight in. "I've gotten curious about Dr. Robinson's house—and the neighborhood, too. I've been reading about Tory Row and some of the other things you've mentioned. Wordsworth Bookstore had a great book, *Literary Trail of Greater Boston*, which includes Cambridge, of course."

"Oh yes, Susan Wilson's book. It's wonderful."

"Did Uncle Ned—I can't think of him any other way—ever give you a tour of the house, mention any interesting anecdotes about the people who lived there?"

"Of course I had to see the house. I love to look at other people's houses. You have to come to mine, and I'll take you to my neighbor's, too. She has a wonderful English stucco house that she's painted a kind of cantaloupe color in the middle of all our stodgy brick and white clapboard. Ned asked me back for tea—too much going on during the New Year's Day party. But I'm afraid no one famous ever lived there. If you're looking for T. S. Eliot or a Lowell or a James, you're out of luck. Margaret Fuller lived on Brattle, but much closer to the Square. Bartlett lived on Brattle, too, but at One sixty-five. He liked to walk to work. His bookstore was at the corner of Holyoke and Mass. Ave. I imagine he must have used the time to think of more quotations. A very energetic man, and what an astonishing memory. He published nine editions of *Bartlett's* before he died in the early 1900s. Justin Kaplan is doing a nice job with it now."

"While it would have been fun to be climbing the same stairs as some notable, I was thinking of more prosaic occupants. Did Uncle Ned ever mention anything about them?"

"No," Bitsy said firmly. "I always had the impression that Ned's house was Ned's house—and now Teddy's, of course. Anyone who had owned it before didn't matter."

The food arrived quickly, but not too quickly. They had both ordered the roasted red pepper soup, one of the lunch specials, and it *was* special—sweet and rich.

They talked about other things—their mutual dislike of Filene's Basement and even greater dislike of the proclivity of their friends to show them all the wonderful bargains they had purchased there. "I can't go through racks and bins," Bitsy said, adding acerbically, "but apparently there are Armanis for pennies and Laurens for a nickel."

Faith steered the conversation back to Brattle Street, moving to plan B.

"Do you know anyone in my neighborhood who might have lived there long enough to have some interesting stories about the house, and those nearby?"

Faith had considered telling Bitsy—and maybe Pix and Niki—about the diary, but somehow it seemed wrong. It was such an intimate piece of writing, so searingly emotional, that at times Faith herself felt guilty for reading what was obviously meant to be private. That's what diaries were—private. Except if you were Virginia Woolf or A Mad Housewife.

Bitsy had scraped the last drop of her soup from the bowl, and it took her a moment to swallow.

"It's not actually *my* neighborhood. And for years there's been a migration to Ten ten."

Faith looked mystified.

"Ten ten Memorial Drive, that tall building smack next to Mount Auburn Hospital. The joke is that you leave your big house on Brattle Street or Francis Avenue for a spacious apartment there, almost literally dropping in at Mount Auburn whenever you need to, and finally make your way a few blocks down the street to Mount Auburn Cemetery. All very convenient."

After laughing at the image Bitsy had conjured up, Faith said, "Mount Auburn Cemetery is beautiful. As you can imagine, it was one of the first places Pix took me to when I moved to Aleford."

Bitsy nodded. "Of course. Prime spot for bird-watchers, and it's heaven in the spring, when the trees are in bloom. Heaven all year round, of course. Only the best people are planted there. Sinners must apply elsewhere. But I do know someone living near you who might fill the bill. What time do you have to pick your little girl up at school?"

"She has a play date today, so I don't have to be home until three." Faith didn't know whether it was the kir, the warm soup, or the lining up of the planets that had arranged for her children to be occupied, but she was filled with a sense of well-being. She hadn't felt this way in awhile. Bitsy was smiling at her knowingly.

"It's hard to keep all those pins in the air at once, isn't it?" she commented.

This wasn't Niki's mother's Vulcan mind meld. This was a kindred spirit.

Bitsy left after their salads—warm endive with bacon, Roquefort, and a poached egg—to call her friend, but she insisted Faith order dessert. When Faith took a bite, she was grateful. It was something called a banana chocolate potpie: warm, dense dark-chocolate mousse with not too much banana, served in a pot de crème container and topped with a thin dark-chocolate wafer—the equivalent of a flaky crust. A dollop of bourbon whipped cream made it perfection. New Englanders were addicted to chicken potpies. They appeared dressed up or down on almost every menu Faith had seen, nouvelle or ancienne. This potpie matched its surroundings. It turned the predilection on its ear—sensuous and naughty.

Bitsy was back. "She's home, and she'd love some company."

"And she is . . ."

"Margaret Ward, your neighbor. I think she's what you're after, and if she isn't, she'll know who is."

Margaret Ward lived on a side street off Brattle, a block away from Dr. Robinson. Her house was from the same period, and Bitsy had said the Wards had lived there forever. It didn't take them long to walk over. Yesterday's storm had dropped a few more unwanted inches of snow all over Boston and more to the west, but today felt like spring—sunny and mild. For a brief moment, the filthy mounds that lined the streets and sidewalks were covered with a sparkling new coat. They arrived at Margaret Ward's house, and when she answered the door in person, Faith's hopes soared. The right vintage. She appeared to be in her eighties, but Faith was sure that after they left, Bitsy would tell her Margaret was 102 or something like that. After Faith had moved to Aleford, she met a youthful-looking older gentleman at a parish welcome party and he told her he had recently taken up spinning. They'd talked about various forms of exercise—he was a cardiologist—and it was only afterward that she discovered he was not the seventy-two-year-old she had taken him for, but ninety-two. Margaret did not have a dowager's hump, but was ramrod-straight, all five feet of her. She and Bitsy made a fine pair. Margaret's hair was white, bright white, without any gray or sallow yellow. It was captured in a neat bun. She wore a soft blue wool dress, the collar fastened with a large cameo. Mother's? Grandmother's?

She led them into a sunny living room crammed with all the objets d'art Faith had come to expect in these Cambridge houses. A good Oriental on the floor, Rose Medallion bowls on the shelves, etchings that might be Rembrandts but probably weren't, a possibly Corot landscape, and some Japanese prints. The wing chairs and sofa had slipcovers, crimson damask for the wintertime, and an abundance of tilt-top, piecrust, drum, and other assorted tables dotted the room. An elderly woman entered after Bitsy made the introductions, and Margaret ordered tea: "Darjeeling, I think, for today."

That accomplished, she turned to Faith and said, "I understand from Bitsy—are you still calling yourself that, Evelyn?—that you want to know more about the history of this part of Brattle."

Before Faith could reply, Bitsy said, "It's not so much that I'm calling myself that; it's everyone else for the last sixty years. But I'll answer to Evelyn."

Margaret gave her a slightly wicked smile, and Faith began to feel she was distinctly outmatched.

"Yes, we're living in Dr. Robinson's house for the semester. I'm from New York City and moved to Aleford when I married my husband." She paused. Of course she'd married her husband—who else? And could she avoid referring to Bitsy by name for the rest of the visit? Now she couldn't decide whether to call her Bitsy or Evelyn in front of Margaret. "I don't know much about Cambridge," she finished bravely.

"Well, you wouldn't, would you? We used to go to New York occasionally. My husband was partial to the old Metropolitan Opera House. He didn't care for the new place. We went once and never again."

Faith presumed by "the new place," Margaret was referring to the one at Lincoln Center, which had opened in 1966. If Faith didn't get back to the city every month or so, she felt oxygen-deprived. Not knowing what to say, she simply nodded.

"I listen to it on the radio, though," Margaret said.

"Are you still getting to the symphony?" Bitsy asked.

Margaret looked shocked. "Of course. The day I have to turn in my seat will be the day they carry me out of here."

Faith could well imagine it would be.

Tea arrived and was served in thin Chinese Export cups. Danish butter cookies, the kind that come in a tin, were passed around. Faith was used to this kind of discrepancy in New England. Margaret would never use a tea bag, but the cookies could be store-bought.

Cup in a hand that looked too frail to hold even its slight weight, Margaret began.

"It is an area rich in history. The Riedesel house is across the street from me—the front faces Brattle—and I'll be happy to arrange for you to have a peek at its famous window. It's a lovely story. In November 1777, we took a number of prisoners of war from Burgoyne's army, including the Hessian general Riedesel, who had his family with him, goodness knows why. They were imprisoned in that house—the Lechmere House—which we'd confiscated from the Tories. His wife, Baroness von Riedesel, was very gay, so the time would have seemed long to her. One day when she must have been exceptionally bored, she wrote her name and the date with her diamond on the windowpane in her room. It's still there, just as she left it."

Faith could not help but think of another woman imprisoned on Brattle Street, many years later and under far worse conditions.

"Do you know anything about the history of our house—I mean Dr. Robinson's? Who lived there before him?"

"Well, it belonged to his uncle, a sweet man. I don't know why he never married. Perhaps because he enjoyed being so desirable. I can't tell you the number of times I had him to dinner here to even out my table. But I never had any skills as a matchmaker. My sister prides herself on her ability, but I tell her it's simply coincidence."

"How about before Ned Robinson? Who owned the house?" Faith knew a sense of urgency had crept into her voice, and Bitsy was looking at her appraisingly.

"We bought this house in 1970. Ned was here when we came. We'd been living in another part of Cambridge before that. The owner of this house was Mrs. Porter—she'd just been widowed and was going to

Weston to live with her son's family. After we'd signed all the papers, she took me for a walk around the neighborhood. I remember it was the end of April and everything was blooming. We stopped to admire that star magnolia in your yard. Back then, it just cleared the fence. Of course now, it's even more spectacular. Just wait.

"She told me that her children always believed there was a ghost in that house, which would have been long before Ned's time. I probably shouldn't be telling you all this. Are you the nervous type, my dear?"

"Not at all," Faith said firmly. "And, although I doubt I'll tell my children, my son especially would be thrilled to live in a place that was haunted."

"Just like my children," Margaret said. "Little ghouls. Well, of course I wanted to hear about it all. Mrs. Porter said she never saw her, but her children used to come home from school and say there was a ghost looking out the window on the top floor. It was a lady. And once, they saw another ghost fly from a tree through the window. That's the only interesting thing I've ever heard about the house, I'm afraid. Except for Ned and Teddy's New Year's Day open houses. They were legendary. After too much eggnog at one, my husband walked into our next-door neighbor's house, thinking he was home—I'd gone on before. I was probably pregnant. I usually was in those days. Needless to say, he startled them, but they were good about it and brought him home."

They had some more tea and Margaret continued to reminisce, taking them to Boston with one remark: "Now you mustn't think my name has anything to do with the Watch and Ward Society. You do know about that, don't you?"

"The 'banned in Boston' people? The censors?" Faith replied.

"Yes. We had more fun outwitting them then we probably would have had without them. During the forties, we would all go to the Old Howard, even women. It wasn't just burlesque; comics played it. The doorman had a buzzer that set off a red light when any of the Watch and Ward came. The girls would put on more clothes and the comics would clean up their acts. We'd go down to the South End for jazz and out to Norumbega Park in Newton to the Totem Pole Ballroom to dance. It was beautiful—banks of velvet couches—and all the big bands played there. No alcohol, couples only, and everybody dressed to the nines. My husband loved to dance. We'd go there and all sorts of other places. It was just after the war and everybody was happy to be alive."

"Women wore hats. My mother wouldn't have gone out of the house without a hat. I even had hats when I was first married," Bitsy said.

"Hats are coming back," Faith added.

"They've been saying that for years," Margaret said sternly. "We're talking about *hats*. Hats every single day."

Faith was chastened. She knew about hats—and gloves. Her grandmother still had boxes of both. She shouldn't have said anything.

They had another round of tea, then Faith realized she'd just make it in time to pick Amy up. Thanking Margaret profusely, she promised to come again. Cambridge was turning out to be full of kindred spirits, even if their horizons ended at the Charles River.

"Good-bye, Faith," Bitsy said. She was staying on and they were switching to scotch. "Maybe someday you'll tell me what this is all really about."

Walking down Brattle in the glancing late-afternoon light, Faith passed their house on her way to Buckingham Street, where Amy was. She stopped and stared up at the windows on the third floor as those children had done. Those children who had seen "ghosts," seen Dora.

The windows were empty now.

March 29, 1946

I can scarcely believe what has happened, and I have had to sit for some time until I could control my trembling fingers enough to write. It has been a week since I have been up here in the nursery, and I was terrified that somehow he had found out about our wordless exchange. I have been seeing it over and over in my mind, like a movie, to the point where

I began to fear that I was projecting it to his mind, as well. But today,
he pushed me into the nursery and I heard the key turn in the lock with
something like happiness.

The sky has been overcast and rain threatens. It has been like this
all week. I have mother's Bible with me and had turned to a passage I
have read often during my imprisonment, Psalm 102:

Here my prayer, O Lord,
and let my cry come unto thee.
Hide not thy face from me
in the day when I am in trouble.
Incline thine ear unto me;
in the days when I call, answer me speedily.
For my days are consumed like smoke,
and my bones burn as a furnace.
My heart is smitten, and withered like grass;
I forget to eat my bread

As I reached this line, I heard a noise, and suddenly there he was!
Phelps! Outside the window, in the big pine! He took a hammer from his
pocket and went to work on the nails that secured the window nearest
to the branch he was crouched upon, then used some pliers, as well. It
seemed to take forever, as he carefully put each nail in his pocket. I was
in an agony of fear, forgetting that my husband would not be home
until Phelps went to get him. I have been increasingly irrational as each
day has gone by with Phelps so near and yet impossible to reach. I
turned the inside catch as soon as I saw him, and finally the window
swung open. In an instant, he was by my side! I know you will
understand that I could not help but throw my arms around him and
sob for joy. I climbed many trees in my childhood and now could
scarcely wait to climb down this one. First, I had to acquaint him with
the truth of my situation. He believed every word, telling me he thought
something was very odd about the arrangement. But tempted as he was

to take me away immediately—and I to go with him—we have decided
we must wait and think of a plan. I cannot let him sacrifice his
education, his chance for a good life, for me. My husband is too well
known, too respected in this community. He would ruin Phelps, and I
would be brought back to suffer unimaginable pain.

But I can bear my life here now, knowing there will be an end to it.
We will wait until Phelps's term of employment is over and his degree
finished, only a matter of this semester, the summer and fall. He seems
to think my husband will keep him on, that he likes to have a driver and
someone to do the heavy chores. But even if he must leave, he will find a
way to come to me from time to time, until he can take me away for
good. Then we will climb down the pine together and go to the West or
South for a new start. This is a large country and we will disappear into
it. Before he left, he took my hand and said, "I thought love at first sight
was something poets dreamed up, but I know now it can happen. It has
happened to me."

It has happened to me, too. Even watching him nail the window
shut did not dampen my spirits. I knew the Lord would hear my prayer.

So these were the ghosts Mrs. Porter's children had seen so many
years ago. Phelps, for all his precautions, had not escaped notice. Faith
closed the little book and pictured the Rapunzelesque scene—Dora's
happiness and hope. But did they finally climb down the tree together?
Did the lady in the tower escape the wicked witch, or, in this case, ogre?

Faith was sitting in the living room. In the morning, light streamed
in and it was a pleasant place to be. Sunbeams filled with tiny floating
dust motes fell in streaks across the rich colors of the carpet, their lan-
guor at odds with the emotions stirred by the diary. How often had Dora
been in this room? It was her husband's domain, not hers. Did she ever
sit before these diamond panes, her heart filled with longing for the
outdoors, fresh air to breathe, earth beneath her feet? Ever have a
moment here alone? Faith picked the book up again. She had to keep
reading, even though she feared the ending would be sad. It was a line

from a song in Rodgers and Hammerstein's *Carousel*—a haunting, plaintive melody, "What's the Use of Wond'rin'?"

Dora and Phelps. Richard. What *was* the use of wondering?

The phone rang and she hastily pushed the book into the drawer of the Queen Anne lowboy that was near the door to the library. She never left the diary out, not only because Ben was insatiably curious—a trait he quite possibly inherited from his mother—but also because she had come to regard the act of reading it as something between the two of them, something between Dora and Faith alone. In the same way—keeping faith—she tried to avoid using the phone in here, although the one from 1946 had been replaced many times. It was just the idea of it.

"Faith, I'm glad I caught you. I'm at Oak Street, and we've had a terrible shock. One of the men was killed last night in front of the shelter. I'll be here all day and into the evening, in case anyone needs me."

"Oh, Tom, that's terrible. Was he hit by a car?"

This was a common cause of accidents, especially on these icy nights—and the men at Oak Street were not always aware of oncoming traffic.

"No, worse. He was murdered. Stabbed. Right outside the side entrance, sometime during the night. He was found at dawn in the doorway."

"Murdered! But why would anyone want to kill someone like that? He couldn't have had any money."

"I know. It doesn't make sense, except he could have quarreled with another man over a bottle, drugs, even over a blanket, and things got out of hand. The police are here questioning everyone who was around, and that's been upsetting. A lot of them have, as we say, issues with authority—there are cops and there are cops."

"I know," said Faith. "But what an awful thing to happen! It's been such a hard winter, and now another fear to add to the ones about finding a warm bed and food."

"I think they're more used to violence, things like this, than we are. It's part of their everyday lives. Still, I've been praying with more men than usual this morning and hearing almost more than I can bear about their lives."

As Tom spoke, Faith was thinking how different this was from the man who had died last week of hypothermia. That had been tragic, but it had been his choice to stay where he was. This time, the victim hadn't had a choice. Maybe it hadn't been another street person. Maybe it had been someone, or more than one—a gang—getting kicks. After all, weren't these people huddled under the moving-company quilts or tattered sleeping bags nonhumans, one step above trash? Or below?

"Was there anything unusual about the crime? Had he been beaten up? Did the police find the weapon?" Her questions spilled out as she felt increasingly angry and helpless.

"Nothing. I haven't heard anything about his having been beaten beforehand. He was just rolled up in a bunch of bedding outside the door, with a knife in his chest—a buck knife. With everyone wearing gloves in this weather, forget prints. No. Nothing unusual—except that a man who was alive yesterday is dead now. Young—only in his forties." Tom sounded bitter.

"Was he someone the people at the shelter knew? A regular?"

"Apparently not, although one of the workers said he thought he'd been here for dinner once. He recognized the jacket. His wallet was still in it—five bucks, a phone card, and a New York driver's license. His name was Richard Morgan."

"*What* was his name?" Faith tried to keep her voice steady.

"Richard Morgan."

7

F aith shoved her fist against her mouth to keep the scream inside
and let her body slide to the floor, her back resting against the
bookcase.

"Honey, they need the phone," Tom said. "I have to go. I'll call you
later. Love you."

Pressing her head against the hard shelves, Faith took her hand
from her mouth and managed to get some words out.

"Bye. Love you, too."

Then she cried.

S he wasn't sure how much time had passed, but the first shock of
grief had lessened. "The endin' will be sad." The line, the tune
from the musical kept running through her thoughts. What had Richard
been doing since she saw him last, that last lunch date? Her eyes filled
with tears again. What had he uncovered that had gotten him killed?
Drugs. It had to be drugs. A whole operation, something big. Had they
figured out that he wasn't who he appeared to be? Taken him for an

undercover cop? Or for what he was—a reporter, a writer? In any case, someone who would inform on them? As she ran these possibilities through her mind, she kept coming back to the fact that she was the only one who knew who he was. She was the one who would have to get in touch with his family. She was still slumped against the bookcase. His family. That meant his sister. What was her name?

Faith closed her eyes. She was in F. A. O. Schwarz on Fifth Avenue. It was December 1989. Richard was teasing her about her preference for the original location, across the street but on the same side of Fifth. That was the "real" F. A. O. Schwarz, with its grand staircase curving up to the second floor, a staircase a beautiful fairy godmother might suddenly descend—gracefully, like Loretta Young, in yards and yards of chiffon. The new store, with its glass elevator next to a gigantic clock that was decorated with storybook characters and played the same tune endlessly, was crass in comparison.

They'd had fun picking out gifts for his niece and nephew; then they'd taken them to be wrapped and shipped. The harried salesperson had had to ask Richard to repeat the name and address. It floated before Faith's eyes: Scarsdale, yes, definitely Scarsdale, and Mrs. Gordon P. Fletcher. The young clerk had spelled it back to them: "*G* as in *good, o* as in *okay*." When she got to *P*, she'd said "*P* as in Ptolemy," and Richard had asked her if she was majoring in ancient history. She wasn't, but she did the *New York Times* crossword puzzle every day. The scene was so vivid—the brightly colored Christmas decorations, the sounds of overexcited children, even the dumb music—Faith didn't want to open her eyes. But she did. She had to call Richard's sister. That was the first thing she had to do. Then she'd call the shelter. Or go down there. Richard would have been taken away by now. But she wanted to be there. Tell them in person. The police were investigating, but when they found out who Richard really was, she knew they'd step up their efforts. His family would put pressure on them, so would his colleagues. It would be all over the papers.

Oh, Richard, why did you have to write *this* book? Why did you have to get yourself killed?

She went into the kitchen and made a strong cup of coffee, then sat down and called information, hoping that the family hadn't moved. Toddlers then, the children were teenagers now, Richard had said. People didn't move when their kids were in high school, especially from a town with a school district like Scarsdale's.

They hadn't. And the number wasn't unlisted.

It was 11:00 A.M. If Richard's sister worked outside the home, there would be no answer, since it was Monday, a workday. Should she leave a message or not? Faith debated. Not, she'd keep trying until she got either his sister or brother-in-law. It wasn't the kind of news anyone should get on an answering machine.

She started to cry again, then pulled herself together and dialed the number.

A woman answered. "Hello?"

"May I speak to Mrs. Gordon Fletcher, please?"

"This is she."

Faith took a deep breath, stood up, and braced herself against the kitchen counter.

"My name is Faith Fairchild, and I'm sorry to be giving you news like this over the phone, but I thought you needed to know immediately that—"

Her voice angry, terrified, Richard's sister interrupted her. "Has something happened to Jessica or Ethan? Oh my God, it's Gordon! He's had another heart attack! Where is he?"

"No, I'm sorry, I should have said right away. It's your brother, Rich—"

Again the woman interrupted, but now there was only anger in her voice. "Look, Faith whatever. I don't have a brother. I *had* one once, but that was a long time ago. Has he borrowed money from you? You loaned him your car and it's gone? Whatever it is, forget about it, kiss it good-bye, and *don't* call me again."

"Wait! Please don't hang up! I don't understand! I must have the wrong person. I'm talking about Richard Morgan, the reporter, the writer."

"Yes, and I'm talking about Richard Morgan the alcoholic, the gambling addict who broke his parents' hearts and even stole from my children when he was last here. The Richard Morgan who did time for using stolen credit cards. The one I haven't seen in seven years. That Richard Morgan."

For a moment, Faith was speechless. Then slowly she said, "I knew him in 1989, then met him again in Boston recently at a homeless shelter. He told me he was doing research for a book."

"That's my brother—or rather, that's Richard Morgan. A plausible story for every situation; plus, he could charm the birds from the trees—and did. I'm not surprised he's hit bottom. It's happened before. The first time, we were sure he would change. And for a while, he did. The second time, our hopes were still high, but by the fifth or sixth time, we'd given up. You must have met him during one of those periods. Nineteen eighty-nine. I remember he came for Christmas that year and wouldn't even touch the plum pudding with hard sauce. It was the best gift he could have given us; unfortunately, he took it back. He's a very talented man. He could have been a great writer."

"He's dead, Mrs. Fletcher." Faith couldn't think of any other way to put it. She was so stunned by this new view of Richard, she could barely think straight. "The circumstances aren't clear, but he died of a knife wound sometime last night or early this morning outside the shelter."

His sister was silent, apparently absorbing the news. When she spoke, she sounded even more angry, more bitter.

"Look, I suppose you expect me to get all sentimental and rush up there to bring him here and lay him to rest, but Richard killed my mother and father. Someone stuck a knife in him, but he'd done that to them, not once, but over and over again. They bailed him out, paid his debts, until finally, the last time, they died instead. I told him never to get in touch with me, *ever*. If you had watched what he did to them, to us, you'd understand. I don't want him near them, even in death."

Faith did understand, although she didn't want to.

His sister continued talking. "I don't know what that shelter does in situations like this, but as far as I'm concerned, he has no next of kin, and I don't want you telling them otherwise."

"I won't tell them about you, I promise. No one actually knows that I knew him. It was just by chance that I was volunteering the night he came in for a meal. I never saw him at the shelter again."

"Then let it go. Are you married?"

"Yes, and we have two children, an eight-year-old and a five-year-old."

A heavy sigh came over the phone. "Concentrate on your family. Forget about Richard. Let the authorities deal with it. I know I sound hard. Believe me, no sister ever loved her brother as much as I did. He was four years older and I thought he hung the moon. When he went off to Harvard and then began his writing career, we all thought he'd get a Pulitzer, make the best-seller list. And sweet, he was always sweet. The drinking started when he was in high school, but that's what guys did, we thought. During college, he'd stay sober when he was home. We never knew what was going on until one of his friends called to tell us he'd been hospitalized with acute alcohol poisoning. The gambling—he was always a gambler, always took a dare. He told me once it was more exciting than sex, because the rush lasted longer—if you were on a winning streak. My Richard died a long time ago. He killed himself. Now, you go and take care of your husband and kids. Forget you ever heard of Richard Morgan. You were duped."

"I'm sorry." Faith started to try to say something more. It was so awful. All those years. All those broken promises. False hopes.

"I'm sorry, too. Hey, my name is Janice. Call me again if you need to. You sound in pretty bad shape. I would be, too, if I found out something like this about an old boyfriend. That's what he was, right?"

"Sort of," Faith said, struck by the oddity of the situation. She had imagined that she would be comforting Janice, not the other way around.

"Okay, then. I've had lots of therapy because of Richard, and some-one else might as well benefit from it, too. Not all families are like the Waltons, although I suppose these days my kids, who are older than yours, would say the Osbournes."

"Thank you, and I *am* sorry. Sorry for it all."

"I know you are, Faith. Take care. Good-bye."

"Good-bye."

Faith hung the phone up, sat down again, and realized she had no idea what she was going to do next.

D uped. Janice said Faith had been duped. Richard had hidden part of his life—most of his life—from her, but had she been duped? He'd never asked her for money or anything else that would indicate he had a gambling problem. He liked to go to the track, he'd told her once, enjoyed playing the ponies. But he'd been so caught up in *The New Yorker* profile he was working on when they met, fascinated by the po-litical climate of the late 1980s as reflected in the career of Michael Stanstead, and equally excited about the book he was working on, she couldn't imagine when he would have found the time to gamble. Was it all a lie? She didn't think so. A functioning alcoholic, functioning at a high level, at least in those days. He *had* been at Tiananmen Square, interviewed Salman Rushdie when he was in hiding, covered Malcolm Forbes's $2 million Moroccan birthday bash. She'd seen the articles. He did drink more than she did. Pictures she'd suppressed popped up— two bottles of wine after a few martinis to start. She'd have a glass or two; he'd drink the rest, always finishing with a large snifter of brandy. And this time, at the Copley, the Ritz, Radius, all the places they'd been recently, he'd always ordered a drink as soon as they sat down—and greeted it, she realized, like an old friend. She had been duped, but, unlike Janice, she could feel only sorrow. Faith hadn't witnessed the other Richard. He was the Richard he perhaps wanted to be when he was with Faith, and he was the Richard she wanted, too, she admitted to herself. Handsome, witty, highly intelligent, and caring. That couldn't have been an act—the way he felt about the street people he'd met. One of whom had killed him. It was probably a fight over a bottle after all.

And the way he felt about her—*that* couldn't have been an act.

Faith's head ached. She couldn't tell anyone at Oak Street about Richard without involving Janice. Besides having promised, Faith couldn't add to the pain that family had already suffered. It was up to them. Perhaps when Janice talked to her husband, Gordon, she would decide to get in touch with the shelter. Bury her brother. But it wasn't up to Faith. Richard wasn't anything to her except an old friend she'd run into again recently.

Even as she told herself this half-truth, she was planning what to do. If she told Tom, he'd want to tell someone at the shelter—and he'd be right. But there was one person who could help her think things out. One person who knew Richard and knew the street. One person who might also know who had killed him. The Monk. The man from Dover who had found peace. The weather was getting warmer. It shouldn't be hard to find him, and she knew exactly where to start. Every Friday, he went to the Arlington Street Church for supper. Like Richard, he liked the meat loaf. She'd go there, and in the meantime, she'd drive up to Maine and visit Dora's friend, Josephine Royce. It was something to do and something that seemed more important than ever now with Richard's death. She could control at least that much of her life.

She could find out what had happened to Dora.

I have a big favor to ask you," Pix Miller said. They were out at the catering kitchen. She was taking inventory and Faith was trying out a recipe for something she'd decided to name Cambridge Tea Cake (see recipe on pages 221–222).

"Shoot—and you know whatever it is, I'll do it."

"Maybe not." Pix laughed. "I want you to cater a birthday party for Millicent. A surprise party at Mother's house."

"Do you think that's wise? She's been in her sixties for so long that any hint we all know she's not could really backfire."

"In fact, she's turning eighty-five, but you know Mother. She has this idea that no one ever does anything for Millicent, and she's done so much for Aleford. No mention will be made of age. Just a few candles scattered across the cake."

If Ursula Lyman Rowe, Pix's redoubtable octogenarian mother, had decided to give a party for Millicent, then Faith might as well get out her cake pans and be done with it. It wasn't that Ursula was tough. She simply managed to get you to think that what she wanted you to do was what you wanted, too. Millicent, on the other hand, was tough and seldom employed tact. Faith and she had gotten off to a bad start when Faith had rung the bell in Aleford's old belfry—a bell cast by a distant cousin of Paul Revere's, a man who also happened to be Millicent's great-great-great-grandfather. The bell was tolled only for the death of presidents and descendants of those fallen on that "famous day and year," and as the call to arms each Patriots' Day during the reenactment of the battle. Faith had had a very good reason for pulling the rope. Baby Benjamin was strapped to her chest in his Snugli and she had just discovered the still-warm corpse of a member of First Parish's congregation. It was highly possible that the murderer was still lurking in the bushes. Millicent Revere McKinley hadn't seen it that way. There were all sorts of other alternatives—her favorite being for Faith to run down Belfry Hill screaming. Being a New Yorker, Millicent had proclaimed, Faith should be good at running and screaming. Then over the course of some years, Millicent had saved Faith's life—twice. Faith had been trying to think of ways to even the score ever since, entertaining visions of throwing Millicent onto the rails of the commuter line, then pulling her back to safety just before the train roared by, or snatching a previously doctored scone from her lips before she took a bite. Maybe catering the party would be a start, although she doubted it. A party was a party, a drop in the punch bowl compared to Millicent's actions.

"When does Ursula want to throw this bash? Because of course I'll do it."

"Sunday afternoon. Sorry for the short notice. Mother only found out that this is Millicent's actual birthday yesterday, and she decided the nonsense about pretending not to get any older had to stop. She was at Town Hall, paying her water bill, when she decided to have a look at some of the town records."

Faith knew that Ursula and other Alefordians routinely mined Town Hall for light reading, in much the same way that others perused the new books shelf at the library or the displays at Sundial Books.

"She says she doesn't know why it didn't occur to her before, but better late than never. And Millicent *has* done a lot for the town. All that research. Keeper of the flame. You know what I mean."

Indeed Faith did. Millicent was still lobbying at Town Meeting to get the town to change its name from Aleford to Haleford. She averred that the *H* had been inadvertently dropped and obscured by the mists of time. She had copious documentation that proved to her satisfaction that the town was named for the Hales, one of its illustrious first families, and not because it was the site of a well-known and well-frequented tavern near one of the best fords of the Concord River. Millicent, or "Thoroughly Militant Millie," as she was known each spring during Town Meeting, was a lifelong teetotaler, and any suggestion that the town she would literally die for had been named for an alcoholic beverage was anathema.

"We'll do a red-white-and-blue cake. She'll like that. And how about a high tea—or maybe Ursula might want to change it to a luncheon? I'd be happy to do a full meal. The party we're doing Saturday night is just a pretheater cocktails fund-raiser for the American Repertory Theatre, so I have time."

"She specifically said afternoon and commented on how difficult it was to have any sort of ecumenical luncheon, what with the Congregationalists starting church at ten, the Episcopalians at eleven, and the Unitarians at ten-thirty, but running over until God knows when."

"And He does," Faith said solemnly. They both burst out laughing. "Tea it is, then, but a substantial sit-down one. I know these old ladies. This way, they'll get something that will stick to their ribs a little better than a poached egg, melba toast, and tea for supper. When Niki comes back, she can start thinking about the cake."

Increasingly, pastry had become Niki's department. She was one of the best pastry chefs in the Boston area and had had many toothsome offers to leave the catering firm for top restaurants. Each time, Faith conscientiously urged her to go, but Niki liked the flexibility she had. She'd worked in restaurant kitchens and knew what the pressure was like. Today, for example, she had headed off for the ski slopes. She was hoping to run into a gorgeous European ski instructor—Norwegian, or maybe French—who would tempt her away from the commitment she was close to making. She hadn't made her list of Phil's good and bad points yet, but she had set up a series of tests for herself, all of which seemed to involve highly pleasurable activities. Saturday night, she'd gone clubbing with her girlfriends instead of with Phil. Today, she was skiing, and she was planning a trip to New York City next weekend. She'd spend time in SoHo, the East Village, and Barneys—all prime pickup sites. Faith and Pix had been watching in amusement. It was all so transparent. In December, or sooner, Niki would be walking down the aisle with her oh-so-perfect mate.

"We'll fill your mother's living and dining rooms with spring flowers—some potted for people to take home. The winter's been so long, so cold, so snowy, everyone needs to believe that spring is officially only a little more than a week away," Faith said.

"I know Mark Twain would be upset with me, but it seems all I can talk about or think about is weather. You know, that introduction to *The American Claimant* he wrote: 'No weather will be found in this book.'"

And he put it all in an appendix for the people who wanted to read about what he considered filler. But this is the coldest winter I can remember, and that's saying a lot."

All New England winters were the coldest Faith could ever remember, but this one had broken several records. She had even been forced to wear a hat—cap hair be damned.

"Barring a blizzard, they'll all come," Faith said, figuring on an even dozen, unless Ursula wanted to put one of the leaves in her dining room table. "Before we sit down, we'll give them an assortment of hot hors d'oeuvres, then soup and quiche, or a frittata, and afterward, the cake. No ice cream. Too cold. Maybe crème brûlée. It may be old hat in the big city, but it's still a novelty in Aleford."

"Since it's Millicent's party, no booze," Pix warned. "Not even sherry, but mother thought some of that sparkling cider would be festive."

Faith could hear Ursula's very words: "festive" and "booze." Knowing Ursula, though, she'd stash a bottle of Amontillado in the pantry and fill a teacup or two. Faith hoped so. It brought much prettier roses to their cheeks than the round circles of rouge Aleford women of a certain age went in for when dressing up.

Pix left and Faith locked up. A party for Millicent. Tom would be amused—and she was happy to have something else to think about. It had been two days since she had heard of Richard's death, and she was still trying to get used to the ache in her heart. When he'd come home that night, Tom had had little to add to what he'd said on the phone, other than reporting there were no leads and a great deal of tension within the Oak Street community.

She drove down Route 2, steering her mind resolutely to a party menu fit for a Millicent. And tomorrow, she was planning to go to Maine.

April 7, 1946

Phelps dares not come too often, although the pine is at the corner of the house, which is set far back from the street, and it would be hard for anyone to see him. Still, he takes great care to be sure there are no passersby and carries clippers with him to make it seem as if he is pruning branches should someone with eagle's eyes look up and spy him.

I am afraid to tell him everything that has happened, for surely he would kill my husband, and then where would we be? As it is, what little he knows enrages him. Instead, we talk about ourselves. And I have teased him about his name. It is a family name and we have come up with a private one of our own. I was right. He is at Harvard on a scholarship. His family was wealthy, but they lost everything in the Crash. They had always gone to Harvard, so he supposed Harvard took pity on him for the sake of all those Harvard men in his family. He feels quite indebted to the college and has vowed to repay the tuition. That is the kind of man he is. He is a city boy, born and raised in Boston. He's never been to Maine. I wish I could take him to the top of Mount Cadillac and show him the way the rounded pine-covered islands seem to rise up from the sea like pincushions. Then we'd go into town for chowder and lobster and blueberry pie.

We talk of escaping to Canada or Europe and starting a new life far, far away. I would go anywhere with him. I will take his name and we will live together as man and wife. I could never get a divorce from my husband, especially in this state, and in any case, he would see me dead before he would grant one. I cannot believe that the Lord would look upon our union as a sin. The union I am in is the one that is sinful. When the time comes, Phelps will leave several weeks ahead of me, if he is still working here. The two of us going at the same time would arouse his suspicion and he'd search for us both. I know he would leave no stone unturned, hiring private detectives and even splashing it all over the newspapers. Phelps plans to hide me somewhere and be available in case my husband calls upon him for information of my whereabouts. When I disappear, my husband will not connect me with Phelps, and, indeed, why should he? As far as he knows, we have met only once, that *first day. I will leave in the night through the nursery window, which Phelps will have left open. He will hang a small bag with a hammer and the nails in the tree so I can secure it again. When my husband awakes, he will have no idea how I escaped. I will have to be quick. He sleeps soundly most nights, but I cannot take any chances. I wish I could drug him, but I have gone over everything in the kitchen cabinets and the medicine chest in the bathroom, with no luck. Perhaps Phelps could leave something hidden for me, but if it was found, the whole plan would be destroyed. I have spent hours working the whole thing out and have convinced Phelps it is the only way.*

I love to go over all this in my mind, testing each detail. Some days, it is the only way I can keep sane.

April 12, 1946

Phelps brings me the newspaper to read while he's here and has tried to catch me up on everything that's happened in the outside world. I knew that meat and butter rationing had ended, only sugar now, although there always seems to be plenty—my husband would never let anything get in the way of what he wants. Everything else is off rationing, not that it does me any good. Even if I could buy shoes, I couldn't wear them. But I will someday. Someday I'll have a closetful of the highest heels I can find. Phelps has been telling me about the trials in Nuremberg. We knew the Nazis were evil, but I never imagined anything like what he's been telling me. A year ago, no less—if you had asked me what I thought of human nature, I would have said we were all basically decent children of the Lord. Some of us may have strayed onto the wrong path, but there was still good there deep down. I know now this isn't true. There was no decency anywhere in Hitler or those other Nazis. There is no good or decency in my husband.

But Phelps is decent all the way through. I can't believe how much we have in common. I never thought such a human being existed. He loves books as much as I do—and movies, too, especially those with

Bogart and Bacall, Tracy and Hepburn. He says he's a sucker for romance, and I told him I think that's swell. He wishes he could put wings on us both and fly out to the Totem Pole Ballroom in Norumbega Park in Newton, a town not far from Cambridge. All the big bands play there—the Dorseys, Artie Shaw. Sometimes he hums a tune and we dance. I feel sad when I think that he'll have to leave this area. He loves it so much. When I told him this, he laughed and said yes, he figured it must be true love if he would leave the Boston Braves for a woman. But I was not to worry, because there were radios everywhere; plus, he was predicting that in a few years from now every house in America will have a television. That sounds like science fiction to me, but he's sure he's right. Today, he showed me the new dime with Roosevelt on it. Phelps says people are spending money like crazy now that the war's over—and not just dimes. I'm glad Roosevelt is on a dime. He was the best president we ever had, and the day he died, April twelfth of last year—I'll never forget the date—we all cried our eyes out. Just a year ago today.

There have been many strikes all over the country and a bad influenza epidemic in December. When I heard that I couldn't help but wish it had hit this house, for maybe I could have gotten to the doctor and convinced him I wasn't insane. Maybe, Lord forgive me, it would have set me free.

We talk a lot about the garden. It's going to look good for a first-year planting, and Phelps agrees with me that the star magnolia will be perfect. We'll never see it in its full glory, but we'll have another beautiful garden with all sorts of trees, flowers, and shrubs to tend together. I want to plant a garden just for herbs in memory of mother.

Phelps's hair is growing out and gets brighter and brighter. When he was a kid, the other kids called him "Carrot top" or "Red." My nickname was "Shrimp," so together we would have made quite a pair then. He says we do now, too.

I've never been so happy in my entire life. I can bear anything now. "Our" song is "People Will Say We're in Love."

April 16, 1946

I want to know everything about him, and he doesn't hold back a thing. He has a sister, twelve years older, who lives in Virginia with her husband and son and daughter. After his sister was born, his parents thought they were done; then Phelps showed up, much to everyone's surprise. Both his parents have passed away. He has happy memories of them, and although the family did not have much money, he never felt poor. The photo album with pictures of the way his parents had lived before and how they had been brought up seemed like fiction to him, a kind of fairy tale. Both of them died his first year at Harvard. His father was quite a bit older than his mother and his death was not unexpected. But his mother's was a shock. Like my poor mother, it was cancer, but it was swift. I don't know which is better—to lose a loved one suddenly or to have them with you longer. You still don't get used to what will happen, but those months with Ma were precious, except at the end, when she was in so much pain. I think sudden is better for that reason.

He enlisted as soon as war was declared, leaving college, and he says although he misses his parents, he's glad they never had to worry about his being overseas. He likes to think of them in some kind of heaven, assuming his life went along the path they knew he'd set out on. They were terribly excited about Harvard, especially his father, who lived to see his son in the same house he had been in during his time there.

Phelps doesn't like to talk about the war, and I don't ask him. His roommate and best friend was killed on Omaha Beach. Phelps was part of the invasion, too. I know what he must have seen, and I'll spend my whole life trying to erase those memories for him.

It's funny. Now that Phelps is with me—for even when he's not by my side, he's in my heart—I don't feel the need to write much. I keep looking out the window, hoping he'll come, and when he doesn't, I keep thinking about the times he has. I guess every girl thinks no one has ever been as much in love as she has, but I <u>know</u> no one ever has as much as this girl right here.

It was after midnight, but Faith hadn't been able to sleep. She'd gone downstairs, made a cup of cocoa, and retrieved the diary from the drawer where she'd left it. As she read, she thought about Margaret Ward. She and her husband had been off dancing in Norumbega Park at this time, living the life Dora and Phelps dreamed about. Again, Faith found herself trying to think of a scheme for them, something foolproof, but, like them, she concluded there was no other way but to wait. She was overwhelmed at the thought of this woman sacrificing her freedom and well-being for the man she loved. But Dora had gotten her star magnolia. Faith hoped she'd gotten much more.

She'd told Tom she was driving up to the Maine outlets tomorrow, and he'd insisted she take her time. He'd pick up Amy and be home for Ben. She knew he assumed she was going with Niki, Pix, or another friend. Or perhaps he didn't. He'd looked a little worried when she told him; she could read his face like a map—each line stood for something, and the tiny one that snaked across from eyebrow to eyebrow meant anxiety. Since Monday, she had been trying to appear as if nothing had happened, but she may not have been as successful as she'd thought.

When she got back into bed, Tom rolled over and pulled her close. The warmth of his body enveloped her and after awhile, she fell asleep.

Faith had never seen anyone use an ear trumpet, but Josephine— "Call me Josie"—Marshall née Royce did. And used the accessory with such flair that Faith wondered why more people didn't adopt the custom. Everyone she knew with hearing aids was always complaining they were too loud or didn't fit properly. Her aunt Chat's were apt to break into a high-pitched tune, unheard by the wearer, but definitely disconcerting to others. Faith assumed that now that most of the boomers had passed through presbyopia—which had spurred optical laser surgery to new heights—they'd be moving on to hearing loss. One little card in the mail offering a free auditory test with an accompanying photo of the devices available was all it would take to galvanize the generation. By the time she needed amplification, they'd be the size of the head of a pin. But there was a certain chic to Josie's trumpet. Greeting Faith, she'd held it to her ear with a flourish, announcing it worked far better than anything else and didn't get lost.

Faith quickly introduced herself and presented a pot of fragrant hyacinths and one of her Cambridge tea cakes, and now they were getting down to business. She could tell that Josie, while happy for the company and the largesse, was eyeing her in that Down East way Faith knew well from her summers on Sanpere Island. Not a full faced stare, but a sideways glance. Mrs. Marshall wouldn't come out and ask Faith what she was doing there. She didn't have to—it was all in that look. Faith answered the question.

"I've been going through some old written material"—she felt protective of the diary, protective of Dora—"and have come across some references to a relation"—she did feel a strong sense of kinship with her—"whom no one seems to know much about."

Josie nodded and encouraged; Faith continued. "She worked at one of the inns in Bar Harbor in the mid-nineteen forties and mentions her friend Josephine Royce. Her first name is Dora. She married a man from Cambridge, Massachusetts, and moved there. That's the last I know."

The old woman put her ear trumpet in her lap and closed her eyes for so long that Faith thought she might have dozed off. Josephine was tall and had led the way to the sitting room with a firm stride. Unlike many of the other residents, she wasn't wearing pastel pants with an elastic waist and matching sweatshirt, but a dark blue corduroy skirt, a floral-print blouse, and a hand-knit cardigan that picked up the soft yellow in the print. Her straight white hair, still thick, framed her face like Buster Brown's. When Faith had given Josie the gifts, her mouth had curved in a generous smile and her blue eyes, without the milky film of so many of those her age, had sparkled. Josephine Royce must have been a knockout, Faith decided.

"Dora—Theodora was her full name, but only her mother called her that," she said. "It meant 'gift of God'—her mother read a lot. She told us that, too. Picked the name from some book. Dora Thibodeau. Her father's family came down from Canada to farm, but they never made a go of it. They all went back, but he stayed and married a local girl. They only had Dora, and a few years after her mother died, she left the farm as fast as she could. I never heard her say anything against her father, but we all got the idea he wasn't much good. I'd been at the inn a few years and was waiting tables. Got room, board, and my wages, and the tips were good. It was hard work, but she had it harder—cleaning the rooms, working in the laundry. If she'd had my job, maybe she wouldn't have accepted the first man to come along."

"Do you remember his name? Remember anything about him?"

"I wish I could help you out, but it's gone now. I suppose I must have known it then. She was such a kid, writing her new name out on every blank sheet of paper she could find. He was some big muckety-muck from Boston—Cambridge, as you said. It was the first time he'd come to the inn. To tell the truth, he gave me the creeps and I switched so I wouldn't have to have his table. He was that particular. Sent the food back and back until it was exactly the way he wanted it. He was much older than Dora. Not bad-looking—a big man, dark hair, thick beard, which wasn't the fashion then."

"Why did he give you the creeps?" asked Faith, directing her question into the trumpet.

Josie paused again, but not for as long. "It sounds crazy now, but I had the idea he was looking us over, measuring us for something. Now, I've had men give me the eye"—she laughed—"but this was different. It was like he was interested but not interested. Shopping around the way you'd buy a car. Maybe his wife had died or he'd decided it was time to get married. But why would he go to an inn in Maine to pick out a wife? You'd think he'd take one of his own kind. Not some girl off the farm. It didn't take him long to settle on Dora. She was the prettiest of us, prettiest girl I ever saw. We all thought she should be in the movies, but she never believed her looks, never believed how smart she was, either, because she'd had to leave school. She was the nicest, too. Some of the girls would have it in for somebody—there was never enough help for all the work—

and they'd start about so-and-so not doing her job or thinking she was too good for it. The kind of things that happen when you're tired and on edge. Most of us had men overseas—fathers, brothers, boyfriends. But Dora just did her job, and often someone else's, too, without complaining. She loved the gardens, I remember, and made friends with the man who worked them. That's where she'd be whenever she had a free moment, and we always had fresh flowers on our dressers. She said it was to remind us we were alive. I remember that. Those were her exact words.

"Anyway, once he made it plain that it was Dora he wanted, he seemed to warm up a little. You'd see them walking in the gardens hand in hand—we weren't supposed to talk to the guests except to ask them how they wanted something done, let alone get up to something like that. But Mrs. Patterson—she was the housekeeper—turned a blind eye. Maybe he'd slipped her some money. That had to have been it, because otherwise she'd have been on Dora like a gull dives for a fish."

Faith remembered that Josie had married a lobsterman, and the image was a familiar one to her, too—the gulls rocketing straight down into the sea. Mrs. Patterson must have been something.

"He gave her a diamond ring that was bigger than anything we'd ever seen and the girls teased her about it weighing her hand down. She quit working, of course, and he took a room for her. It was like a fairy tale, like Cinderella, where one minute you're scrubbing toilets and the next somebody else is doing yours. He took her to Bangor and fitted her out with new clothes. She looked so smart. He'd gotten a license and they were getting married in Augusta on their way back to Massachusetts. Dora would have liked a church wedding, I think—she was religious, been raised in the church—but whatever he said was fine with her. She didn't have anyone except her father. I don't know if he was there or not. I always thought it was a little sad that she didn't have anyone to stand up with her, but we'd gotten used to all kinds of weddings in the war, so we didn't think about it much. Mine was a time, though. We waited until December—a Christmas wedding. My husband was in the air force and brought home enough of that silk parachute cloth for me and, later, his sister when she got married. Our daughters wore those dresses and maybe our granddaughters will."

"Did you hear from Dora after she left?"

"No, I didn't, and that surprised me, because she said to all of us she'd write, and since we had shared a room, we were especially close. They were going out to California for their honeymoon, and we thought at least we'd get a postcard. I was afraid I'd made her mad, because the night before she left to go to Augusta, I told her I wasn't sure she was doing the right thing. That she ought to wait awhile. I never had a sister and I guess I'd started thinking of her as my little one. So I wrote to her at the Cambridge address she'd given us, apologizing. I've always been known to speak my mind. She even teased me about it, but I decided to say I was sorry just in case she took offense, although Dora was the last person who ever would. The letter came back and I tried twice more, but they all came back. I thought they must have settled someplace else, so I called her father, but he didn't have much to say. Just that she was busy with her new life. I couldn't figure out where she was."

Josie took the trumpet from her ear and placed it in her lap again. Outside the window, there was still snow on the ground in what Faith hoped was a garden. The placc wasn't bad—clean and bright, but it still wasn't home.

"I wish I could tell you more. I'm sorry you came all this way for nothing."

"It hasn't been for nothing. Please don't think that." Faith slipped the photograph from her purse and put it in Josie's hand. "I just had this picture, but you've made her real."

After staring at it, Josie gave the picture back without a word and stood up. They walked toward the door together.

"If you find out what happened to her, will you let me know?" She put her hand on Faith's arm. "I've been worried about Dora for fifty-seven years."

8

Nineteen forty-six had been the city of Cambridge's one hundredth anniversary and *Manning's Cambridge Numerical Street Directory* devoted its first page to "Firsts" in Cambridge. Among those "worth enumerating" were the first printing press, 1638, and hence, the publication of the first book in America, 1640. Apparently equally important was the first commercial varnish in 1820, the first pressed glassware in 1827, and, truly important—the first sewing machine in 1845. Then, in 1876, Thomas Watson was at the Cambridge office of Walworth Manufacturing Company when he spoke on the telephone to Alexander Graham Bell all the way over the Charles River in Boston. Faith was amused to see the "Firsts" end here with a line to the effect that as outstanding as the above were, Cambridge has many other accomplishments as well. The researcher either got tired or ran out of room.

The main branch of the Cambridge Public Library was a wonderful Richardsonian-style building, its warm red stone exterior a sharp contrast to the gray cement of the much more recent Cambridge Rindge and Latin High School next door. Outside the buildings in the park that surrounded the library and the school, students were everywhere. The groups were instantly identifiable—pierced punks, letter-jacketed jocks, geeks playing games on personal organizers, the popular girls chattering away on cell phones, the unpopular ones in groups of twos or threes, clinging together for comfort and protection. High school: the best years of your life? I don't think so, Faith almost said aloud as she passed one particularly sad-looking girl eating a sandwich alone as she read *The Bell Jar.*

Inside the library, the reference department had been instantly helpful, setting Faith up at a microfilm scanner with the directories— and, even better, threading the film for her. Faith loved librarians.

The Cambridge Directory had been privately published, and from 1954 until 1972, when it ceased completely, the issues had been sporadic. When Faith had asked how she could find out who had lived in a partic-ular house in the mid-forties, the librarian had suggested beginning with the directories. "Then, if that doesn't help there are the poll-tax lists and the police's residents lists. You could also trace ownership by going to the Middlesex County Registry of Deeds, but let's start here."

"Here" turned out to be fine. Without a last name, Faith went to the back of the 1946 issue, where the street listings were. "Carver, Chauncey B." was listed as residing in the house. There was a tiny icon in the shape of a bell after his name and those of several others on the page. She turned to the front of the book for a key. The symbol stood for a phone—that it was an unusual enough occurrence to warrant an indi-cation was startling. She thought of the kids outside glued to their cell phones. They would find it hard to imagine a time when there hadn't been a phone in every house and every pocket. But there had been a phone in this one. Armed with the name, Faith looked up "Chauncey B. Carver" in the front of the directory. There he was, along with the address. In parentheses after his name was "Theodora T." Wives in parentheses appeared in many listings. Some listed professions, and after Mr. Carver's name, "lawyer, 97 State Street, Boston" appeared.

Quickly, Faith went through the directories for 1947, 1948, 1949, and 1950, her heart sinking as she turned up the entries for Chauncey but none for Theodora. The books were issued in August and compiled after the first of the year. Nineteen forty-six was the only year Dora had appeared.

The librarian came back. "Found what you need?"

"Yes, I'm afraid I have," Faith said slowly. She put the spool of film back in the box and returned it to its drawer. As she left, she stopped at the desk.

"Do you know how the information was collected for the directories? If someone was in one year—say a wife—then in the following years just her husband was listed, what would that mean to you?"

"I don't know how they collected the information, but I can look into it. As a guess, I'd say there was a form you sent back in, or they may have gone door-to-door. The directories are not the most accurate listings. You'd have to try the other places I mentioned. If a name was left out of later additions, I'd say the person had either moved or died."

There was an exhibit of Maurice Sendak's illustrations in the glass showcases lining one wall of the reference room. Faith looked over the librarian's shoulder at the little boy in the Night Kitchen falling through the sky and knew exactly how he felt.

L et's get a sitter and go to a movie tonight," Tom suggested. "We haven't had much time alone together lately."

Tom had left a message on the machine, and when Faith came back from her research at the library, she returned his call.

"We *never* have much time alone together and won't until the kids are in college, and maybe not even then, from what I hear from Pix. Samantha likes to come home to study most weekends and enjoy the benefits of the Miller pantry, washer, and dryer," Faith told Tom. "I'd love to go out, but I don't know where we can find a sitter on such short notice."

Faith had planned to ask Tom to keep an eye on the kids while she helped out at the Arlington Street Church's Friday Supper, but he was right—they did need some time alone together. Finding the Monk could wait. It was the old "ships passing in the night" thing, and when this happened to the Fairchilds, those ships tended to go aground.

"I'm sure one of my students would oblige. I can send an E-mail out."

"Give it a try," Faith said, "and I'll look in the paper and see what's playing."

When she'd left Josie yesterday, Faith hadn't felt like shopping, and she was not a great fan of outlets, in any case—last season's stuff at this season's prices. Waiting for sales at Bloomies, Bergdorf's, and Barneys made more sense—plus, she got to go to New York. Tom had asked her what she'd bought and she'd told him she hadn't had any luck, feeling guilty about the half-truth—or half-lie. Suddenly, she wanted to go out tonight a lot, wanted to be with Tom, wanted their lives to be the way they had been before Cambridge. Before Richard.

"I'll be here until it's time to get Amy, so let me know," she added. "Try to avoid someone who hears divine voices, but other than that, anyone will be fine. I mean, it's *Harvard*."

Tom laughed. "Okay, honey, I'll get back to you as soon as I can."

Faith went into the kitchen and made herself a sandwich. She'd missed lunch and was hungry. As she layered roasted peppers, caramelized onions, and fresh mozzarella on top of sourdough bread, she ran through all the movies she hadn't seen. The Academy Awards were coming and she needed one to root for. She drizzled a little olive oil on top of the cheese and added a little ground pepper and salt, then crowned it with the second piece of bread. *Panini* were all the rage now and it was a fad she endorsed. She'd always filled her toasted cheese sandwiches with a variety of fillings, but now that they had an Italian name and were pressed, not toasted, she had added several to her catering menu. Her own *panini* press was one of the items that had accompanied the Fairchilds from Aleford. She took the fragrant fin-ished product out and poured a glass of milk. Instead of sitting in the formal dining room, she ate at the kitchen counter, standing and looking out through the small window at the side yard. There was still snow on the ground, but the forsythia bushes were swelling. She didn't think Professor Robinson—Teddy—would mind if she brought a few branches into the house to force. Chickadees, nuthatches, and a pair of cardinals careened through the air. She thought that maybe she ought to start one of those life lists Pix carried around with her—a small red notebook with the names of every bird she'd ever spotted. Pix had given Ben his in first grade and would give one to Amy, too, when the time came. It was very New England, very Pix and Ursula. The continuity of it all was tempting, but aside from the three she'd just named, Faith knew she could reliably add only about five more, and of those five, *seagull* was probably not the precise nomenclature.

Had Dora stood gazing out this same window? Dora Thibodeau Carver? Faith finished eating, cleaned up, and went into the living room to read more of the diary while she waited for Tom to call back.

April 25, 1946

I will remember this day for the rest of my life. Phelps came through the window and declared he must let me breathe the air of freedom or go crazy. He went first and I followed, forgetting none of my tree-climbing skills. At the bottom, I was so excited, I thought I would faint. The blue sky looked enormous, like a tent over us, and the sun was so bright, it hurt my eyes. He had a sandwich in his pocket and we shared it. Our first picnic. It was ham and cheese, but it tasted better than a fancy steak dinner. I have never dared tell him about my meals. The ones I prepare for my husband and the ones I am forced to eat while I sit in that spacious dining room with him each night. Once he discovered me eating some leftovers as I was cleaning up in the kitchen, and after what followed, I would never let another morsel of what he calls his food pass my lips. He will not have a glutton for a wife and believes that women should eat differently from men, genteel food like poached eggs, bouillon, and toast. I stopped caring what I ate with him many months ago.

Phelps had his camera and took dozens of pictures of me. He picked

*one of the pansies he has planted. It is deep purple and the petals feel
like velvet. I always think pansies look like kittens' faces, and when I
told him that, he said we'd have kittens and puppies and as many
children as I wanted to go with the menagerie. Then he told me that the
name "pansy" comes from the French word for "thought." Phelps knows
so many things but, unlike my husband, does not need to show it all
off. I picked a pansy and put it in his buttonhole. The gardener at the
inn called pansies "heart's ease." A guest from England told him that's
what they called them there. Phelps is my heart's ease, and when I
said that, he kissed me and whispered some French to me. It sounded
something like "Pensay amwah" and it means "Think of me." When
you give a French lady a bouquet and it has pansies, this is what it
means. I know about the language of the flowers. Ma would say,
"Rosemary for remembrance." She always grew a bunch of it and other
herbs in her vegetable garden. I think the English and the French have
us beat when it comes to names, though. My heart's ease, I hope you are
thinking of me this moment, as I am of you.*

*We dared not stay long, but each minute seemed like a year. I
didn't mind climbing back up, because I know for sure that I will be
climbing down someday for good. It's real now, and that was exactly
what he had in mind with all his talk of fresh air and freedom.*

May 1, 1946

*I thought he had found out about us for sure. It has been so long since
he has locked me in here, instead of the spare room. But if he knew, he
would kill me, and Phelps, as well. But first he would torture me in
some way that only he could think of, and he has not done so. At times,
he seems to forget I exist, and once he locked me in the spare room and
left me for two days. I could hear him moving about, so he did not go
away. One night, he gave a dinner party. People were laughing and
talking downstairs. "Poor man," they must have said to one another,
"burdened with a wife like that. How good he is to her."*

Not being able to be with Phelps has robbed me of all my energy. I

feel myself becoming a listless shadow of the girl I used to be. At times, I
wonder if I am ill. It is all I can do to keep my hopes up.

The phone was ringing. Faith ran to answer it, the book in hand. As she had expected, it was Tom.

"Good news, honey. Mindy's free and will be glad to watch the kids. What do you want to see? Something new, or shall we go to the Brattle? They're doing a whole 'Oscar's Oversights' series."

Faith had stopped paying attention to anything he said after "Mindy's free." She struggled to keep from saying what was crossing her mind, things like "How could you even think about asking her to come here?" and others of the "Are you living on another planet?" nature. Instead, she settled for the very civilized, very neutral "I don't think I'm comfortable with this, *Tom.*" Emphasis on "Tom."

"She doesn't hear voices, divine or otherwise," Tom said.

"Yours is apparently enough," Faith commented dryly.

"I thought you were over this. Mindy is my graduate student. Period. A competent, mature young woman, whom I would certainly trust with my kids." He sounded exasperated.

"Who happens to have her eye on you, and wants to have her arms, et cetera, as well." The words had burst out of Faith's mouth.

"Now, Faith, you're just not making sense. Mindy isn't interested in an old man like me. Half the guys in my seminar are in love with her. Besides, I won't even be here."

It was hopeless. Faith sighed.

"I'll get Danny or maybe Samantha for next weekend. If you can get home in time, I'd like to go over and lend a hand at the Arlington Street Church Friday Supper."

"I'm sorry you feel this way."

"I'm sorry, too."

Tom didn't say anything.

"Will you be able to get here in time for me to go?" Faith asked. "I'll leave dinner."

"Yes, I'll be there. Faith . . ."

"What?"

"Nothing. See you later."

As she hung up the phone, Faith realized she had a death grip on the little blue diary. She went back to the living room and continued to read in an attempt to keep from thinking about anything else.

June 5, 1946

It is suffocating up here. It has been unseasonably warm. The whole house is like an oven, but this room is the worst. My husband has taken to leaving me up here for the entire day while he has Phelps drive him to Cape Cod or Rockport, a place on the coast, north of Boston. He is visiting those of his friends with houses in these spots, returning refreshed. My days may be unbearable, but the nights are worse. Each outing seems to invigorate him, and it is agony for me to know that my beloved is under the same roof, but I cannot let him know by even a small sound what is going on so close to him.

I can bear it. What I could not bear would be the destruction of all our planning, which is what would happen if Phelps ever walked into the room, for if he did not strike my husband dead, he would surely injure him. When I first came here and was trying to find a way out, it occurred to me I could climb up one of the fireplace chimneys. There are fireplaces in each bedroom and a very large one in the living room. Once on the roof, I would surely attract someone's attention. But I soon realized I would only be returned to my captor, for no one would ever think that this respectable Cambridge man would treat his wife this way. It would be the same at any trial, if Phelps were to harm him. No one would believe us. There are no witnesses, and he has always been careful to stop short of disfiguring me or leaving bruises that could not have come from a common fall. It is hopeless. And besides, like me, Phelps has said he cannot take a life. He has taken enough lives in combat, and no matter how justified, neither of us can kill my husband.

He has kept Phelps on, buying a fancy new Cadillac, which lets him

treat Phelps like his chauffeur, a servant. He made a lot of money
during the war and now he can spend it. He knows Phelps needs the
free lodgings and is giving him a small wage in addition, as he asks
him to take on more and more chores. It is only because of me that
Phelps is staying. Aside from the hatred he has for him as my husband,
he says he is an odious man with contempt for everyone but himself.
He does not let his friends see this, but he regales Phelps with his views
of them behind their backs as they drive home.

On these outings, Phelps is forced to stay with the other servants,
who are always busy, so it is no fun for him, but he takes his books. He is
determined to finish his degree and set me free. The thought of this is the
only thing that keeps me going. I've felt so ill from the heat lately. Most
food disagrees with me and all I can keep down is water. He leaves a
pitcher and a glass here, but it is never enough. I sleep a lot—and dream.

June 30, 1946

I am pregnant.

Faith put the book down. She couldn't bear to read any more and it
was also getting late. Dora must have known. Must have suspected. She
was feeling so ill. Morning sickness, not the heat. A baby. She was going
to have a baby. Not an occasion for rejoicing. Not like Hope's news.
What had happened to Dora? What had happened in this house? And
where was that baby now?

It was a relief to have the children around, a welcome distraction.
Since Ben had started school, Friday nights were Faith's favorite
nights of the week—not a school night and not a "church" night—a
relaxed time, usually reserved for family. Even the fact that Ben was
frantically telling her he had a "major" project on the Mayans—"You
know who they were, right, Mom?"—due on Monday didn't faze her.

She'd been there before. At least it wasn't one of those shoe-box dioramas. She reassured him that she did indeed know who the Mayans were and, even better, had become well acquainted with the Cambridge Public Library, where she would take him the next morning when it opened. Appeased, Ben agreed to read to his sister while Faith threw together an "everything pasta" casserole to leave for her family. When Tom arrived, he was treated to the idyllic scene of Ben reading *Charlotte's Web* to his sibling on the big living room sofa and the tantalizing smell of good food in the air. Faith had her coat on.

"There's a casserole in the oven—broccoli, chickpeas, a little tomato, onion, béchamel sauce with Parmesan, and penne. Ben will want to know. Be sure to tell him no mushrooms whatsoever; otherwise, he'll take an hour dissecting what's on his plate. Baths if you feel like it, but I should home by then. Sorry for the rush; I don't want to be late. See you." The tight knot in her stomach seemed tied around her words, too. She knew she sounded abrupt.

As she walked down Brattle, grateful for the approach of the equinox, which would mean each day would be brighter—and warmer—she tried to sort out what she was feeling. Maybe she was overreacting to Mindy, but it was because Tom was so stupid about it. Naïveté, thy name is Man. Obviously, he enjoyed the relationship—a bright young woman who shared his interests in a way Faith didn't. Why should she begrudge him that? Because Mindy was a young predator, a—what had Natalie Compton called her at the party?—"little minx."

As she put her token in the slot and pushed the turnstile, Faith also admitted that there might be some who'd say her relationship with Richard hadn't been all that different from Tom's with Mindy—shared interests, common views. But they'd be wrong. The two situations weren't at all similar.

No, Richard had been an old friend—and an older friend. If death had not intervened, Faith told herself, she would have introduced him to Tom and Tom would have been impressed by the book. But wait—She shook her head. Richard hadn't been writing a book about the homeless. He was homeless himself and an alcoholic. Janice had said that her brother, Richard, died a long time ago. Faith's Richard had never existed.

A tall woman with a Modigliani face was playing the guitar and singing a song Faith didn't recognize, something about "wanting memories." She stood on the T platform, her guitar case open for contributions. It was a beautiful, haunting melody and the woman's voice was clear and true. The train arrived and Faith put a dollar in the case before getting on. She looked back and smiled at the woman, but the singer didn't react. Her eyes were fixed on some other scene, turned inward. She was someplace else.

Despite her hurry to leave, Faith realized now that she had plenty of time, so she got out at Park Street instead of changing to the Green Line for the Arlington Street stop. The walk to the church wasn't long—across the Boston Common, then through the Public Garden, home to the Swan Boats and the bronze statues of Mrs. Mallard and her eight offspring, replicas of the characters in Robert McCloskey's *Make Way for Ducklings*.

When she climbed to the top of the stairs from the subway onto the Common, she saw that the pushcarts selling T-shirts, caps, and sweatshirts with Boston Celtics, Red Sox, Bruins, Harvard, and MIT logos—the local Big Five—had multiplied, a sure sign of spring. Some teenagers, obviously on their senior class trip, were having their picture taken against the backdrop of the golden-domed State House. One of the chaperones kept urging them to calm down: "Remember, people, this will be in the yearbook. Do you really want your grandchildren to see you like this?" Faith could have told him that time for these kids was a concept for old people and that the only clock ticking was how many weeks to the prom and graduation.

Ben and Amy would be in this picture sooner than she cared to think about. Ben was already a pre-pre-adolescent, and it wasn't always pretty.

She passed the Frog Pond. No skaters now, although the ice was hard. She'd have to ask Bitsy, equally knowledgeable about Boston as

Cambridge, if it was true that you could still graze a cow on the Common, as Ralph Waldo Emerson is said to have grazed his mother's herd. Faith did know that it really was a common, owned by every Boston resident, which amounted to a few blades of grass or inches of paved path apiece. It was the oldest public park in the world and couldn't be sold, leased, or built upon without the consent of the entire citizenry.

After she'd first moved to Aleford, before the kids were born, Tom was eager to show off his turf, and when they weren't exploring the South Shore, land of his youth, they walked all over Boston. Tom had noted the Common as not only a pasture in those early days but also as the site of those punishments the Puritans were so enamored of—the stocks, the pillory, cropping ears, slitting noses, branding cheeks or hands, and, of course, whippings and hangings. These punishments were meted out for things like kissing your wife in public, eavesdropping, neglecting work, scolding, sleeping in meeting, repeating a scandalous lie, selling at too great a profit, and being a Quaker or a witch. They didn't differentiate between the latter two. One poor man was sent to jail for life for stealing squirrels from the Common for food.

It all looked quite peaceful now, although it had always been an active place. The Common had been the scene for the Sacco and Vanzetti demonstrations; Martin Luther King, Jr., had spoken to a crowd of fifty thousand civil rights protesters in 1965; and the Vietnam era had provoked massive turnouts. She wondered what would be next.

The wind picked up as the path sloped down to Charles Street. She crossed into the Public Garden—not owned in common, but by the city of Boston—and into the world of Beacon Hill/Back Bay privilege. Even the wind died down as she started toward the elegant small bridge that crossed the man-made lake. The formal flower beds, usually filled with blooms throughout much of the year, were still buried under a blanket of snow, a few blackened stems poking through the surface. It was very quiet, very still. No tourists, and still too cold for the foot traffic of those leaving work late on a Friday afternoon. Avoiding the subway, or taking the long way around, past General Washington on his horse and the flower beds, was still a pleasure several weeks away.

A man was walking slowly in front of her, his head turning from side to side, as if he were trying to memorize the view. Just before the bridge, she overtook him. She glanced over at him and screamed.

It was Richard Morgan.

He drew back, but she grabbed the sleeve of his jacket.

"Richard! Richard! My God, I thought you were dead. Your wallet, your license! They were in the man's pocket. . . . Richard!"

He was pulling away from her. He was unshaven and his hair lay matted under a greasy woolen cap. But his eyes were clear. He knew who she was.

"Go, just go," he said softly.

Faith was crying. "Please, let me help you. I talked to your sister. I know—"

He wrenched away and started to run down the stone stairs that led to the path below the bridge. Faith followed him. He'd exchanged—or lost—the green jacket for a beige one, lighter in weight.

"Don't go! Richard! *Please*, talk to me," she called after him.

For a while, she pursued him, their two figures caught in an absurd race along the dark, icy path. He was heading toward the Charles Street entrance, past the ducklings, their backs and heads shiny where small hands had lovingly stroked the bronze feathers.

"Stop!" she shouted, now close enough to see that his footing had become uneven and his pace was slowing down.

She tried to think. Not Copley Square. It had to be someplace far away from where he might be recognized. It had to be inside, safe. Harvard's Peabody Museum was free on Sundays until noon and it opened at 9:00 A.M. Richard had asked her if she'd discovered it, and they'd talked about its idiosyncratic collection of artifacts from expeditions launched all over the globe.

"I'll be at the Peabody the next few Sundays at nine and will wait until quarter to eleven. There's no charge then. By the totem poles on the ground floor! Richard! Please come! Please!"

He looked over his shoulder; he'd heard her. The light changed and he sprinted across Beacon Street. She didn't follow, collapsing onto a bench instead, heedless of the neat ridges of snow on the seat. Heedless also of the curious looks from several onlookers, particularly one man, who seemed to study her intently before moving on across Beacon Street himself.

Faith lifted her head and wiped her eyes with the back of her hand. The glove didn't do the job, so she fumbled in her pocket for a tissue.

Richard was alive! But who was the dead man—and who had killed him? Who had placed Richard's identification on the corpse? The only answer that made sense was one she couldn't bear to think about.

After awhile, the damp penetrated her coat and Faith stood up. She looked at her watch. It wasn't too late to go to Arlington Street and help out. Aside from being uncomfortable with the notion of again letting Tom believe she'd been someplace she hadn't been, she needed to keep busy—needed to calm down. Her heart was racing and she felt panicked. Preparing and serving food would go a long way to help.

The harsh winter and accompanying illnesses had thinned the ranks of the volunteers everywhere, so they were happy to see her at Arlington Street. Faith was soon busy doling out paper cups of soup and coffee to the men and women who had been waiting. The tables were filled. Unlike those at Oak Street House, the people here were served and could go back for seconds. Some area churches prepared food, and recently Arlington Street had put in a state-of-the-art industrial kitchen, so finally there would be enough mashed potatoes, the most popular item. After the rhythm of the familiar and comforting job—feeding people—had slowed her heart rate and cleared her mind, she realized she needed to find the Monk now—not to *find* Richard, but to find out what he might know about Richard. The Monk was the only street person Richard had ever mentioned by name. Faith was sure he identified with the man and perhaps envied the peace he'd found. It made sense that if Richard were in trouble, he might seek him out. Richard had told her that the homeless community was a tight one in many respects. Maybe the Monk knew what had happened. During a lull, she asked one of the volunteers, who seemed to be a veteran, if she had ever come across a man people referred to as "the Monk."

"The Monk? Sure. He's been around as long as I have. Someone told me that he used to live out in Dover—big house, high-paying job, a lawyer, I think, wife, family—then it all fell apart. First the job, then the family, or maybe the other way around. The interesting thing is that he has made a life for himself on the street. He exudes a kind of inner peace, contentment. That's why they call him that. I don't know that he's tied into any particular religion, but he has found something, and maybe it's God—by any name."

"Could you point him out to me? I'd like to meet him," Faith said.

"I haven't seen him yet, but I'm sure he'll be here. He never misses us. We joke about how it's the meat loaf, but I like to think it may be something more. He doesn't eat and run, just sits and talks to people here."

"A kind of ministry?" Faith asked.

"Maybe. I've got to get more salad. Can you hold the fort here? I'll be right back."

When the woman returned, she scanned the new arrivals and those who had been served while she was away.

"Sorry, he's not here yet. I hope he's not sick. With the bitter cold, their immunity is low and anything going around hits them."

The Monk had not appeared by the end of the supper. As Faith was about to clear an empty tray, a woman approached her. There was one table set aside for those women who felt more comfortable sitting together. The woman had come from that table. She was wearing several knit hats, each layer pulled down tightly over the next. It was difficult to tell how old she was—not a strand of hair was showing, but she'd pinned a bright yellow plastic daffodil jauntily onto the topmost hat, proclaiming spring and her own femininity. Faith smiled at her.

"I like your flower."

The woman shrugged. "Accessories can make or break an outfit."

Clearly, we're on the same wavelength, Faith thought, wondering how the woman had ended up here.

"I heard you asking about Daniel—'the Monk,' most people call him. He hasn't been around since last weekend, but he sells *Spare Change*, the newspaper. A new issue came out yesterday, so he'll be at one of his usual spots over in Cambridge—outside the Fresh Pond Bread and Circus, the Porter Square CVS, or the Harvard Coop. I'm assuming you want to find him for a good reason." She looked straight into Faith's eyes, and the message was clear: If Faith did not have a good reason for tracking down the Monk, Daniel, she'd have to answer to Flower Power.

"Yes, we have a friend in common, and it's him I'm worried about."

"Is he on the street, too?"

"Yes. His name is Rich—" Faith broke off, hesitating a millisecond. "His name is Goodman." Goodman. Why hadn't it struck her before? Goodman. How Richard thought of himself, wanted to be? "He's originally from New York. He hasn't been in Boston long." As she said this, Faith realized she didn't know when Richard had come here. "Since January, or maybe earlier."

The woman shook her head. "I don't know the name, but Daniel has been with a guy the last month or more. Nice-looking. Usually, Daniel goes his own way, but the times I saw them together, you'd almost think they were brothers. Well, I have to be going. Hope I helped." She gathered an assortment of canvas bags from under a table, bags with the names of banks, bookstores, even one from a Harvard reunion.

Faith put out her hand. "Thank you. It was good to meet you. My name is Faith. Hope things get better for you."

"Good to meet you, too, Faith. I'm Nancy. And things aren't that bad for me, not compared to some. Don't worry."

She turned and walked out the door, the daffodil bobbing with each step.

Faith left after helping clean the kitchen. When she entered the house back in Cambridge, she felt a sense of comfort for the first time. Whatever its past had been, its present was hers: Ben, Amy—and Tom. There had been a woman with a child tonight, unusual at Arlington Street, the volunteer had said, and that reminded Faith of the grim statistics Tom had quoted recently—40 percent of the homeless population consisted of families with children; in Massachusetts alone, over thirteen hundred families, which included three thousand children, were in Emergency Assistance family shelters every night. Faith realized that she, like most people, thought of the homeless as a guy with a cup outside the subway or Dunkin' Donuts. It just wasn't true. And while the coming of spring meant better weather, it really didn't change anything for these families and individuals.

It was after 8:3o, and as she went upstairs, she could hear the sounds of bath time—happy sounds. She quickened her steps so she could go and help.

Saturday morning was devoted to the Mayans and a story hour for Amy run by the library. Then Faith went out to Aleford to get ready for the American Repertory Theatre event, dropping the kids off at the Millers'. Tom would pick them up later, in plenty of time to see the spring lambs at the Audubon Sanctuary, Drumlin Farm, in nearby Lincoln. Faith was envious. Ever since Pix had taken her years ago, before Ben was born, this had become a rite of spring. And every year, she thought and said the same thing: "They look exactly like stuffed animals! Adorable, cuddly toys!" Having protested "cute" all her life, she succumbed when it came to the lambs—and a few other things, like Burdick's chocolate mice, patent-leather Mary Janes, and even her children on occasion.

"They are really going for this asparagus!" Tricia Phelan exclaimed.

She and her husband, Scott, had worked for Faith for years—Scott tend-
ing bar, and both as wait staff. Faith quickly handed her another tray.
The asparagus was a popular item, and she was planning to offer it to
the ladies at Millicent's party tomorrow: the tip and an inch and a half
or so of the stalk cooked al dente, then wrapped in a small crepe with
smoked salmon and crème fraîche. She'd also done bruschettas with
wild mushrooms; prosciutto and ricotta in phyllo puffs. And instead of
making the crab cakes that had become ubiquitous at these affairs, she
had skewered shrimp marinated in a citrus vinaigrette with tiny tomatoes before running them under the broiler for a few seconds. She was
happy to see that the cheese station, usually ignored at these things,
with its cubes of orange and yellow rubberized cheddar, needed
replenishing. Their stay in France had completed her degree in *fro-
mage*, and she prided herself on discovering new kinds from both sides
of the Atlantic—and farther afield. Two current favorites were Mothais
Fermier, a raw-milk chèvre from Poitou, and Ladotiri, made from a
combination of sheep's milk and goat's milk, from Crete. The idea of
serving cheese from Crete was part of it, she knew, a link with those
elegant ancient Minoans with their frescoes of acrobatic bull dancers
and their beautiful snake goddess statuettes.

People were making their way to the desserts, and some had started
there. You had to have strawberries dipped in dark chocolate in New
England, but Faith had added other fruits, too. She'd also let Niki loose,
and the result looked like the window of a pastry shop.

The crowd was definitely artsier than the Cambridge Div School
crowd, but the men retained their penchant for wearing mufflers or
long scarves wound carelessly around their necks or hanging over the
shoulders of their corduroy jackets. The difference was mainly with the
women, who had been to New York often enough to have adopted black
as the color that does the most for anyone of any age. Faith laughed to
herself as she remembered Nancy's quip yesterday about accessories. It
was certainly true. One woman had destroyed whatever chic she was
trying to project by wearing a fuchsia vest and matching beads over a

perfectly decent black wool sheath. Niki had a T-shirt that proclaimed WHAT SEPARATES US FROM OTHER ANIMALS IS OUR ABILITY TO ACCESSORIZE. The best-dressed woman tonight wore a black sweater, black pants, and a broad necklace of tiny gold beads, which caught the light and did kind things to her face.

By 8:00 P.M., they were cleaning up and almost ready to go home.

"Nice to have an early night for a change, huh, boss?" Scott said.

"Very nice. Now, why don't you take your wife dancing?"

"Got the sitter. Got the plan." The Phelans had a two-year-old son, Dana, the apple, peach, and plum of their eye.

By the time Faith got back to Brattle Street, both kids were asleep and Tom was watching a tape of golden moments in the history of the Celtics basketball team. He was in one of the beanbag chairs, and before she could sit in the other, he pulled her onto his lap. She felt her body relax against his as he wrapped his arms more tightly around her.

"Glad you're home."

"Me, too."

"Your sister called." His eyes were riveted to the screen. Faith had given him the tape for Christmas a few years back and was surprised it hadn't been destroyed from overuse by now.

"What did she want?"

"You. Wow! There'll never be another Larry Bird."

"I mean, did she say it was about the wedding, the baby, or something else?"

"None of the above. We talked about how terrible the winter's been and she said she'd try you again, but probably not until tomorrow, because she's busy making money."

"She didn't say that!"

"Words to that effect. She's not home now, because they were going to the opera with your folks."

The four bonded regularly over libretti, and little whoever would be warbling arias from *La Traviata* before "Row, Row, Row Your Boat."

Tomorrow was going to be a busy day, and if Hope didn't reach her, Faith would call her. It was unusual for her sister to call on a weekend. That was quality time with Quentin.

They went to bed and Faith fell sound asleep, only to awaken an hour later. After fifteen minutes in which she tried to convince herself she'd fall back to sleep, she got up, put on Tom's warm robe, and went down to the kitchen for some Sleepy Time tea. While the water was boiling, she got out Dora's diary. So far, she'd managed to keep herself distracted from the memory of seeing Richard, from the memory of him racing away from her. She'd told Tom she had something to do at nine o'clock the next morning, but he hadn't asked her what. They were treating each other with fragile care. She would tell him. She would tell him everything when it was over. Right now, she just had to push on through.

What this house needed was a comfy chair. The only place to curl up was on the window seat. She pulled one of the little tables next to it and placed her steaming mug on top of the day's paper. Then she started to read. They were the same words she'd read yesterday—no, Friday now— after she'd come back from the library. The same words that had stopped her from reading on. But this time, Faith kept going.

June 30, 1946

I am pregnant.

I wrote these words and stared at them for what must have been an hour. I am staring at them still. I am pregnant. I have known for some time, but did not want to admit it to myself. I can't avoid the facts any longer. I am pregnant, but I do not know who the father is. The thought of one brings the deepest joy, the other deepest misery. I have not told either man, nor have they seemed to notice anything. There is not much to notice now, but that cannot last forever. I think the baby will come sometime in early January, but it could be sooner. Much sooner and I will know for sure whose it is, and that does not bear thinking of.

But what should I do? If I tell Phelps, he will want to take me away immediately, and I cannot let him do that. This child may not be his, and I can't let him sacrifice everything for someone who is not his own flesh and blood. Nor can I lie to him and let him think it is his.

Since the first night of my marriage, pregnancy has been my greatest fear and if there were not the chance that I am carrying <u>our</u> child, I would kill myself at once. The hell I suffer is nothing compared to what any child would have to bear. I am positive of this. I know him so well. He would control his or her every waking moment with impossible demands, until he had reduced the child to the level of an animal.

For now, I will say nothing to them and let each think what he may of my ill health. I am so thin that if I make a show of eating, I may be able to get away with my condition until the fall. My husband is revolted by my times of the month and I have continued to announce them to keep him from me and now to keep him from finding out, as well. It will be harder with Phelps. I cannot bear not sharing every thought with him, but he has his whole life ahead of him and I can't burden him with mine until I am sure the baby is his. How will I know? All I will have to do is look at the baby's face—those tiny eyes, mouth, little cheeks, and nose. I will see my beloved mirrored there or I will see the devil.

September 9, 2003

I have almost completely lost track of time. In early July, my husband announced he was spending the summer in Europe. I almost cried when I thought of the promises he made to me. Can it be only a year or so ago? He would take me to Paris, to the top of the Eiffel Tower and dinner at Maxim's, then Rome and London—even Athens to see the Parthenon and Egypt for the pyramids. That gullible girl died long ago and a bitter woman has taken her place. I did not cry. I would not give him the pleasure.

"I have discharged the young Harvard student, who worked out quite well, and have provided him with a reference. I'm sure he will have no trouble finding another place like this to live."

But he won't, my heart said, never a place like this.

"You will not starve, my dear. Someone will bring groceries and other necessaries once a week. And I would not leave you without anything to occupy your mind, such as it is."

It is his belief that I am only slightly above the level of a retarded person. He refers constantly to what inbreeding in rural communities produces. I cannot imagine why he wanted to marry me except to provide himself with a convenience, much the way he has with his wine cellar and imported cigars. An instrument of pleasure. Perverted pleasure. He would be surprised at my vocabulary, increased even more now after these months of reading. He left the dictionary and my Bible. I know he meant it as a joke. He laughed heartily. But these two books have been wonderful companions.

I did not know who the woman was who brought the food, but I knew from the moment I saw her that I could not trust her. I had thought to bribe her with my wedding band and the few pieces of jewelry that he has not taken back, and thus buy my escape. I planned to hide somewhere until Phelps could join me. Get some kind of job. However, I knew from the way she looked at me that she was of the same ilk as my husband and that he must have been paying her more than my tawdry pieces could fetch. She never spoke to me, only rang the bell, unlocked the door, shoved the bag at me, and departed, locking it again from the outside.

Before he left, he locked the door to the top floor. I think he placed some valuables in the attic and did not trust the woman not to search for them. The silver that was in the dining room is gone. This cut me off from Phelps. I feared they would be no way to communicate, but one day I saw him outside the small kitchen window. He held up a sign—"Tuesdays 4:00"—then another—"Are you all right?" I nodded, for now I was, and pressed my face to the window. He could not press his in return. The window is too high and the shrubs too thick, but he held his arms as if to put them around me. We stayed like that for a long time. His face was filled with sadness. He appeared each Tuesday with more *messages to keep my courage up. Each one ended the same way: "I love you." I know he would come more often if he could, but it was not safe. He was taking a chance as it was, but I had to see him, if only for those brief minutes, so I didn't tell him not to come.*

I hope the baby will be healthy. I should be eating better. The first time I felt this new life stirring, I could not help but feel happy. A kernel of this remains every time I feel something, but I am so distracted by the larger question that I cannot think clearly about the human being growing day by day inside my womb.

I have my sewing basket, without the scissors, which he removed, and over these weeks I have let out my skirts and dresses, so that it appears that I have merely gained weight. My husband returned a week ago, and instead of being disgusted, he appears to find me more attractive. "You have become quite a cow lounging about, but it suits you," he said, grabbing my breasts. I do not know why the obvious does not occur to him, but it has not.

My life has returned to the way it was before. My only solace is you, little book, and the hope that Phelps will come to the nursery soon.

s locked me in again until he comes back from his office but I did you Diary, tucked into the waistband of my skirt under my sweater. That sunny summer when I was buying my trousseau in Bangor, I had the sudden tho

A my, have you been playing dress-up with Mommy's things again?" Faith looked straight into her daughter's big blue eyes. Amy was a terrible liar and invariably looked to the left or right when confronted.

"No, not since we moved to this house," she answered, her gaze puzzled but unswerving.

"Okay, peanut—it's just that I thought some of my things looked a little mussed up, but I was in a hurry when I put away the wash and must have done it myself."

Faith was in a hurry now, too. She had told Tom she was meeting a friend at nine o'clock and would join them at church at eleven. Memorial Church was a five-minute walk from the Peabody Museum; she wouldn't be late. Tom didn't ask her whom she was meeting or why. Just nodded and said, "Okay, I'll save you a seat."

The *why* was what Faith was thinking about herself as she cut across the Cambridge Common to the museum. It was a beautiful morning, much warmer, almost mild. No Almighty would have dared to rain on Millicent's birthday, so Faith shouldn't have been surprised. Everything was ready for the tea party, and she hoped Miss ("Not Ms., thank you very much") McKinley would be happy, or, failing that, at least gracious. The Cambridge Common was much larger than Aleford's and wasn't surrounded by as many original houses, but it retained a strong sense of the past—a plaque marked the spot where the "Washington Elm" had stood, the tree under which he assumed command of the army. A monument to those who died for the Union, a statue of Lincoln under its dome, was the largest memorial; a smaller, more recent one to the Irish who had perished in the Great Hunger stood nearby and was equally moving—all these reminders that for three hundred years this had been the center of Cambridge. It was almost deserted now, though.

There wasn't a soul in the museum, either. Cambridge mommies and daddys were still in the arms of Morpheus, unaware of the milk cascading over the sides of cereal bowls as unsteady hands prepared for an orgy of cartoons before the grown-ups woke up and turned the channel to PBS.

Faith smiled at the guard at the desk, hung up her coat, and walked through the exhibition space devoted to the bushmen of the Kalahari, heading for the totem poles. She'd thought about meeting Richard at the Ware Collection, the Glass Flowers, but it was less private—located right by the gift shop—and always made her slightly nervous. The botanical specimens—some four thousand of them—were composed entirely of glass, a tour de force from the late nineteenth and early twentieth centuries, which enabled study of the species year-round. They were always in bloom. Faith had made the mistake initially of bringing Ben and Amy, and the visit had been brief. As soon as she entered the gallery, she could see the headline: MOTHER HOLDING CHILD FALLS INTO CASE, DESTROYING PRICELESS BROMELIADS. The models were so delicate that on subsequent visits she tiptoed and kept well away lest a vibration destroy a stamen or pistil. No, the Glass Flowers were not the place to meet, although the lights were kept low and she knew that at this point it would make Richard comfortable.

The spot she had picked was not a bright one, either, and had the virtue of being isolated at the far end of the Hall of the North American Indian. She had it all to herself at this time of day. And she sat down on a bench that faced an exhibit of ceremonial masks from the Northwest coast. They were flanked by two tall house posts—totem poles were memorials. These appeared similar, but house posts functioned to support the roof beams of the places where sacred rites were held. A tape played songs from the tribes of the Northwest. Faith quickly took out the "Sunday Styles" section from the *New York Times*, before the unease she was starting to feel mounted. There was nothing like looking at Bill Cunningham's photo piece, "On the Street," which chronicled what trend was hot during the prior week on the sidewalks of New York, or reading the "Vows" column, which highlighted a unique wedding, to take one's mind off just about anything.

By 10:00 A.M., she had resorted to reading each and every wedding announcement—they were so much chattier now and told more than you needed to know about the bride and groom: "She had spinach in her teeth on our first date and I thought that was so cute"; "He asked me so many times, I felt sorry for him and finally said yes."

An hour had passed and no Richard. No anyone. The carved figures of men squatting on top of the grizzly bears on the house posts were looked resigned, their hands folded. The masks in the case were looking more and more lifelike, too—their mouths open, about to speak to her. Telling her what? Give up? Go home? Go to Harvard Square? Get some coffee? What did she hope to accomplish? That she could somehow get Richard to go for help, transform him, even though his family and no doubt other friends had failed repeatedly. There was a Kwakiut transformation mask directly in front of her—a raven, opening to reveal an anthropomorphic face with a hooked nose. Masks. Richard had worn several. Which was real? Or maybe they were all false, the man himself long since an empty husk.

There were two entrances into the room where she was sitting, and she'd been keeping an eye on both. She got up and walked through the adjacent galleries. Still empty, but she wasn't surprised. It had been

this way when she'd come another time before church, that time with
Ben and Amy. This had been why she'd thought of it as a meeting place.
She went back to her bench. The music with its haunting melody and
words she did not understand intensified her sadness. She couldn't do
anything about Richard, for Richard. He wasn't going to come. She
knew she'd come back next week, but she also knew that that, too,
would be futile. It was 10:30. She could stay only fifteen more minutes.
She heard a door close. Probably one of the staff. The only way down
here was via the main stairs. She opened the paper again to distract
herself. She hadn't read all the ads.

It happened so swiftly that for a moment she thought she had fallen
over by herself. She was sprawled on the floor facedown, the force of
the push hard enough to stun her for a moment, knock the wind out of
her. Tears stung her eyes. She touched her nose, still not sure what had
happened. It was bleeding. The sight made what had happened real. In
one swift motion, she pushed herself to her knees and jumped up, running out the door. A figure in a beige jacket was disappearing around
the corner.

"Richard!" she called, racing through the galleries, but he had too
great a lead. She didn't catch another glimpse of him. It was as if he had
vanished into thin air, air that felt moist and smelled slightly stale—the
odor of antiquity. "Richard!" she called out again, but softly this time. It
had to be Richard, but why? Why come to meet her and attack her? Why
not simply not come at all? She retraced her steps and returned to the
bench to get her pocketbook.

It was gone. That was why.

"Oh, Richard," she said to herself. "I would have given you money.
You didn't have to steal it."

With a heavy heart, she made her way upstairs. A family was entering the gallery. "I know you'll like the totem poles," the father was saying to his son, who looked about four years old. He was gripping his
dad's hand, dancing up and down in excitement. "Can you say *totem*?

Toe-tem," the father instructed, his face a professorial mask. Child rearing was serious business in his house, apparently.

She went to the rest room and washed her face, wiggling her nose gently. It hurt, but it wasn't broken, and the bleeding had stopped. Without her purse, she used her fingers to comb her hair.

As she left, Faith debated whether she should report the theft. She decided not to—she knew who had done it. Instead, she asked the guard if she had seen a man in a beige jacket. In his early forties, about six feet tall, brown hair. She was supposed to meet a friend, she told the woman.

"Yes, I did. He came in, and he hasn't left."

"Are you sure? I mean, I was supposed to meet him, but . . ."

But what? He grabbed my purse and ran off, so he must have left?

"You might want to go back and look. I know he came in, and I've been here the whole time. Tan jacket, tall, could use a shave. Maybe he didn't see you."

He *did* see me, saw me sitting there, an easy mark, Faith thought bitterly as she explained that she didn't have any more time.

"I leave at noon, but if he comes by before that, I'll tell him you were looking for him. Do you want to leave your name?"

"It's Faith."

"Okay, Faith, you have a nice day now. I'm sure he'll be sorry he missed you."

Faith thanked the guard, who had tried so hard to help, and went to get her coat.

Outside, the sky was blue and it was warmer than before. All should have been right with the world. She walked down Divinity Avenue and stopped dead in her tracks. There behind a low hedge, on top of the melting snow, was her pocketbook—the maroon leather Longchamp Tom had given her for Christmas. She retrieved it and quickened her pace. She would be late for church, but not too late. As she hastened along, she opened the bag and looked to see what was missing. She'd have to cancel her Visa. She couldn't imagine he'd have taken anything else but that and the cash she'd had—about thirty dollars—more than she usually carried. A gender difference—men always had to have a bunch of cash on their person; women walked around with a credit card, a bank card, and a dollar in change.

The Visa was there; the ATM card too. And even more mysterious, so was her thirty dollars.

Maybe it hadn't been Richard after all, but if it hadn't been, then who had it been? And why, why, why?

Millicent Revere McKinley's eighty-fifth birthday party was already a roaring success. Used to Ritz crackers with cream cheese and piccalilli or anchovy paste on triangles of toasted Pepperidge Farm white bread, the guests devoured Faith's hors d'oeuvres as fast as she refilled the trays. Pix had pressed her daughter, Samantha, into service and she was passing the treats.

"You'd think these old ladies hadn't eaten in days!" Samantha exclaimed.

Pix and Faith exchanged looks. For some of the partygoers, this was close to the truth. Living on fixed incomes, and with the increase in taxes on all levels, cutting down on food was the first thing they did. And they'd be too proud to go to the Aleford Food Pantry run by the local churches. Faith resolved to tell Tom that they had to cast their Meals on Wheels net wider. For future reference, she took note of who was present and really loading up.

While the women sat down to their first course, cream of asparagus soup, Faith, Pix, and Samantha had theirs in the kitchen.

"Oh, I told Reverend Fairchild that any night this week was fine," Samantha said.

"Fine for what?" Faith asked.

"He called me to see if Danny could baby-sit next weekend," Pix interjected. "He said you hadn't been out in awhile and he wanted to take advantage of big-city life. I told him he didn't have to wait until the weekend and to call Samantha. She has a car this year on campus and it's easy for her to get into Cambridge—she seems to spend half her life there anyway."

"I do not," Samantha protested. "Nick comes out to Wellesley a lot, too. Anyway, anytime is good." Nick, a junior at MIT, had become a major presence in Samantha's life, much to her father's chagrin ("She's still a child") and her mother's approval ("A nice steady boy").

Faith was touched by Tom's effort. Obviously, there weren't going to be any more Mindy suggestions. When she'd slid next to him in the pew earlier that day, he'd looked at her with concern. "Are you all right?" he'd whispered.

No, I'm not all right, she'd wanted to say. Wanted suddenly to tell him everything, but as they stood for the first hymn, she'd replied, "I'm fine. I had a nosebleed, which kept me, so I'm a little out of breath."

"We'll call you tonight," Faith told Samantha. "Now, let's see if anyone wants seconds and then serve the tart."

The second course was the Alsatian tart, which had gone over so well with the Uppity Women—a group not unlike the one in the next room, it occurred to Faith. She was serving the tart with a salad of mixed greens and pear slices. The sweetness of the fruit provided a nice contrast to both the greens and the onion/bacon tart.

Niki had outdone herself with the cake, recreating Old Glory in marzipan and draping it over the top, leaving room for "Happy Birthday Millicent" in red, white, and blue script. The cake itself was lemon—two tangy lighter-than-air layers with lemon curd in between and creamy butter frosting on top. There were plenty of oohs and aahs when it was set down in front of Millicent, who cried, "For me!" and promptly blew out the candles in one breath. Ursula shot Faith a triumphant glance that said, I knew she'd be pleased. Then she turned to Millicent and said, "Of course it's for you, birthday girl. Now, Faith, you, Pix, and Samantha pull up some chairs. You've worked hard enough."

Teacups were filled and refilled. Talk turned to the upcoming Town Meeting and town elections. Faith began to relax. It was all so familiar. Like stepping back into a favorite picture—one that had hung on the wall for a very long time.

"Well, Faith, we'll miss you," Millicent said cheerfully, no hint of regret in her voice, although it could have been the party that induced the chirpy note. Faith found herself wondering which it was; then suddenly the words sank in.

But it was Ursula who picked up the cue. "You mean you miss her now, of course. Everyone does," she said firmly.

"All right, Ursula, I don't want to spoil my own party, but you've heard the same things I have, and I just want to say that we'll miss poor Tom and his little ones, too."

Millicent had formed the habit of referring to the Reverend Thomas Fairchild as "poor Tom" shortly after his marriage to "that girl from New York," then later tacked on the children, always with the suggestion in her voice that somehow they weren't Faith's doing, but Tom's alone—like Athena springing from the head of Zeus.

Faith fortified herself with the dregs of her tea.

"I don't know what you've heard"—and no one knows better than I how rumors get started in Aleford, she added to herself—"but I can assure you that the entire Fairchild family will be returning to the parsonage at the end of May."

Millicent looked down at the crumbs on her plate. She'd had two large pieces of cake. "Whatever you say, dear."

It was all Faith could do to keep from slicing Millicent.

"More tea, anyone?" Pix appeared with a fresh pot, and cups were raised all round. These ladies had the innate capacity to drink gallons of tea without the need to excuse themselves from the table. They would make camels jealous.

Faith took the empty pot back into the kitchen. She knew her cheeks were flaming and that she looked upset. It was all getting to be more than she could bear. The incident at the museum had been pushed firmly to the back of her mind. Millicent's words, touching upon another matter Faith had resolutely filed, brought this morning's fear and confusion roaring back, followed by the rest of the contents of Pandora's beautiful but deadly box, currently residing in Faith Sibley Fairchild.

Pix followed at her heels like the faithful friend she was and firmly closed the door in Samantha's face, suggesting she keep her grandmother and her friends company.

"Don't pay any attention to Millicent. You know what she's like," Pix said.

"Yes, which is exactly why I *am* paying attention to her. Nobody in this town has an ear closer to the ground. I'm surprised it hasn't formed roots. What is she talking about? You must know."

Pix looked uncomfortable. "Willard Moore ran into Tom in Cambridge a week ago and asked him when he'd be back, and apparently Tom said, 'When pigs fly.' But you know that Willard has absolutely no sense of humor, and Tom was making a joke, of course. He's told the vestry he'll be returning at the end of May, as you said, and that's that."

Willard Moore didn't have a sense of humor and Tom knew that as well as anybody else did. What was he doing saying "When pigs fly" to Willard, of all people? She knew the answer. It must have been on one of those sunny, mild days. Tom had probably just finished his class and was off to Oak Street or someplace else. He was free as a bird—or a pig with wings—and then there was Willard, a grim, literally, reminder of what he'd be returning to in a short time. Faith sighed.

"I don't know what Tom will decide eventually. He's committed himself, so we'll be back, but it may be that it won't be for long. He may decide it's time to move on to something new."

"And how does that make you feel?" Pix asked.

"I have no idea," Faith replied.

---

aith sent the ladies home with fragrant pots of purple hyacinths, bags of assorted scones, and some of her wild-strawberry jam. Niki had baked a small version of Millicent's cake for the guest of honor to take home, as well. At the door, Millicent had hugged Faith, an event so rare that Faith reflexively hugged her back, wondering if this marked some new stage in their relationship.

"It was the best birthday I've ever had. And I *will* miss you, no matter what anyone says."

Maybe it wasn't a new stage.

Faith thanked her—for what, she knew not—and said good-bye to the others. It was the loveliest birthday party they'd ever been to, they called out as they were leaving, their arms full, showering her, Pix, Ursula, and "darling Samantha" with thanks.

It didn't take long to put Ursula's house back to rights, since it was so very close to them to start with. Faith was back in Cambridge in plenty of time for supper and the kids' bedtime.

"It's been a busy weekend for you," Tom commented when they were finally alone in the living room, the Sunday *Times* a mountain of newsprint between them on the sofa. "The thing last night, Millicent's party today, not to mention all that Mayan research."

She was exhausted, Faith realized, and her own bedtime was going to be pretty close to the kids', but first she regaled Tom with a description of the birthday party, not omitting what Pix had told her about Willard Moore's encounter with him.

"*Merde!*" Tom exclaimed. They'd switched to swearing in French, in the vain hope that Ben and Amy wouldn't catch on. "I don't know what I was thinking of. Yes, I do know. I was thinking, Oh *merde*, here's Willard, and then he was going on about First Parish, Aleford, and asking when I was coming back. I was feeling a little peeved, so I said something I admit was stupid, particularly since I should have remembered his wife is one of the biggest gossips in town."

"It really doesn't matter," Faith said. And it didn't.

She stood up and stretched.

"I'm going to try Hope. There was a message on the machine. Calling yesterday and again today means that something's up. Then I'm going to turn in," Faith said.

"I heard it when we came back from the park. Don't leap to any conclusions. She sounded fine. And she sounded fine when I talked to her yesterday, too. It's probably to let us know the wedding date."

Was her weltschmerz so apparent? And Tom was right. Hope *had* sounded like her usual happy self.

But she wasn't.

"Fay, I'm so glad you called. I was just about to try you again."

"What's wrong. It isn't anything with the baby is. . . ?"

"No. Apparently, I'm healthy as a horse—or mare, I should say. It's just that I've been getting attacks of the blue meanies lately. What do I know about being a mother? What do I know about being a wife? And all this stuff is for life!" Hope wailed.

Faith relaxed. Here at last was something she could deal with—prenuptial, prenaissance jitters. Been there, done that—doing that. Admittedly, her sister's life, unlike her own prior to marriage and motherhood, fell into a fixed pattern—and it had suited Hope very well all these years. She loved her work. She loved her corner office with its fabulous view. She loved her duplex co-op with its fabulous view. She loved Quentin and the life they shared—intense periods of work, followed by equally intense periods of relaxation in Mustique, Gstaad, Santo Domingo, Megeve, depending on the season—plus, they always had Paris (for a long weekend). Hope had already fit Quentin into her life. It wasn't marriage; it was mostly the baby that was making her teeter on her Manolo Blahniks.

"Everybody feels this way," Faith reassured her sister. "You're getting a double dose, that's all. Believe me, there's something about hearing 'I do' that goes straight into your bloodstream and stays in your heart forever. The same for the first little coo."

"That's very catchy, Fay. You should have had a career on Madison Avenue instead of going to that cooking school." She paused for a moment.

"I feel like I'm unnatural. I mean of course I want this baby, but it's a whole new country, and I don't have a map."

Hope was turning a pretty nifty phrase herself, and Faith knew what she meant about not having a map. Pix had been her trusty guide so far, and it looked like Faith would be passing on her words of wisdom to her sister. Hope's words continued to flow, rushing after one another in a single panicked sentence. "I only know a few kids, and they're very cute, except that boy on the third floor who keeps kicking people when he's in the elevator—I always wait for it to come back down again—but I don't have to live with them."

"When it's your own, you tend to overlook runny noses, snotty attitudes, et cetera. The danger is overlooking too much—obviously those parents on the third floor are—because you get so crazy about them."

"I *do* love Ben and Amy," Hope said thoughtfully.

"And they love you. You're a terrific aunt, which is very good training for motherhood. Besides, you're not on a desert island. You will have a map—me, Mom." Faith paused a millisecond here at the picture of her mother offering child-rearing advice to Hope. It would never happen. Not that she didn't adore her existing grandchildren, but aside from coming for a week after each birth, during which time she took excellent care of all of them very efficiently, Jane stuck to gifts and planned excursions. "And Quentin's mom." Quentin was an only child, and his mother had greeted the news of his impending matrimony and patrimony by sobbing hysterically and saying, "I'm so happy! I'm so happy!" This from a woman, like her son, with never a hair out of place and emotions held in check so long, they were in danger of being auctioned off as lost property.

Hope's voice lost its trepidation. "I'm going to have a nanny. Someone at the office is finishing with hers just in time, and she's a jewel.

English, even, and older. Not the type to go and write about us. I don't care if *The Nanny Diaries* ended up on the best-seller list, it was extremely inappropriate."

"Extremely inappropriate" was tantamount to a felony in Hope's lexicon.

As Faith talked to Hope, she was flooded with memories of the kids as babies: those tiny finger- and toenails, Pearly like the insides of seashells; that sweet baby smell—it should be bottled—and their little mouths—they really were like rosebuds. Lord! Did she want another baby?

Quickly, she moved Hope on to matrimony. Faith had even more experience here. There had been plenty of wedding receptions delayed by last-minute doubts at the altar. At one wedding in a beautiful house out in Lincoln, when the wait began to stretch close to an hour, Faith served coffee and sent Niki to Donelan's, the local market, for Danish.

"Have you set a date for the wedding?"

"Didn't I tell you? My mind is turning to mush these days, and it better be my hormones. April twenty-sixth. Daddy will be busy with Easter before then, and besides, the weather will be better."

"And you still want to get married at Aunt Chat's?"

Faith had been surprised by the couple's decision to get married at Chat's house in Mendham, New Jersey—Jersey, for goodness sakes! Chat's friends and relations were still coming to terms with her hegira from the city when she retired several years ago, and now Hope and Quentin, native New Yorkers, were going to get married there—in the country!

"Absolutely. Everything will be in bloom, and whatever isn't, we can bring in in big pots. We've arranged for vans to take people from the city out to Chat's. That way, no one will get lost. Quentin didn't feel we could ask people to try to find it out there on their own."

Hope was making it sound like tracking down the source of the Nile, but Faith concurred.

"I should drive down and help you find a dress."

"All done. Vera is doing both of ours. Think Barbizon, but not too much like shepherdesses. Although we may go that way for Ben and Amy."

"I don't think Ben will want to dress up as a shepherdess—or a shepherd, for that matter. Amy, however, will love it. Put her in a leghorn bonnet and give her a basket of rose petals, plus a dress with lots of crinolines, and she'll be in seventh heaven."

"I wish you could come down. Talking to you has made me feel so much better. It really is going to be all right, isn't it, Fay?"

"It's not simply going to be all right; it's going to be wonderful," Faith said—and it would be, although if Vera Wang was going to put her in a dirndl as matron of honor, there could be a problem. On second thought, any dirndl Vera Wang came up with would bear very little resemblance to either Fragonard or Heidi.

They talked awhile longer. Their father would perform the ceremony, as he had Faith's wedding, but Hope wanted Tom to say a blessing. Faith was sure he would be delighted, but she left the phone for a moment to get his approval anyway, which was, as predicted, "I'd be delighted."

"I'm so sleepy all the time. I don't know if it's work or little beanbag"—the couple's only name for the baby so far, and one Faith hoped would not stick; they had a cousin who'd been called "Rabbit," until finally at age ten he'd announced he was only answering to Bob. "Big crunch time now." It was always a big crunch time for Hope.

"Well, just be sure you get plenty of rest. You like your doctor, right?"

"She's wonderful. That's what I mean about being unnatural. Sometimes I think she's more excited about the baby than I am."

"It's her job to be excited. She wouldn't be doing it if she didn't adore babies, and nothing you're feeling is unnatural. Read the books I sent. And I'll send some more."

"Penelope Leach is almost falling to pieces. And Quentin came home with Brazelton. Brazelton and Dr. Seuss. I think he meant to get Dr. Spock. He insists he just wanted to start our child's library, but I'm pretty sure he got confused all around, because he did say he didn't think little beanbag would be ready for *Star Trek* for a while."

Faith hung the phone up and went to the calendar to figure out when she could go to the city and see her sister. It would have to be a weekend, so the kids could sleep over at a friend's house at least one of the nights.

Once again, she fell asleep immediately—soundly, deeply, dream-lessly—and awakened an hour later with the full knowledge that trying to return to that blissful oblivion would be a fruitless endeavor. Cocoa time.

And time again for Dora's diary.

Thanksgiving Day, 1946

My husband is hosting a large dinner downstairs for friends, apparently an annual event, missed last year—he told me—because he had only recently discovered that the young jewel he had married was tragically flawed. He enjoys relating this tale, which he tells with feigned reluctance and to only a few, knowing they will spread it all over Cambridge, which appears to be a smaller village in some ways than where I grew up! He says that when my symptoms began to appear, he took me to specialists as far away as Switzerland, but my condition is hopeless, a hereditary curse. Swept off his feet, he had married me without meeting any of my family, knowing only that they were wealthy New Yorkers. He keeps me comfortable, the story goes, in my rooms with an attendant. He is an object of pity in Cambridge and held up as a model of spousal devotion. It makes me sick to think about it.

Up here in the nursery, I cannot hear them—or they me, which was the idea, I'm sure. He will toast me at some point, I was told, and I'm sure some of the women will have tears in their eyes. How surprised they would be to know that I have been slaving all week cleaning the house, baking, and preparing the meal. He has hired someone to serve, but I know the dishes will be left for me.

I am so weary, it is all I can do not to sleep, but I need to write. It has been a long time since I've been here and an age since I've seen Phelps. He came once in September and stayed until just before my husband came home. It was crazy of us, but we couldn't help it. He teased me about putting on weight, but he said it suited me. He doesn't want a woman who is a bag of bones. I should have told him then, but I could not. I am haunted by the fear that the child I am carrying is not ours, but my husband's. Until I know, I will keep my secret.

I have prayed and given my thanks. Thanks for the love that has come into my life and thanks for the love of God that has always been with me.

I must sleep now. It will be a long night.

December 1, 1946

Oh, how I wish I had known this sooner!! But to know now is enough. I will be free. Somehow I'll get word to my darling! I must! At breakfast this morning, my husband grabbed me as I was trying to clear his place, and after a revolting kiss, he said, "You are looking so fecund that had not a bad case of the mumps in my twenties rendered me sterile, I might imagine you to be with child." Then he roared with laughter. I must have looked shocked, as I was, for he continued. "You don't think I would have married someone like you if I had thought to breed?"

I stood in the kitchen for some time, trembling with joy, and had to hasten to clean up before he left for the day. It would be too much to hope that Phelps will come. As soon as I see him, I will tell him. I know he will be as happy as I am. We are going to have a baby!

December 15, 1946

The pains started early this morning. I know it's too early. It must be a false labor. I'd heard of this from Ma, who helped bring many babies in the village into this world. People would call her before the doctor.

I have not seen Phelps, nor have I been able to think of any way to get word to him. Deliveries are made in the morning or early evening. I

*am never allowed to see the deliverymen. Had I the chance, I would
thrust the note I have prepared into a hand or pocket, make of it what
they would.*

*It has been some hours and the pains are much closer together. I
fear this is the real thing and that he will come upon us, killing us both.
Oh Lord, why are you not with me now? I have prayed all day for a
miracle.*

Dora's handwriting had started out unsteady, and by this point, the
words sprawled across the page. When the entry continued, it was
almost indecipherable. There were several dark brown smears on the
side of the page. Blood. Dried blood.

*He is beautiful. Our son. I bit the cord, like an animal does, and tied it
as best I could, cleaning him with my blouse and wrapping him in my
sweater. The pain was sweet. I have known much worse. He is eagerly
nursing, and the sight of his head at my breast fills me with joy, even as
I know the end is near. He is very small. His eyes are large, deep blue—
and best of all, his hair is pale red, soft and downy like an Easter
chick's. I am drowsy and he will sleep soon, too, I know. He is a good
baby, crying out only at the shock of entering the world.*

*I am weak. I have not been able to stop my bleeding. I took the
cushion from the window seat and we are lying on it. I can see the pine
and blue sky above. I have said the "Our Father" and I do not pray for
me, but only that he will watch over our child. Amen.*

Poor little boy. I fear we will both be in the arms of the Lord soon.

Faith closed the book. The remaining pages were blank. She was too
shocked to cry. Too devastated. Phelps had not arrived in time. Dora
had not escaped. They had never danced together again. And the baby.
He would not have escaped, either. Had he died that night? Had
Chauncey Carver, coming upon the scene, found his wife dead—or near
death? Had he made her last moments an agony? He would not have

summoned a doctor to witness the scene, his humiliation. And the baby? Had he conveniently died also? Carver would have known instantly who the father was and would never have let the proof of his wife's infidelity survive. The librarian had told Faith she could look up births and deaths at City Hall. All she needed were the names and approximate dates. She had them, but she didn't need to look them up.

Faith knew what she had to do. She put on a jacket, crept upstairs, got her shoes and some tissue paper that she had used to put in the bags with the scones and the jam. She'd bought a package that had a rainbow of colors, and now she selected deep purple—purple, the color of mourning. Purple, the color of Dora's pansy. Faith wrapped the little book in the paper and went out the front door and into the yard. It was a hazy gibbous moon and the sky was almost dark, but with the street-lamp, she had enough light for the task she'd set herself. She had brought a soup spoon from the kitchen, and now, kneeling down, she started to dig in the earth at the base of the star magnolia. Its branches arched above her, silhouetted and swelling with buds that would soon transform it. Dora's tree.

The spoon wasn't strong enough and it bent. Faith sat back on her heels, frustrated. It wasn't that the ground was frozen; the warm weather had thawed the surface. It was the spoon—one from an inexpensive bistro set that she'd brought from home.

Home. Whenever she'd thought of home, she'd always thought of New York—the place where she was born, raised, and had lived until her marriage to Tom. She was a New Yorker. An expatriate, an exile. Now, as she looked at the spoon, she realized the home she'd been thinking of was Aleford. The parsonage. It had taken a long time, but it had finally happened.

Slipping the spoon into her pocket, she considered digging with her hands. Or she could go back inside and get one of her heavy cooking spoons. Then she thought of the garage. She'd look there first. If there were any garden tools, that's where they'd be.

Faith walked back along the side of the house, heading toward the garage, a night animal. Her eyes had adapted to the dark now. She could see her breath, but she didn't feel cold.

The old garage doors had never been replaced. No remote control, just heavy old-fashioned doors that met in the middle. She pulled them open just enough to slip through. They kept Tom's car in the garage, hers outside. He had become a true urbanite, walking or using public transportation for the most part. They should have left his car in Aleford.

There were shelves at the end of the garage, and on one was a big sturdy wicker basket filled with garden tools. The assortment would have fetched a good price at an auction or flea market—"Vintage basket with garden implements." She took a spade and a trowel and returned to the front yard. Looking at the handles, whose green paint had almost completely worn off, she realized with a start that these could have been the tools that Phelps had used to plant the garden so many years before. These were the kind of things that stayed with houses as they changed owners—wallpaper rolls in the attic, boxes of replacement tiles and odd drawer pulls in the basement, hoses and garden tools in the garage.

She loosened the soil at a spot behind the trunk and began to dig. She wanted to go well below the surface. Satisfied at last, she placed the diary in the hole and buried it, aware of the faint odor of the promise of spring. She spread the dead leaves and other remnants of winter back over the grave; then she said a prayer for Dora and her child.

When Faith went back to bed, she slept. She had found out what had happened in that room on the top floor. And she had not been wrong. The woman who'd been imprisoned there had been murdered as surely as if her husband had shot her straight between the eyes.

10

B en, have you been doing your homework at my desk?" Tom asked.

They were having dinner. It had been a glorious day, the temperature having soared into the sixties. Faith had taken the kids to the playground on the Cambridge Common, then to Harvard Square for ice cream at Toscanini's. Ben had stuck with his favorite, creamsicle. Faith had wavered for a nanosecond between chai and Belgian chocolate before saying to herself, "Chai over chocolate! What am I thinking!" And Amy, the wild card, had chosen *nocciola* frozen yogurt. It was possible to pretend that it was summer. Harvard undergraduates had ditched their pea coats and parkas for cutoffs and tank tops. Tom had come home early with lamb chops from Savenor's Market, declaring he would broil them himself. All Faith had to do was provide a side dish or two. She'd steamed some broccoli, tossed it with olive oil and a hint of garlic, then given in to Ben's pleas for twice-baked potatoes.

"No, Dad. Honest to God. See?" Ben held up his hands and wiggled his fingers. They had had a run of blatant falsehoods before discovering that he thought he had immunity if his fingers were crossed.

Tom helped himself to another potato. "That's funny. I could have sworn I left Mindy's rough draft on top of *Gospel Parallels* in the top drawer. They're vice versa now."

"Maybe we have poltergeists, or house elves," Ben said excitedly. "It's possible. A lot of stuff has been out of place, right? My books got moved to the shelf above, and Amy couldn't have done that even standing on a chair."

"I did not!" she exclaimed indignantly, displaying a mouthful of broccoli.

"Don't speak with your mouth full, darling," Faith said automatically.

"I just said you *didn't* do it, dummy," Ben said, looking disgusted.

"Don't call your sister a dummy," Tom said automatically.

Faith looked at him. No one, not even a poltergeist or an elf, could get into the house. With such valuable contents, they were extremely careful about setting the alarm whenever they left and then again at night when they went to bed. Tom was apparently as distracted as she was, and as for Ben's books, she had probably done that when she cleaned his room last.

It had been a beautiful day, but there had been one odd interlude. She'd been walking back down Massachusetts Avenue with the kids, all three of them contentedly licking their cones—a recent achievement for Amy, who was proud not to have to have a cup anymore. Faith had spotted a vendor selling *Spare Change*, and as she handed him a dollar, something about his face convinced her he was the Monk. It wasn't that he looked blissed-out. Just relaxed, calm. She remembered the woman, Nancy, at the Arlington Street Church had said this was one of his locales.

"Daniel?" she asked. "Is your name Daniel, the Monk?"

He smiled. "Why yes, it is. Do we know each other?"

"No. I met Nancy at the Arlington Street Church and she said you sometimes sold the paper here, so I took a guess. But we do have a friend in common, Richard Goodman, or he may have said his name was Richard Morgan."

"Both good folk. Know them well." He had looked at her intently.

The children were busy with their cones, and Faith pressed on.

"I'm trying to find Richard. Do you know where he is?"

"He could be a lot of places. Why don't you wait until he finds you? Yes, sir. Thank you, sir." He'd turned to another customer, then back to the Fairchilds.

"Enjoy your ice cream; enjoy the day."

"Thank you. We will," Faith said, vowing to return.

Now she looked at the scene in front of her, her family gathered around the table. "Strawberries for dessert. They're starting to come in from California and taste like real fruit, not sawdust."

"Why would anyone eat sawdust?" Ben asked.

"It's a phrase," Tom explained patiently. Faith's had given out at about 4:00 P.M. "Just a phrase."

"Bobby's mommy says he's going through a phrase," Amy informed them solemnly.

D o you know that man?" Niki asked. She and Faith were in Starbucks. "What man?"

"Damn, he's gone. Tall, wearing a watch cap and a beige jacket. I didn't get that close a look, but he walked in, started for the counter, saw you, and hightailed it out of here. Or maybe it was me. It had to be one of us. No one else is around."

Faith was about to say, "It's me, not you," but then she realized it would mean a great deal of explaining, something she wasn't up to at the moment. She was going through a "phrase," too. Richard again—and he'd bolted again. It would be pointless to follow him; the Square would have swallowed him up by now. He could have ducked into any one of the countless shops and restaurants, or dashed down the entrance to the T.

She took Niki's hand instead. The ring that had been around her neck was now on her finger, sending tiny rainbows across the wall in front of them.

"Yeah, I'm doing it. Getting hitched. Putting on that old ball and chain. Tying the knot. Taking the plunge. The leap. Whatever."

"You don't fool me for a minute. You're thrilled. Come on, admit it."

"Yes, boss, I am. Totally, completely, ecstatically happy."

Faith gave Niki a big hug. Phil was almost good enough for the assistant who had become her treasured friend.

"I'm surprised I didn't hear shouts of joy from the Constantine household. We're not that far from the Watertown-Cambridge border."

"I'm surprised, too. A couple of neighbors called. They thought the shouting didn't sound like the usual—you know, 'Why are you destroying my life?' I tried to get my mother to put a sock in her mouth before I told her, but good luck there."

"Was Phil with you?"

"Are you kidding? I'm never going into the house again without him. He's like Gardol—you know, that plastic shield that kept Mr. Tooth Decay away. I always wondered about the little kids who were in the half of the class that got the toothpaste without the magic ingredient. They have to be in their forties or fifties now. Root canals, crowns, implants—couldn't they sue? Anyway, Pop produced some ouzo—not hard at my house—and the place began to fill up with everyone of Greek origin within a ten-mile radius. Actually, it was pretty cool. But Mom and I have already started a major war over the wedding dress."

"Right. She wants you to look like you've stepped off the top of a cake."

"Except puffier sleeves, fuller skirt, longer train. I have a plan, though. You and I will go pick one out, and the bridesmaid's dresses and yours. I'll give them a nonrefundable deposit. That should do it."

They finished their coffees, went next door to the bead store—Niki made her own earrings, the longer the better—then said good-bye at the corner of Appian Way and Brattle. Faith walked slowly along the brick sidewalk, feeling happy for Niki. She *had* made the pros and cons

list, but she said she'd decided not to share it with Pix and Faith after
reviewing some of the items in the "Pro" column. By the time she was
on the second sheet of legal-size paper and still had almost nothing
under "Con," she was "hooked." Faith smiled as she thought about all
the traditionally masculine marriage descriptions Niki had appropri-
ated. "Ball and chain" was for grooms; orange blossoms and Mendels-
sohn were for brides, except Niki wasn't going to be just any bride. No
bride ever is, Faith thought, smiling to herself. Two happy weddings—
Niki's and Hope's—good matches, not the kind where you wonder if the
couple will make it through the honeymoon.

It was overcast and yesterday's summer had disappeared without a
trace. She shivered slightly and wrapped her scarf around her neck
more securely. She heard footsteps behind her and moved over on the
narrow sidewalk to allow the person to pass. No one did. She turned
around. The walk was empty, but the hedge next to it was quivering.

Stop it, she told herself. It was broad daylight. She was in a city of
over 100,000 people. She started walking again, faster, telling herself it
would be nice to pick Amy up early for a change. Again she heard a
noise, but she didn't turn around. She was almost running now. At
Mason Street, she stopped to let a car go by. On the other side, almost at
Amy's school, she turned around. A flash of beige—the jacket. Richard
was following her.

Stalking her?

Faith looked at the Lobstering Women of Maine calendar she'd hung
on a hook projecting from the kitchen wall. The squares were filled
with appointments and reminders of birthdays, as well as her catering
schedule. Tom had squeezed in his dates, too. Will there ever be a
square left blissfully empty? she wondered as her life stared her in the
face. March was going fast. And where had February gone? It seemed as
if they had just arrived in Cambridge, but their time here was almost

half over. Since laying Dora's diary to rest, Faith had felt a kind of relief. It had been the not knowing that was such a torment. Someday soon, she would drive back up to Maine and tell Josie Marshall in person that her friend had died long ago—an edited version. Before that, though, she'd check the records at City Hall. The diary had ended abruptly. If Dora had lived, she would have written more—or taken it with her when she left. How long had she lain on that cushion on the floor, waiting for death, or a miracle? Was it one of the times that Carver had been gone for days? And the baby. It was unlikely he had survived, especially if much time had passed. And he'd been early, a preemie. Even in the hospital, he might not have lived. The extraordinary equipment available now was unheard of then. And Phelps. What of him? He would never have known of the baby. At least Faith hoped not. Hoped he had not happened upon the scene. But it would have been unlikely. No, she was sure she knew now what had happened in that room. Chauncey Carver had turned the key, summoned help, which arrived too late, of course, and played the bereaved widower—the scope of his inventions given full rein.

"Oak Street—Faith" it said in Wednesday's little box on the calendar. They were having trouble finding volunteers again. There was a symposium at the Divinity School, and Tom had been involved in the planning, which meant going out to dinner with the speakers afterward. She'd been envious when he told her they were going to Rialto. After a meal there, Faith always left with the same thought—that Jody Adams, the chef, might be reason enough for leaving New York City.

She had committed herself to dinner duty at Oak Street and also the cleanup, but sitters weren't a problem now. A call to Bitsy had turned up a stellar list, mostly nieces and nephews or a cousin's children. Faith should have thought of her Cambridge guide immediately; it would have saved all that Mindy trouble.

The sitter, a senior at Brimmer and May, appeared shortly after the kids got home. The three bonded at once, and, feeling totally unnecessary after Sophie had assured her she was capable of managing dinner—"I've worked in Le Grenier's kitchen on the Vineyard for ages"— Faith left.

At Oak Street, she searched every face, stared at every beige jacket, but in vain. Again she was struck by the differences in age, appearance, and manner of the people who came here. The fact that they were in Boston, Massachusetts, the United States of America, the wealthiest nation on the globe, sickened her. She thought of where and how she had lived her life, what she had taken for granted until relatively recently, things she had thrown out that someone might have used—or eaten. Tom was right. This was what they should be doing. Not preaching to the choir, but ministering to those who really needed them most. She would make time for Oak Street and the other kitchens.

The warm weather had been a tease. It was cold again and the line was long. Once more, she was alone cleaning up. The others had had to get back to the suburbs; there was just the one van. But she didn't mind. The hot sudsy water felt relaxing, cleansing. She had come to a decision. She'd talk to Tom. Tell him leaving Aleford would be all right. The kids were young. They would adapt. And besides, the only thing that mattered to them was that they would be with their parents—parents who were happy with each other and with themselves.

She left the shelter and walked toward the T stop in Chinatown. She'd discovered it was much simpler to take the subway than deal with Boston streets and Boston drivers. Unlike those who had planned New York, which was so logical, whoever had mapped out Boston's byways had done it all as the crow flies and all as one-ways. Bostonians drove fast, assumed the orange light meant speed up, welcomed crosswalks as guides for mowing down pedestrians, and, in general, took pride in the idiosyncrasies of their city's "can't get there from here" traffic patterns.

It was twilight, that pause before nightfall, beginning to stretch out as daylight saving time neared. Faith started down an alley shortcut to Harrison Avenue.

"Faith!"

Someone was calling her. He was wearing a beige jacket and a watch cap pulled down over his hair, his head lowered against the cold wind.

"Richard!" She ran back toward him, filled with joy—and relief. He *hadn't* run away.

She stopped, but before she could say a word, his hand was over her mouth, her nose. A glove, a cloth, the smell. She was going to be sick. Her knees buckled beneath her. Then nothing.

The room whirled about. She tried to sit up, but it made the sensation worse, so she lay down again. Her head was on a pillow. She was lying on a bed. Someone was sitting in a chair next to her. The last thing she remembered was leaving Oak Street House.

"Tom?" her lips were dry and felt funny. She knew she had spoken, but she couldn't hear anything.

"Tom?" she said, louder this time. "Tom!" She was screaming, but her voice was a whisper.

The figure in the chair stood up and held a glass of water with a straw to her lips. She drank, and the room gradually came to a standstill. She had never been here before. She knew that much. It looked like a hotel room. The shade on the window next to the bed was up. She could see the CITGO sign in Kenmore Square. She was in Boston. But where in Boston?

With the return of consciousness came a rush of adrenaline, fear—and remembrance. The alleyway.

"Richard? Richard, what's going on? Where are we?"

The room was dark except for the light from the window, the light from the city at night.

He snapped a lamp on, and Faith sat up completely.

It wasn't Richard.

It wasn't anyone she knew.

She could see the door, and without thinking, she shot off the bed, grabbing the knob. It was locked. The man watched her, not moving, not saying a word. She turned the dead bolt and reached for the knob again.

"I'm afraid I can't let you do that, Mrs. Fairchild. But don't worry. You won't be here long."

It was an educated voice, a voice that spoke of money—good schools, an important job, elite circles. A Cambridge voice, distinct from the Boston Brahmin's slight drawl and deliberate mispronunciations.

He'd grabbed her from behind and was forcing her into the chair next to the one he'd been sitting in. She fought back, screaming, aware that her voice was still but a rasp and that most of her strength had been sapped by whatever he had drugged her with. Swiftly, he tied her hands and legs to the chair with ropes already in place.

Wrong place, wrong time. Why had she been such a fool? She, streetwise from birth, had strode off alone at night in an unsafe neighborhood, away from traffic, away from streetlights.

"Please. I have two small children. I know there wasn't much money in my purse, but if you'll take me to an ATM, I can get you more. Much more," Faith pleaded frantically. The man didn't look like a thief. He didn't look homeless. But by now, she knew that there was no such thing as looking homeless. Or desperate. All ages, all appearances, all manners.

She tried to keep the thoughts of what else he might want from her mind. If she didn't, she would lose what little hope she had.

"I trust you are not feeling overly ill from the dose. It was a very small one and should wear off completely soon," he said matter-of-factly, then continued. "You don't know who I am, do you?"

The question surprised her.

"No, I don't. Should I?"

"I packed up all my photographs, but you might have seen my picture in something from the Divinity School."

"Dr. Robinson?"

It was too bizarre. Dr. Robinson. Teddy. Yet, the man in front of her was the right age, and glimpsing the red plaid lining of his jacket, she realized it was the one she had mailed to California.

California. "Why aren't you in California?" It was an absurd question, but the first that occurred to Faith. They were house-sitting for him while he was on sabbatical in California; ergo, he should be in California.

"It's spring break and I had some business to clear up here, although you've made it overly difficult. But that's neither here nor there. Where is the diary?"

"The diary? Dora's diary?"

Dora. Theodora. Theodore Robinson. Like the tumblers of a lock, the pieces were lining up.

"I've searched the house several times, and it's nowhere to be found. And I must find it. I'm sure you see why."

"Actually, I don't," Faith confessed. "Why don't you untie me and we can talk about it? Then we can go to your house and I can give you the book." She spoke in as calm and measured a tone as she could muster. Clearly, Dr. Robinson was insane. But she felt safer. Harvard professors, even nutty ones, didn't kill people, at least they hadn't, to her knowledge, since Dr. Webster did away with Dr. Parkman.

Dr. Robinson stood up and began pacing about the room.

"I assume you read it. You did, didn't you?"

Faith nodded. She didn't see the harm in his knowing. But it was an invasion of privacy. Dora's privacy. His mother's privacy.

"I'm sorry. I should have sent it to you as soon as we found it. But I had no idea she was your mother. I thought her name was Carver."

He stopped and stood over Faith.

"How did you find that out? Never mind. It doesn't matter. Tell me where it is and we'll be on our way."

You'll be on *your* way, Faith thought with a start. His face was contorted, a mask of control losing a battle with rage. He wanted the diary. Only she knew where it was. But why? He was born illegitimately, but that was fifty-seven years ago. No one would care about it now.

He walked over to the window and stood with his hands on the sill, his head bowed down, silhouetted against the neon light blinking slowly on and off as the gasoline company's logo filled in, then disappeared. The CITGO triangle, a landmark.

"You have no idea what it was like growing up in that house, or maybe you do. One of Chauncey Carver's favorite activities when I was in my teens was to regale me with accounts of what he had done to my mother, 'the whore,' he called her. But he wanted an heir, a son, more than revenge, so I was allowed to live. He had had mumps and was sterile. Then I arrived. She was dead. No one would ever know. His name wouldn't die out. His precious, precious name. Chauncey Brandon Carver and Chauncey Brandon Carver, Junior. Father and son."

Chauncey Brandon Carver, Junior, had become Theodore Robinson. He'd taken his mother's name for his first name, and for his last . . . Faith was pretty sure she knew—and she also knew now why Teddy had to have the diary.

He was still facing the night sky, lost in a morass of dark memories. She slipped her shoe off and tugged with her toe at the knot on the rope around the opposite ankle. As she'd hoped, Professor Robinson was no Boy Scout, and soon her feet were free. At least she'd be able to kick. She slipped back into her shoes. He turned to face her.

"She was a wonderful woman."

He had given her what she needed. A way to buy time. His mother. Faith could tell him about his mother.

"I know. And a very intelligent one. Her diary is beautifully written, especially when you consider she came from a rural background in Maine. But she was a reader. . . ."

Faith continued on, telling him all the good things Dora had written about, her love of the outdoors, gardening, dancing, and finally she got to Phelps.

By now Teddy Robinson was sitting on the side of the bed, hungrily listening to Faith's every word.

"Yes, they truly loved each other," he said, "and Uncle Ned continued to love her until the day he died. He's buried next to her in Mount Auburn. There's no stone. I took the box of ashes and did it myself."

Uncle Ned. Uncle Ned? Teddy didn't wait for the question.

"Ned was her pet name for him. His family always called him Phelps. I lived with his sister for a while down in Virginia after. . . . well, after. But Mother thought it was a funny name and took the nickname 'Ned' from his first name, Edward—E. Phelps Robinson, Junior. I'm the third, except I couldn't be."

"But how . . ."

Teddy Robinson wanted to talk. Desperately wanted to talk.

"How did I hook up with Uncle Ned? He used to climb the big pine to get into the nursery when my mother had been locked in. He saw Carver leave one day not too long after I was born and took a chance that my mother was there. He hadn't been able to get to her for some time. Instead, he found me and one very terrified nurse. He knew right away I was his and he also knew instantly that the nurse didn't like her employer. From the very beginning, he would meet us in Longfellow Park. I think she may have been in love with him. Ned had finished his degree, but he wanted to stay clear of Carver, who would have killed him—or at the very least, ruined him—if he'd seen him. I was one thing; Ned was another. Oh, and my mother. Carver was glad she was gone. 'Pathetic and retarded, quite a mistake. Pretty enough, though.' That's what he said."

"I'm sorry," Faith said quietly.

He looked startled, as if he'd forgotten she was there.

"Ned went to Columbia for a law degree and started a practice in Providence. If it hadn't been for seeing him a few times a year, I never would have made it. Even as it was, when he left each time, I couldn't be sure he'd be back. He told me he was my real father when I was ten and showed me pictures of my mother. She wasn't 'pretty'; she was beautiful."

Faith was steadily lifting her wrists as hard as she could, loosening the ties.

"Yes, I found a picture, taken under the star magnolia, but before it was in bloom."

"She never got to see it. That was only one of the things Ned used to mourn. He blamed himself for not getting her out. But he didn't know she was pregnant. Didn't know what Carver was like. Chauncey Carver was a lawyer, too. His family owned the parts of Cambridge Harvard and MIT didn't. There was no way my mother and Ned could have won. I never did. Not until the end, that is." He paused. "But Ned did win. He got the house and he got me. That's what he used to say. That he was a lucky guy. I sold him the house when it came to me—he wanted the garden, 'Dora's garden'—and then I enlisted. I was just out of college. When I came back, I went to Virginia for a while and became Theodore Robinson, Ned's nephew. Chauncey Carver, Junior, died during the TET Offensive—at least that's what got sent into the alumni notes and told to one or two other people. As he got older, Carver didn't work much and was something of a recluse. No one had ever paid much attention to me anyway. It was easy to 'die.' "

He paused and continued somewhat dreamily. "Virginia was nice. I liked it there. Maybe Ned's sister knew, maybe not. She never let on. I feel guilt every day of my life for what happened in Nam, but not an ounce over what—"

He stopped talking abruptly.

"Tell me where the diary is and I'll let you go. Tell me at once."

There was something of Chauncey Carver in the voice of his "son." Something menacing, bullying. The voice of a person who always got his way.

Come closer, she prayed. Come on, closer. I can't get you over there.

He took out a switchblade, opening it.

"See," he said. "Tell me where it is and I'll cut you loose."

Closer. Come closer.

The blade was brighter than anything else in the run-down room.

Closer.

He took a step nearer. Faith didn't say a word.

And nearer.

She kicked up hard, catching him squarely between his legs. As he doubled over in pain, she stood up, the chair on her back, and reached for the knife, which he'd dropped in his agony. But he stepped on it in time, so she went toward the door instead, wrenching one hand loose and desperately trying to free the other. He yanked the leg of the chair and pulled her to the ground, the knife in his hand again.

"Tell me or I swear I'll kill you right now!"

The door to the hall opened and banged against the wall.

"Professor Robinson? Remember me? Richard Morgan, the Bible as Literature? If I recall correctly, you gave me a *B* plus." As he spoke, Richard was barreling into the room and had his former teacher pinned to the ground before the end of the sentence, forcing the knife from his hand, which Faith immediately grabbed. She cut herself loose.

"Did he hurt you? Are you all right?" Richard turned his head toward Faith and saw her nod. The last few seconds had robbed her of all speech.

"Okay, can you give me the rope from the chair legs?" Richard asked. Faith could and did, then watched him quickly tie the professor's hands together. There wasn't enough rope for his feet, but Teddy didn't seem to want to go anywhere. He lay on his back on the floor, his eyes closed.

Faith was stunned. Very stunned, but she'd found her voice.

"How did you know where I was? What's—"

Then Tom walked in.

"My God, Faith! Are you all right!" he cried, reaching for her.

Faith looked at him in amazement, then behind him to make sure everyone she had ever known in her life wasn't lined up there, too, to ask the same question.

"I'm okay now," she said, and kissed him hard to prove it to both of them.

Holding his wife's hand, Tom turned his attention to the two other men in the room—the man he knew, and the one he didn't.

"You must be Richard Morgan," he said, and Faith realized she had been forgetting her manners, but then the situation was not one covered by Emily Post or her more recent incarnations.

"I don't know how to thank you," Tom said. "If you hadn't called . . ."

"It's all right," Richard said. "I called and you came, but what about the professor?"

"The police are downstairs and they have an ambulance. Do you think he'll go quietly?"

Richard nodded.

They made an odd sort of procession, the four of them: Richard and Tom on either side of Dr. Robinson, with Faith bringing up the rear. The hall was silent. It was the kind of hotel where people minded their own business. There was no one in the elevator, either. In the lobby, Teddy became agitated. "The diary. I have to have it. Where is it?"

Faith put her hand on his arm and looked directly into his face. His eyes were bloodshot, rimmed with angry red skin, as if he'd been rubbing his face with his fists. He blinked several times and his lips were twitching in agitation.

"It's gone. No one can ever find it."

He relaxed visibly. "I wasn't sorry that I killed him. Uncle Ned and I took the body to the Combat Zone. That's where they found him. I was never sorry. Ned wasn't, either." Then he allowed himself to be led away.

"I want to stay with him until the dean gets there; it shouldn't take long," Tom told Faith.

She nodded. Now that the danger had passed, all she could think about was that poor little boy, Dora's baby—Teddy. She wanted Tom to stay with him, too. There wasn't any more time for Dr. Robinson, Harvard Divinity professor and scholar, but there was plenty of time for the Fairchilds.

"I'd rather not go along, and I want to talk to Richard about what's happened. I have no idea how he knew I was here. So I'll see you at home," Faith said.

"You're sure you're all right?"

"I'm sure." She gave his hand a squeeze.

Tom looked at Richard, tried for a smile, then just shrugged. "Whatever you want."

C offee?" Richard asked. "I think I can treat."

He needed a shave, and a bath, but she was very, very happy to see him.

Her words tumbled out: "How did you find out where he'd taken me? And the door—oh, he must not have turned the lock back again, so it was open. But—"

"Coffee. I need it and you need it," Richard said, steering her out the door and onto the sidewalk. The air was frigid, but it felt wonderful.

They ended up at another McDonald's. Richard was emptying several packets of sugar and containers of cream into Faith's coffee, although she normally took it black.

"Are you sure you're feeling okay?" He'd been asking her this, picking up where Tom had left off, since they were at the hotel. "Are you sure you shouldn't be checked out by a doctor?"

"I feel fine, mostly," she insisted. "My throat is a little sore, I have a slight headache, and I'm tired—that's all. And I'll feel even better when you've told me everything. *Everything*."

"That's not so easy, Faith. But I'll give it a shot." He also gave her a smile, and the Richard she knew, her Richard, was in it.

She sipped her coffee. It was surprisingly good. She held the cup in both hands and leaned back in the chair. Tonight's events could wait for a bit; she wanted Richard to start from the beginning—or almost the beginning.

"Can you tell me what happened that night? The night that man was killed outside the shelter?" she asked.

Part of her didn't want to know the answer, but more of her had to find out.

"That's why I've been looking for the Monk. To find out. I gather you've been looking, too—found him before I did."

"He didn't tell me much, though." Faith thought back to their brief, elliptical conversation. He'd obviously been protecting Richard, and now she was about to find out why. He'd also been right; Richard had found her.

"That night, the Monk met up with me down by the expressway. I'd been drinking for days. Maxed out my last credit card but had some cash. I got a post office box when I first came up here, had my mail forwarded from a couple of places I'd lived, and the 'You've been preapproved' offers rolled in. I'm pretty good at filling out the forms. Nobody ever turned me down. Then I'd clean up, get some cash, and head to Connecticut. Sometimes I'd get lucky at the casino there, sometimes not. But I'm avoiding the subject, right?"

"Right," Faith said. While she had wondered where the money had come from, the Platinum Visa card, all this was skirting the main issue.

"Anyway, he found me and was taking me to Oak Street, so we could get beds. It was one of those bitterly cold nights. But we were too late; the shelter was closed. We wanted breakfast there the next morning, and he knew where there was a heat duct near one of the doorways, so we stayed there. Two other guys came along, and with four of us, it warmed up a lot, especially because they had a bottle. The next thing I knew, I was cold, colder than I've ever been, and only the guy next to me was there. I shook him, and that's when I realized he was dead. He'd been stabbed, but you don't want to hear about that. I panicked. Suddenly, I was completely sober. It's hard to describe, but the whole world came into focus, like when the eye doctor turns the knobs and all the letters look sharp and clear. I even thought that, thought of the eye doctor, and when I did, I realized I was losing it. Losing my mind. Finally. Not incrementally, the way I'd been thinking I was all these years, but totally and completely in that split second. I took out my wallet, threw Richard Goodman's identification down a storm drain, and left Richard Morgan's on the body. I was dead.

"Then I ran. Ran all night, trying to find the Monk. I figured he must have seen me kill the guy and I wanted him to tell me why I did it. Once I knew that, I could be dead for real."

Faith thought her heart would break.

"When did you find him?"

"Not until yesterday. And, Faith, I *didn't* do it. I didn't kill that man. It was the other guy, his drinking buddy. I'd passed out and they began to fight over the bottle. The Monk was asleep—he doesn't drink—and he woke up just as the knife appeared. He tried to stop it, but it was too late. The guy ran off when he realized his pal was dead, and the Monk followed him. By the time he came back, I'd gone."

Her relief was enormous.

"So you didn't stop when I found you, because you didn't know what had happened? You still thought you'd killed him."

He nodded. "The terrifying thing is that I could have done it. Done it and blacked out. That's what I thought had happened. Only the Monk helped me remember."

"But if you were trying to avoid me, why have you been following me?"

"It wasn't so much that I was following you as following the guy who was following you. Professor Robinson. Sunday, I went to the museum. I thought maybe I could convince you to just forget all about me." He drank some coffee. "No, that's not true. After I saw you in the park, I wanted to see you again. I was feeling pretty desperate."

"Then you saw him push me and take my purse. He must have thought the diary was in it."

"I was in the next room, trying to decide whether or not to go in, and he came flying out. I recognized your purse right away, but I didn't get a close look at him. Tonight, I remembered that he always had some sort of association with the museum, so he had keys to those downstairs doors, the other ways in and out. I could hear you following me, so I knew you were all right. I managed to follow him for a while; then he locked a door from the other side. The only way I could get out was through the Natural History Museum. I decided to try to keep an eye on you. I didn't know it was Robinson, of course, but I knew something was wrong."

"I don't know what he used to knock me out, but it must be something he took from labs in the Natural History Museum. Some sort of chloroform," Faith said. It was all making sense. "He'd searched the house. Things were out of place, but they're always out of place in our house, and of course I thought he was in sunny California, instead of breaking into his own house."

"What was so important about the diary?"

Faith remembered Richard didn't know the end of the story, and she told him briefly.

"So that's what that was about killing somebody," Richard said. "He killed his father. No, wait, Ned was his father. He killed Carver. But Robinson would have been pretty young."

"From what he told me he would have been just out of college. Then he enlisted and came back as Ned's nephew. We'll probably never know what happened between him and Chauncey Carver that night. It doesn't sound as if it was planned. Carver finally must have pushed him too far. In effect, he got rid of Chauncey Carver, Junior, too. Then he killed himself off for real in Vietnam, leaving everything to Ned. He'd already sold him the house."

Faith realized, once Chauncey Carver was dead, Ned—Phelps—and his son had planned things very well. Ned would have had no need to practice law anymore if the estate was as large as Robinson had indicated. Father would have managed it for son. Bitsy thought Ned was from New Jersey; she'd mentioned that at lunch. It was an impression Ned had been sure not to correct. Few would have recalled his family, especially as they had been forced to the wrong side of the tracks during the Depression. Teddy stayed with Ned's sister in Virginia and entered the scene as a beloved nephew, the two spending a good life together, traveling, collecting porcelain. The only thing missing was Dora. And it would have been impossible to fill that empty space—for both father and son.

Richard's voice broke into her thoughts. "Leaving Carver in the Combat Zone, the red-light district in those days, was a pretty safe bet. It was a dangerous place. But no wonder he wanted that diary so badly, and that's why you had to go, too, since you'd read it. I'm sure the idea was to leave you in the hotel room, overdosed on something, and slip back to California. The diary was proof that he wasn't who he'd said he was all these years, and perhaps proof that he'd inherited illegally. Aside from being a murderer, he had no claim to the estate, unless his father had stipulated him as heir. Carver couldn't have legally adopted him as his son, because then he'd have had to reveal that he wasn't."

Faith could see the novel taking shape in Richard's mind.

"But tonight! What about tonight?" There was still so much she didn't know.

"I saw you go to the subway in Harvard Square and followed you to Oak Street. I wanted to tell you what the Monk had said. And tell you I was leaving—again. But I didn't want to go into the shelter for a meal. I guess I thought I'd see your husband and . . . well, he's a man who doesn't make me feel great."

"Actually, I think you'd like each other."

"Actually, I don't think that will ever happen. But hold on—I need more coffee. You?"

Faith nodded. While he was gone, she thought about the two men. Richard, when she knew him in 1989, had been a kind of dress rehearsal for Tom. Both men had a passion for justice; both were men who used words, written and spoken, to try to make the world sit up and take notice. But the one man's passion had become self-immolation.

Back now, Richard picked up the thread.

"I saw someone else waiting outside, and this time I *did* recognize Robinson. He has the kind of face that looked old when he was young and never changed."

Faith knew what he meant. She couldn't imagine Professor Robinson ever looking any different than he did now.

"I didn't really think too much about it, even though he had the same jacket as the man in the museum. . . ."

"And yours," Faith said. This was a major problem with menswear: It was so generic. And Teddy must have memorized her calendar on the kitchen wall. That's how he knew she would be at the shelter—without Tom.

"I assumed he was waiting for you both. Remember, I hadn't seen his face or much more than the jacket in the museum. While I was waiting, I went a few doors down to that new place, the warehouses they're turning into galleries and artists' studios. I had a clear view of the street and the shelter, but I almost missed you. By the time I caught up with you, the professor was putting you in his car, and you seemed okay. He must have propped you up with the seat belt. I figured he was probably giving you a ride back to his house, but still, the whole thing seemed strange, so I grabbed a cab on Harrison and followed you. Call it my old reporter's instinct. When he stopped at the hotel and took you in, I could see that something was wrong. He was holding you up. You were weaving. He probably told the clerk at the front desk you'd had too much to drink, not that they'd pay much notice in a place like that. I went to a pay phone and called your house. As you might imagine, I had a hard time making your husband understand—I mean, who the hell was I? Finally, I told him to call the police and the dean, then hung up and went in. It also isn't the kind of hotel where they are too particular about who's coming and going. I said I'd been with my friend and his wife, and when she began to feel sick, they'd told me to follow them to the hotel. The night clerk gave me the room number and I went up. I was about the bash the door down, then decided to try the knob first. The rest you know. And your husband did call the police—and the dean; you know that, too. So, now you know everything."

Faith shook her head.

"I don't know what you're going to do now."

"Neither do I, my sweet, sweet Faith. Neither do I."

Tom was waiting up in the kitchen. It seemed later than it was. It should have been three o'clock in the morning, but it was only a little past midnight.

He stood up and Faith walked straight into his arms. They held each other the way soldiers home from battle hold their loved ones.

They were both crying.

J ane Sibley had tears in her eyes. Faith darted a glance at her mother as she preceded her sister up the runner that had been laid on Aunt Chat's freshly mown meadow. The sight of the tears had almost stopped Faith in her stately walk to the altar, her matron of honor's walk. Jane never cried—or if she did, it was in private.

The weather was perfect. April in New Jersey, unlike in Massachusetts, really *did* mean spring. The Fairchild children had performed nobly, Ben carrying the ring on one of Chat's Moroccan velvet throw pillows, Amy methodically scattering rose petals up the aisle. Quentin and his best man stood next to the Reverend Fairchild, all three men beaming. Faith had been fine so far, but her mother's misty moment brought a lump to her own throat. Her little sister was getting married—and having a baby.

The couple had chosen Purcell's "Trumpet Voluntary" for their wedding march. The joyful notes rang out clear and true. Faith reached the altar (a large folding table covered with one of Chat's damask cloths and masses of spring flowers) and turned around. She had a perfect view of her sister and father. Pregnancy agreed with Hope. Under her veil, her dark hair shone. Her skin glowed. She had never looked more beautiful, and the full-skirted strapless satin bridal gown emphasized her growingly Rubenesque figure. Hope had thankfully abandoned the Barbizon School, and Faith's own creation was a simple delphinium blue crepe chiffon sheath, cut in a low vee in front. Hope and Quentin had given her a silver necklace—a solid band that rested on her collarbone. She and Hope were both wearing the earrings their grandmother had given them; the diamonds picked up the sunlight and were totally appropriate today.

Hope handed Faith her fragrant bouquet of Iceberg roses, white Madame Lemoine lilacs, and light peach Mary Rose roses. These, supplemented by Queen Anne's lace, cosmos, and peonies in a mixture of shades, adorned the tables and filled the urns in the garden. Faith carried a slightly larger version of Amy's nosegay—lilies of the valley and roses, surrounded by a mass of baby's breath—not the two sorry sprigs that usually accompanied a "mixed bouquet." Garlands of more baby's breath defined the aisle. The flower had been a deliberate choice on Hope's part, as the ceremony was a celebration of both happy events.

Hope's father kissed his daughter, made way for Quentin, and assumed his role as the Reverend Lawrence Sibley. "Dearly beloved, we are gathered together here in the sight of God and in the face of this company, to join together this Man and this Woman in holy Matrimony . . ."

"Dearly beloved." Faith had been to so many weddings, but the words struck her anew. Those here—witnesses to the love of these two about to be united as husband and wife—were the dearly beloved. It was such a tender expression. A community of the beloved—relatives, friends—a community you carried with you throughout your life. She thought of her own dearly beloveds, a group that had been expanded tenfold by her move to New England.

After they returned to Aleford next month, the Fairchilds would be staying there for the time being. Tom intended to maintain his connection with the Urban Ministry, but he felt that it was also part of his calling to stir up his own congregation. In the last weeks, they had talked endlessly about how to go about this. Tom had come to the conclusion that he was blaming First Parish for some of his own failure to inspire, to lead. He was excited now about the tasks that lay ahead and his role as a gadfly. Faith knew she would be a part of all this in a way she hadn't been at the church previously. But she would not take on the Christmas pageant or the annual May Fair. Lines had to be drawn.

She would miss Cambridge. Not the house. Never the house, but definitely Harvard Square and the friends who would now be a drive away, instead of just a few blocks.

And she would miss Richard. She already did. He had disappeared again, calling once after that night to make sure she was all right. He told her he was leaving Boston. She'd asked if he would be getting in touch with his sister, or if he wanted Faith to call her. It would be wrong to let her continue to think he was dead.

"It might be easier for her," he had said. "Whatever she told you was only a fraction of the hell I put my family through. She is absolutely right not to want anything to do with me. And the thought that I might cause her any more suffering is a terrifying one."

Faith recalled Janice's advice to her: "Concentrate on your family. Forget about Richard." But she doubted Janice had, despite all her bitter words.

And Faith knew she never would, either.

The star magnolia was in full bloom the day the Fairchilds left Brattle Street for Aleford. Dora's diary would mix with the soil and become part of the tree. Faith cut a small branch to take home with her, and wondered if one of the Longfellow poems Dora had learned as a pupil in Maine was "Curfew":

The book is completed,
And closed, like the day;

And the hand that has written it
Lays it away. . . .

Song sinks into silence,
The story is told,
The windows are darkened,
The hearth-stone is cold.

Darker and darker
The black shadows fall;
Sleep and oblivion
Reign over all.

HAVE FAITH
IN YOUR KITCHEN

BY FAITH SIBLEY FAIRCHILD

A Work in Progress

BUTTERNUT SQUASH SOUP

1 medium-size (approximately 3 pounds) butternut squash
1 medium-size yellow onion
2 cups chicken stock
Water, if necessary
½ cup half-and-half
¾ teaspoon freshly grated nutmeg
Salt and pepper to taste

Peel and seed the squash. This is easier to do if you cut it into several pieces first. Cut the prepared squash into chunks and place them in a stockpot or similar large pot. Peel the onion and cut it into four pieces. Add these to the pot. Pour in the stock, unsalted if you are using canned stock. If the stock does not cover the vegetables, add water. Cover, bring to a boil, then turn the heat down to medium low and simmer until you can pierce the squash with a fork. Puree in batches in a blender or food processor and return to the pot. Add the half-and-half,

nutmeg, salt, and pepper. Serve with a dollop of crème fraîche and grate
a hint of nutmeg on top. Serves 8 as a first course or 6 as a main course.

This soup may be made the day before and refrigerated. It is also a
base for other squash soups. For curried squash soup, add a peeled and
seeded apple cut into quarters with the onion and replace the nutmeg
with curry powder. For squash and roasted red pepper soup, add two
roasted red peppers with the onion and replace the nutmeg with ⅛ teaspoon of red pepper flakes.

As a heart-healthy recipe, this soup also tastes delicious without the
half-and-half and with no salt at all.

ALSATIAN ONION TART

PASTRY:

1 ½ cups flour

Pinch of salt

12 tablespoons unsalted butter, cut into pieces

3 tablespoons ice water

Place the flour, salt, and butter in the bowl of a food processor and add
the ice water through the tube with the machine running. Stop as soon as
the dough forms a ball. Wrap it in Saran wrap and refrigerate for 30
minutes.

You may also make the pastry by hand, cutting the butter into the
flour and salt, then adding the water and shaping the dough into a ball
before refrigerating.

You may also used prepared piecrust.

After refrigerating, roll the pastry out and line a 9-inch pie tin or
quiche pan. Refrigerate again while you are making the filling.

FILLING:

2 slices bacon, cut into pieces

1 ½ cups onion (approximately 2 medium-size yellow onions thinly sliced)

2 tablespoons flour

2 cups milk

3 large eggs

½ cup light cream

¼ teaspoon freshly ground pepper

⅛ teaspoon freshly ground nutmeg

Fry the bacon until it is crisp. Add the onions and sauté for 3 to 4 minutes. Sprinkle the flour over the mixture and stir. Add the milk and bring the mixture to a boil, stirring constantly. Turn the heat down and simmer for 3 to 4 minutes.

Remove the pan from the heat and let it cool for 10 minutes. Beat the eggs and cream together and add them, the pepper, and the nutmeg to the onion, bacon, and milk mixture.

Preheat the oven to 400°F. Pour the filling into the pastry shell. Place it on a cookie sheet. Cook the tart in the middle of the oven for approximately 45 minutes, checking after 40 minutes. The crust should be lightly browned and the filling firm. Serves 8.

Faith caramelized the onions for her luncheon, but it isn't necessary for the dish. Try it as a variation if you wish. You may also add some freshly chopped parsley or other herbs to the filling after you have sautéed the onions. Whole milk makes for a creamier tart, but 1 percent or 2 percent tastes fine also.

COUSIN LUISE'S LINGUINI WITH ASPARAGUS

1 pound fresh asparagus

1 medium-size yellow onion

3 teaspoons minced garlic

4 tablespoons olive oil

2 tablespoons unsalted butter

12 ounces dried linguine

2 tablespoons water (from the pasta pot)

4 tablespoons white wine

2 tablespoons fresh lemon juice

4 tablespoons grated Parmesan cheese

Salt and pepper to taste

Break off the woody ends of the asparagus. Asparagus breaks naturally at this point. Hold a spear and bend it. It will snap at the point where it becomes too tough. Then slice the spear diagonally into approximately 1-inch pieces. Set aside.

Boil water for the pasta while you are sautéing the onion and garlic in the oil and butter until golden. Cook the pasta according to the directions on the package and drain, reserving 2 tablespoons of the cooking liquid.

Add the asparagus to the onion and garlic mixture and cook for 2 minutes, stirring if necessary. Remove from the heat and add the water, wine, and lemon juice. Mix it with the pasta in a warmed bowl, adding the Parmesan cheese, salt, and pepper—or you may serve it mounded on top of each pasta portion. Serve immediately. Makes 4 portions. The butter may be omitted and replaced by olive oil.

This is one of the best preparations for the first asparagus to appear in the spring, an elegant yet simple recipe.

CAMBRIDGE
TEA CAKE

1 cup unsalted butter

1 ½ teaspoon mace

Pinch of salt

1 ½ cups sugar

5 large eggs

2 cups sifted cake flour

Grease and lightly flour a loaf pan, approximately 9 inches by 3 ½ inches and set aside.

Note: Do *not* preheat the oven. This cake goes into a cold oven.

Cream the butter with the mace and salt. Gradually add the sugar and beat until fluffy. Add the eggs one at a time, beating well in between. Stir in the flour and mix. The batter should be very smooth.

Fill the pan and place the cake into the oven. Turn it to 300°F. Check with a cake tester or broom straw after 1 ½ hours. It should be done or close to done.

Try toasting slices of Cambridge Tea Cake and topping them with fresh fruit, ice cream, or both.

HARVARD SQUARES

1 cup softened unsalted butter

¾ cup firmly packed brown sugar

¾ cup white sugar

2 large eggs

½ teaspoon vanilla

2 ¼ cups flour

1 teaspoon baking soda

½ teaspoon salt

1 cup chocolate chips

1 ½ cups peanut butter chips

Preheat the oven to 350°F. Cream the butter, then add the sugars and beat until fluffy. Add the eggs and vanilla, mixing well. Combine the flour, baking soda, and salt, then add to the batter. Combine the chocolate and peanut butter chips. Stir them into the batter.

Spread the batter evenly into a well-greased jelly-roll pan (approximately 15 ½ inches by 10 ½ inches).

Bake in the oven until golden brown, 25 to 30 minutes.

Cool in the pan, then cut into squares. Makes 48 squares.

You may substitute butterscotch or other kinds of chips for the peanut butter chips.

This is a good bake-sale recipe.

AUTHOR'S NOTE

It has been a long, cold winter in New England. The weather and the war have dominated, sapping our spirits and energy. It has been an indoor winter; only the heartiest venturing out for winter sports—or the newspaper. During these months and months of below-freezing temperatures, burst pipes, and constant anxiety, I found myself thinking about—and turning to—comfort food and comfort books.

Comfort food is highly individualistic. One person's meat loaf is another's Mallomar. Often we associate comfort food with specific events or people. Where did we first eat it? Who made it? Try as I might, even with their recipes, I can't reproduce either my aunt Ruth's or Horn & Hardart's macaroni and cheese. Taste buds altered with age? Or are some foods time- and place-specific?

When we were sick, we got ginger ale and "pink pills for pale people"—children's aspirin. Progressing back to health, we advanced to cinnamon toast and/or beef bouillon on a bed tray with very wobbly legs. The thought of the flat soda, the toast, and the soup still invokes the sickroom's happier qualities—Mom all to myself, no school, and Betsy McCall paper dolls from the latest issue of the magazine. Either because we were extremely healthy children or because my mother came from a Scandinavian background where illness was not encouraged—"Let nature take its course"—these sick days were rare and the comfort foods that accompanied them have acquired mythic powers.

Triscuits, Wispride cheese spread, and a glass of Almaden sherry were what awaited my father after work as he decompressed during that Cold War ritual known as the cocktail hour. Occasionally, there would be Planter's mixed nuts. There was a cachet, a glamour to these comestibles, forbidden treats for adults only. To nibble a Triscuit now is to commune with that long-ago feeling of being a child watching and waiting for life to happen. Crackers and cheese and sherry—this was sophistication. Forget Nick and Nora Charles and their martinis—food, of course, never played a great role in *The Thin Man*—in New Jersey, we knew what adult comfort food was.

Every once in awhile, it's nice to spend a day in bed with a slight cold or a touch of the flu. "The pleasant land of counterpane," Robert Louis Stevenson called it. If you're very organized—and up to it—you can put a large thermos of cocoa, mint tea, or a bottle of ginger ale next to you to sip during a day that stretches out much longer than a workday. A box of crackers or vanilla wafers is all that is needed to complete the menu. Lovely if someone's around to bring chicken soup or cinnamon toast, but it's not necessary. A really good quilt is, as well as several down pillows. Then it's time to turn to comfort books.

Jane Austen and Agatha Christie are good comfort authors, because you can read them over and over again, never quite remembering the plots. Nancy Mitford—*Love in a Cold Climate, The Pursuit of Love, Don't Tell Alfred*—is ideal also, but because of the familiarity, the anticipated jokes, not the forgetting. In a similar fashion, Mary Roberts Rinehart's nonmystery *Tish* books are a panacea for all ills.

Another book for what ails you is Janet Gillespie's account of her childhood summers in Westport, Massachusetts, *A Joyful Noise*. It combines an appreciation of the natural world with an equal appreciation of her eccentric relatives. It's back in print now—from Partners Village

Press—and copies often turn up at library book sales—a great place for obtaining all sorts of comfort reads. It's also available at the Common Reader, www.commonreader.com.

Mysteries are natural comfort books, and if you feel a bug coming on, you can go to the library and select a stack of them to take home, happy in the knowledge that if one doesn't grab you, there are a dozen more in the pile.

Vintage mysteries are perfect, both those by the authors you may know—Dorothy Sayers, Arthur Conan Doyle, Wilkie Collins, the Baroness Orczy—and those by the ones you may discover—Craig Rice, Frances and Richard Lockridge, Joan Coggin, Elizabeth Dean, Phoebe Atwood Taylor, Constance and Gwenyth Little, Charlotte Murray Russell, and John Stephen Strange. (Many of these authors' books are available from the Rue Morgue Press in Boulder, Colorado.)

And finally, there are children's books—definitely a misnomer when it comes to Madeleine L'Engle's *A Wrinkle in Time*, Jane Langton's *The Fledgling*, and Lucy Maud Montgomery's *The Blue Castle*. Then there are the Harry Potter books, or whatever your favorites may be—and never forget Nancy Drew. These are books for a lifetime.

Comfort is the key word. Whether it's milk toast or Milky Ways, murder or mirth, may you be comforted.